LIF.

MOMENT

TEN FLIGHTS INTO DARKNESS

JAMES MAXEY

WORD BALLOON BOOKS!

LIFE IN A MOMENT

TEN FLIGHTS INTO DARKNESS

JAMES MAXEY

LIFE IN A MOMENT
TEN FLIGHTS INTO DARKNESS

Publication Credits

"Lonely Hill" first appeared in *Asimov's* November 2022

"I Wear Devils" first appeared in *The Devil You Know Better* edited by RJ Carter, May 2022

"Clockwork Melting" first appeared in *Artifice and Craft* edited by David B. Coe and Edmund Shubert, July 2023

"Mercy is for Morning" first appeared in *James Gunn's Ad Astra*, Dec 2020

"Suzie Durham, Reaper of Souls" first appeared in *Dark Doorways*, Oct 2023

"Angst of an Atomic Ant" first appeared in *Beware the Bugs,* June 2022 under the pen name Rufus Formica

"Angel Hunted" first serialized on Kindle Vella beginning Jan 2022

"Queen of Mars" first appeared in *Paradoxical Pets,* Nov 2022, under the pen name California Lee

"The Map of the Drowned City" first published as a novella July 2021

"Life in a Moment" first appeared in *Corvid-19,* edited by Mike Pederson, June 2021

Table of Contents

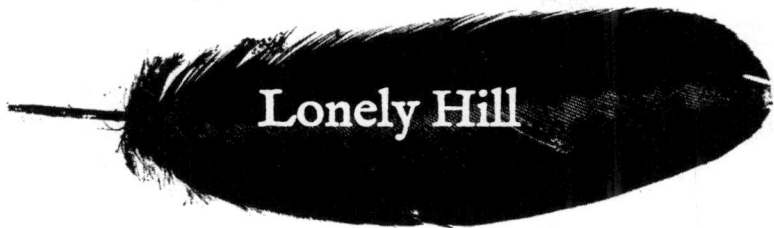

Lonely Hill

Buck Heglund, aged sixty-one, of Burnt Stump, North Carolina, had been living in the RV behind his house for a year. He woke to unwelcome silence. The generator had conked out again, which meant the electric heater had cut off. So much for his plan to get an early start digging out his flying saucer.

With the current cold snap, Buck couldn't put the generator off until a more convenient time. He could see his breath as he unzipped his sleeping bag. If circumstances were different, these freezing nights were bad enough that he'd gladly apologize to Kate and move back into the house. Even though, by any fair-minded assessment of the situation, Buck didn't feel like the fight had been totally his fault.

The year before, he'd gone out hunting before dawn on a cold November morning. He'd trudged home around nine and clomped straight into the living room to warm up next to the woodstove. He hadn't taken off his boots, caked with red clay. Honestly, there hadn't been that much mud on the floor, certainly not enough to justify Kate's drama. Kate had accused him of being drunk, which was true, but it wasn't on purpose. He'd been sipping Cousin Johnny's homemade rotgut while waiting for a deer that never showed up. If the deer had been punctual, he wouldn't have finished the flask.

When Kate had voiced her opinion that Buck's failure to remove his boots was proof he had shit for brains, he took it hard. He'd suggested they refrain from further conversation until she cooled off. Alas, while it was solid advice, he'd worded it poorly, growling, "Shut your fuckin' mouth."

That night, and all nights since, he'd slept in the RV.

Now, November had rolled around again. All he needed to do to sleep under his own roof was to have Kate accept his apology.

The primary obstacle was that Kate had died two nights after their fight, only a week shy of her sixtieth birthday. The last time he'd seen her alive she'd brought his dinner out onto the back porch. He'd come up to eat it, thinking the meal might be a peace offering, that she was ready to talk to him again. She had spoken, briefly.

"I've got a headache," she'd said, sounding weak. "I'm taking somethin' and turning in."

"Okay," he'd said. "Feel better."

She'd died that night in her sleep. An aneurysm, the doctor said. She'd shut her mouth forever.

Buck tried to stop thinking about Kate as he got dressed and stepped outside to check the generator. The twisted wire he'd used to jury-rig the carburetor had rusted in two. A bread-tie would be a perfect replacement. He walked over to the house, hesitating a moment at the backdoor, then opened it and stepped into the kitchen. The air smelled stale and dusty.

He went to the junk drawer and dug through the stray screws, old keys, jar lids, clothespins, batteries, and pencil stubs. For decades, an endless number of engineering problems on the farm had been solved with these miscellaneous contents, but he suspected the junk drawer might not deliver the goods he needed to get his flying saucer airborne. Still, one could hope.

Buck found the bread-tie he needed. He closed the drawer and stood in the silent house a moment more, gazing at the floral curtains Kate had sewn by hand. He ran his rough fingers along the ceramic ears of the flour, sugar, and coffee canisters shaped like cats. Like half the objects in the house, Kate had picked those up at a yard sale.

Buck turned, his eyes flickering toward the living room. He could still see his red boot prints in a meandering line from the door to the woodstove. Not literally, since Kate had cleaned up the prints the same day he'd made them. Mopping up the mud hadn't mopped up the memory.

He shook his head as he went back outside. The house was too haunted to occupy. Even with a working generator, the thought of another winter in the RV wasn't appealing. Buck had to wonder: If he ever found the door, could he maybe live inside his flying saucer?

Buck had owned a flying saucer his whole life, but hadn't known this until about a week ago. His family farm included forty acres of bottomland along Occaneechee Creek. This floodplain was flat as a pancake, save for an odd, perfectly circular hill that bulged up maybe thirty feet above the surrounding land. The hill had terrible soil, all red clay and rocks. Nothing took root there but briars and wild grasses. Since long before Buck was born, people called this forlorn place Lonely Hill.

Ten days ago, Hurricane Tilda had turned the bottomlands into a lake. When the floodwaters drained away, the river had carved a deep gully in the side of Lonely Hill. When he'd gone down to check out the flood damage, he'd spotted something weird in the gully. Buck found a wall of stacked river stones emerging from the red clay, too evenly arranged to be a natural formation. Part of this clay-encrusted wall had collapsed. Behind it was another wall of what looked like a single, smooth sheet of what might have been ceramic, shimmering in pale blues with hints of pink, like the inside of the oyster shell Kate had found that one time they went to the Outer Banks. The surface was sloped and curved, matching the overall slope and curve of the hill. Buck rapped the shell with his knuckles and it sounded hollow.

Leaning closer, he realized the surface wasn't completely smooth. It was covered in small, irregular divots, thousands of them, some skinny, some fat, some squiggled and swirled, running in closely spaced parallel lines. It looked almost like chiseled letters, but not from the alphabet he knew. For something that had been buried in the earth since long before he was born, the surface was strangely clean. Red clay was the stickiest muck known to man, but it looked like someone had been out before him with a bottle of Windex and a squeegee.

Running his hands along the divots, the surface felt familiar, though he struggled to identify the texture. It didn't feel like a tile or a shell, nor was it glass, and it definitely didn't feel like metal. It was soft and firm at the same time, and slightly warm.

Buck swallowed hard. The thing it reminded him of, honest to God, was the way Kate's thighs had felt in the darkness on their wedding night. Kate had grown up on a neighboring farm. She was strong enough to throw a calf over her shoulder and carry it a hundred yards. On their honeymoon, he'd marveled at the paradox of her body, the way her thighs were hard as stone, yet softer than the silk of her gown.

Buck pulled his hand away, staring at his fingers. When a person finally went crazy, how did they know?

Only about ten feet of the surface was exposed, and maybe twice that much of the stone wall. Local legend said the hill was an Indian mound, though his cousin Johnny insisted it couldn't be an Indian mound, since the Occaneechee didn't build mounds. Looking at the alien squiggles, Buck decided that Johnny was right. No humans had built the object before him. Assuming that the curved ceramic filled the whole hill like a big hubcap, there was really only one thing it could be. He'd found a flying saucer.

Probably.

Maybe.

The only way to be sure was to dig that sucker out.

There was still frost on the ground when Buck tossed his mattock and shovel into the bed of his ATV and drove down to Lonely Hill. The path took him past the beds where Kate used to grow sunflowers, now full of brown, tangled weeds.

Buck felt guilty about the ruined flower beds. As the ATV rattled down the hillside Buck kept thinking of how, at the funeral, most of Kate's family had given him the cold shoulder, blaming him with their eyes if not their words for having failed Kate.

Buck and Kate had forty good years together, but when they fought, they fought hard. Buck could never have fallen in love with someone who wasn't a tiny bit vicious. Who could understand that their shouting matches weren't a break in their love, but a pure expression of it? The only person who'd ever shared in this understanding was now buried in the family plot near the old barn.

Buck hadn't visited Kate's grave since the day they put up the tombstone. He didn't farm on a commercial scale anymore, but he kept himself busy. Once he had his flying saucer dug up, he'd find time come spring to bring back the sunflowers.

His ATV grumbled and growled through the muddy ruts along the creek. The blackberry vines covering the field around Lonely Hill were pushed down like a giant had stepped on them. Mud, leaves, and trash clung to the thorns.

A dozen blue tarps were visible on the hillside. The branches he'd placed over the tarps didn't do much to hide them. If some nosey teenager came poking around Lonely Hill, he was sunk. All his neighbors — including Kate's family — had long ago sold their land to developers. Big housing developments surrounded his acreage on three sides. Bored teens inhabiting the cookie-cutter McMansions mistook the "No Trespassing" signs on his property for an invitation. You couldn't walk far on Lonely Hill without finding beer cans and condoms. He raced an invisible clock to dig the saucer out before it was discovered.

Working for him was the fact that whoever had buried the saucer had apparently done it by hand. All the river rocks he'd taken off the hill had topped out at twenty or thirty pounds, not all that heavy, but Jesus, there were a lot of them. Fortunately, the smooth mother-of-pearl surface acted like it was greased. Once he dug out a lower section of the rock wall he'd climb up and kick the earth above it. The whole slope would slough off and slump up, a bit like snow coming off the hood of his truck in one mass.

Working against him was the fact that he was just one man with some hand tools. He'd sold his tractor and other heavy equipment over a decade ago when they'd lost their tobacco allotment. But who could he trust to help with this? His cousin Johnny? Johnny would keep his mouth shut, but he'd also show up with a mason jar full of his latest batch. The two of them would get less work done together than Buck would on his own. Twenty years ago, when he still had farming neighbors, there were a dozen people he might have trusted, and men who could have done the hard work. Alas, most had used the Judas silver they got for their land to hightail it to Florida.

Buck parked his ATV next to a pile of muddy stone. He let out a long, weary sigh as he faced reality. There was no one he could turn to for help. Lonely Hill was his lonely burden.

Buck groaned as he lowered his aching body from his ATV and grabbed his shovel. He pulled a tarp away to examine his handiwork. After five days of excavation, there was no longer any doubt this was an alien spacecraft. When he'd first started digging, no matter how careful he'd been, he kept banging the surface with his shovel. He never scratched it. A few days ago, he'd finally given in and whacked it with his mattock hard enough that he felt the jolt all the way down his spine. Nothing. No dent, no crack, not even a scuff.

As he studied the ground where he'd dig next, he noticed a chunk of red clay had fallen off the surface, dried out like an old flower pot. He picked up the clump to study the impressions of the engravings, now reversed and raised. He was more certain than ever it was an alphabet. There were thirty or forty symbols that appeared pretty often, always mixed in different sequences. Thin, swooping lines ran up and down from some of the engravings, connecting symbols to symbols five or six lines away. If these were letters, there were no gaps to mark where one word ended and the next began. His initial impression of parallel lines was giving way to a new theory as more of the saucer emerged. Instead of multiple lines, he suspected this was all one line, spiraling out from some still hidden spot at the peak. He imagined that, if you could look at a phonograph under a microscope, you might see a pattern like this.

Knowing his brain was never going to solve the mystery, Buck turned to more dependable organs, his muscles and lungs, his healthy heart and calloused hands. He sank his shovel into the dirt and dug, uncovering rocks, tossing them aside, then digging some more. His shoulders, back, and thighs united with his shovel shaft and blade, forming a single machine. His aches and pains faded as he warmed to the work.

Buck labored well into the afternoon. The day was cool but cloudless, and the naked sun left him drenched with sweat. He'd taken off his coat hours ago. Now, he took off his shirt. The sun seeped into his muscles, bringing new life. Revitalized, he worked harder, and far longer than was safe for a man his age. Stopping now wasn't an option. He felt something stirring inside him, not just the excitement of discovery, but a feeling like he'd been asleep for an unfathomable time and was only now awakening.

Grabbing his mattock, Buck climbed to the crest of the hill. He looked around at all the blue tarps, covering at least a thousand square feet. His excitement changed to worry. After all this work, he'd uncovered no more than an eighth of the saucer, assuming it filled the whole hill.

This hard reality drained all energy from him. He lowered himself to the ground. At this time of year the sunset came early. It was already skirting the ridge of the hill beyond the creek, casting long shadows through the mostly leafless forest. The shadow of the ridge crept toward the edge of the saucer.

Buck started getting cold but couldn't summon the will to put on his shirt and jacket. He kept staring at the ridge. Here and there, through the trees, he glimpsed red and gray rooftops from the development beyond the hill. These houses were built over Kate's family farm. Buck always swore he'd die penniless before he'd see his land spoiled. So far, that vow was working out.

When Buck was twelve, and his parents let him start hunting on his own, he'd leave the house before dawn and come down to Lonely Hill. He'd used his machete to hack his way to the top, since it was a good vantage point to watch for deer, and because if you entrust a twelve-year-old boy with a machete, he will find an excuse to use it.

In those predawn hours, he'd sit surrounded by the peculiar, noisy silence of wind whispering through trees and grass, birds calling and frogs chirping, the creek burbling, and the whine of mosquitoes. There were no human sounds, and no human lights. Back then, being thirty miles outside of Raleigh was like living on a separate Earth. The skies would be frenzied with stars. As the world turned toward dawn you could almost see the wheel of the universe rolling. The Milky Way spilled across the sky on crisp, cloudless nights, until it was washed clean by pink dawns.

That was long ago. Now, the lights from the surrounding neighborhood washed out all but a few bright stars. Night was an eternal dull gray and seldom silent. Though the nearest road was a quarter mile away, you could hear SUVs and minivans rolling in and out of neighborhoods. Heat pumps hummed and dogs barked and when someone on the ridge opened a patio door, the distant whisper of television sounded like the murmurs of ghosts.

With the night growing colder, Buck stretched out on the grass. He stared at the dingy haze overhead and counted stars. One, two, five, a few more. He closed his eyes, no longer having the strength to gaze upon the corrupted heavens.

The hillside gave up the heat of the day in gentle waves. Buck felt as if he was sinking into the earth, down past the grass roots and grub worms, down past bone and teeth and antler, down through clay and river rock, into the dark, slumbering womb of the ship beneath the hill.

He, too, slumbered, half aware of dreams flickering through the darkness, all shadows and formless motion. He felt once more the ache of Lonely Hill and knew, somehow, that the saucer hadn't come to Earth on its own. A second saucer had been beside it, no mere machine, but a... friend? Brother? Mate? Human words didn't quite fit the emotional connection Buck now felt. The ship had come here with a second part of itself, and now that part was gone.

The faded images grew clearer the longer he dreamt. The saucer landed next to Occaneechee Creek long ago, when there were no roads or square-walled houses, just the stick huts of the local natives. The sibling/spouse/companion saucer had flown on, searching. Men surrounded the saucer, men with black braids, dressed in buckskin, bringing blue-gray rocks from the water to pile on top of this alien object that had appeared on their land. To protect it? Preserve it? Or to hide it and forget it? The saucer wasn't a part of the natural order. It was uncomfortable for men to gaze upon.

Buck's loneliness and the loneliness of the saucer merged into a single hollowness. Buck didn't belong in this world any more than it did. Born into a land of forest and fields, Buck hadn't traveled through space to reach an alien planet, but through time. The suburban inhabitants of this transfigured world gazed upon him with disquieted eyes, a trespasser on the soil of his own birth. It was only a matter of time before someone buried him, so that the new breed of men could move on untroubled by his memory.

*"**Of course you** didn't take off your goddam boots! You've got shit for brains!" Kate shouted, her eyes flashing, her fists clenched. A vein in her temple throbbed, purple and angry. Deep within her skull, unseen, other veins bulged with each pulse.*

"Shut your fuckin' mouth," he snarled, on the defense when he had no defense. His right to leave a trail of mud through his house wasn't a hill he was willing to die on. She'd won the argument, had won it before she'd said a word, simply by looking so disappointed.

Why hadn't he said, "Christ, you're right, I'm drunk, and wasn't thinking, and I'm going to go get the mop?"

Shit for brains. He'd let the only thing in the world that ever mattered slip away in the night. She'd been alone, all alone. The red mud could never be washed clean.

When Buck finally opened his eyes, he wondered if he was dead. The sky was a sullen blue. He felt the way a corpse must feel, cold as ice and unable to lift a finger. Back-to-back days of hard labor and sixty-two years of hard life had caught up to him. Sleeping on bare ground half naked should have finished him off.

Alas, it was not the Lord's will that Buck die mercifully in the quiet morning. Buck perceived the Lord's will that he carry on by his growing need to pee. Grunting, he managed to sit. He rose on trembling legs and undid his fly. He had a vague sense he was desecrating hallowed ground, but an even deeper instinct that there was nothing offensive in the act. Any water within him had come from this land and would eventually return to it, just as he'd arisen from the soil of this farm and would one day be lowered beneath it. The land itself was his last link to the living world. Well, that and his cousin Johnny.

As the sun crept above the trees, Buck spread his arms and faced the golden orb. The insides of his eyes glowed as the sunlight penetrated him. He felt stronger each second he stood there, absorbing the light. He felt an overwhelming compulsion, despite the chill, to take off his boots and pants and bask in the sun as God had made him.

Buck opened his eyes. He surveyed the quilt of blue tarps covering the hill below him. Somehow, the saucer was talking to him, not in words, but in desires. The saucer wanted sunlight on its skin. He limped down the hill, stiff, his knees and lower back feeling full of broken glass. He grasped the closest tarp and peeled it away. His pain receded a little when he did this.

The tarps fluttered and ruffled as he dragged them off. He placed them all neatly on a pile. When they settled, only the rustle of the breeze through the briars remained. It was then he heard purring. He looked around, certain that a cat had to be standing right at his feet. Nope. He looked up, wondering if he might be hearing a plane. Nope again. The ground beneath him was trembling ever so slightly. It was like standing on the floor of the RV when the generator kicked on.

The saucer was waking up. The sunlight had revived it.

Buck stepped toward the saucer. He placed his hands on the pearly shell, trying to feel the vibrations. His mouth dropped open as the surface began to flow and buckle beneath his calloused palms. Buck stepped back as the mother-of-pearl bulged and folded. His eyes grew wide as the saucer immediately before him took on a new shape. Where there had once been a relatively flat, sloped wall, there was now a recognizable replica of an isolated portion of human anatomy.

A vagina. He was looking at a vagina. Though it was made of pearl and eight feet tall, there was really no mistaking the shape. Two parallel bulges with a depression dividing them, and delicate folds like flower petals peeking from between them.

Buck wondered if he was still dreaming, but knew he was awake. He was beyond awake. The closest feeling he could compare it to was when he was twenty-five, on a Sunday morning at the Burnt Stump Church of God. The preacher had started speaking in tongues, then the choir, then the whole congregation. He'd been swept under by this holy wave, flooded with God's love, and for the briefest, fleeting moment, he'd felt connected to the divine. His mouth had uttered words he'd never heard and couldn't translate, but he'd grasped their meaning all the same.

He understood the saucer's meaning even if he didn't understand its language. The fact that he was in the presence of a space vagina wasn't sexual. On some instinctive level, he knew the saucer was inviting him inside. The saucer had searched Buck's mind for something appealing to enter and had overshot the mark.

"I think the shape you're looking for is a door," said Buck, not knowing if his ape-grunts had any more meaning for the saucer than the squiggle alphabet had for him. The connection had been formed via his night of sleeping on the hill overcame the language barrier. The female organ flattened out, growing more angular, until it formed a distinct rectangle with a visible seam all the way around it. A handle bulged out, leaving a nearly perfect reproduction of the door of Buck's RV.

His hand trembling, Buck pulled the door open. It was pitch black inside, and smelled like damp soil. He had the impression of movement in the shadows, of dim, fluid shapes flowing into new forms. The room filled with light as windows formed in a circle along the upper rim. Buck stepped into a space that resembled the interior of his RV, only instead of it being a narrow rectangular box, it was a wide open dome, maybe fifty feet across. The walls and every object within were made of the same pearly, curved ceramic as the exterior. There was a bed near the back of the room, a stove and refrigerator to his right, and a big round table in the middle, surrounded by chairs.

Buck walked to the table. He pulled out a chair and sat down. He let out a long, low whistle.

He stopped mid-whistle as he gazed back at the door. He'd left a trail of red footsteps all the way to the table. He knew what Kate would have to say about that. He wanted, more than anything, for her to be here, right now, berating him for his carelessness. He was surprised how much he missed that. He longed for her non-stop, nagging insistence that he should be and could be and must be a little bit better than he actually was.

As if sensing that the footprints caused Buck distress, the floor shimmered and the mud flowed together into a single red blob that undulated toward the door then dropped outside. With the mud gone, Buck's longing for Kate lost enough of its edge that he grew aware of the second thing he missed most at this moment: Breakfast.

These days, Buck lived on frozen pizza and snack cakes. Now, the thought of junk food left him a little queasy. He wanted the kind of breakfast Kate used to fix for him, bacon and eggs, fried potatoes, and fresh biscuits rich with lard.

Just as the saucer had made him feel an urge to take off his clothes as a way of conveying its desire that he take off the tarps, he suspected his ravenous cravings weren't solely his own. The saucer amplified his hunger to show it needed a more substantial meal than sunlight. On a common sense level he grasped that the craft wasn't actually hungry for bacon and biscuits. What did a flying saucer eat?

Buck drove his pickup over to Alamance County to see his cousin Johnny. Johnny lived in a hole in the ground, a fallout shelter the size of a two-car garage. The only above-ground structures on his property were a couple of ratty sheds and dozens of solar panels. Johnny didn't like paying power bills. He didn't pay for gas, either. He had numerous plastic drums full of used fryer oil mellowing beneath tarps. Every vehicle Johnny owned burned homemade biodiesel.

Buck knocked on the hatch leading down into Johnny's bunker. He had to wait ten minutes for the hatch to creak open so that Johnny could stare at him with bloodshot eyes.

"Took you long enough," said Buck.

"You're the one waking up a fella in the middle of the night," grumbled Johnny.

"It's three in the afternoon," said Buck.

"That's what they want you to think," said Johnny. "They keep adding seconds to the clock, leap seconds they call them, then expect us all to pretend like nothing's changed."

Buck chuckled. He appreciated Johnny's warped humor. At least, he hoped it was humor. The alternative explanation was that he had a mentally ill relative hiding from the world in a dank pit. That seemed like something Jesus might hold a person accountable for.

Johnny motioned for Buck to climb down. Buck did so, groaning as his tendons plunked and plinked like breaking guitar strings. Johnny came by the farm now and then, but Buck hadn't been inside Johnny's bunker in years. The place had a composting toilet that gave it a noteworthy aroma.

Johnny's bunker looked like he'd commandeered the basement of a library. There were bookshelves everywhere, though they mostly held guns, tool boxes, and canned food. The books themselves were piled in precarious stacks with no obvious rhyme or reason, though there was a rectangular, neatly stacked slab of random encyclopedias leveled off with plywood and a sheet of foam rubber that served as Johnny's bed, dining area, and computer workstation. From the covers of books, spaceships hovered in alien skies and red-eyed robots menaced women in bikinis. Johnny had what must surely be every science fiction novel published in the 1950s, along with towering collections of *Popular Mechanics*, *Scientific American*, and more than a few comic books.

"What brings you by?" Johnny asked, pulling a mason jar off a shelf to fill two chipped coffee cups.

Buck took the offered cup. His eyes watered from the fumes. "I, uh, got some questions. About fuel."

"Finally converting your truck to biodiesel?"

"No. I—" Buck frowned. He took a sip of the shine, wincing as it burned across his tongue. How was he going to say this crazy thing he had to say?

"This about your flying saucer?" asked Johnny, grinning.

Buck's eyes went wide. "How the f—"

"I helped you set up your game cameras along the creek, dummy," said Johnny, sounding pleased with himself. "I went out to check on them after the hurricane. Saw the tarps. Took a peek."

"And you didn't come find me to ask what was going on?"

Johnny shrugged. "Figured you'd mention it in your own time."

"You're taking the news I have a flying saucer on my property really well," said Buck.

Johnny took a long sip of his shine, then licked his lips. "Not my first trip to this rodeo."

"Right," said Buck. "You've got tons of experience with UFOs."

"Technically, you have a UBO. It's a buried object, not a flying one. And you know what I did in the Navy."

Buck sighed, rubbing his eyes. Before Johnny had dug a hole on his land and moved into it, he'd served in the Navy for six years. Claimed he'd found out that the Navy didn't have submarines to fight a cold war. Said that their real purpose was retrieving alien ships that had crashed in the ocean and sank to the bottom. Of course, it had been more than thirty years since Johnny left the Navy. These days, Johnny mostly harangued anyone in earshot about how the government monitored people's brainwaves via their cellphones. Johnny hadn't gone on a crazy UFO rant in years.

Crazy? Buck wondered why he still had that word in his vocabulary. What if everything that Johnny said about the UFOs was true?

"Right about now, you're realizing everything I told you about UFOs is true," said Johnny, grinning ear to ear. "I told you! I told you!"

"Yeah, you told me," said Buck.

"Now you've found a flying saucer but it's out of gas," said Johnny.

"You think it burns gas?"

"Don't be stupid," said Johnny. "Gasoline can't even get a rocket into orbit. It ain't got the energy density to move a spaceship between the stars."

"The saucer likes sunlight," said Buck. "Maybe it's solar powered?"

"You ain't serious?" said Johnny, shaking his head. "Solar power's useless in interstellar space. To fly between stars, a spaceship needs to bring along its own sun. It's probably got a fusion reactor."

"So we need to get it some uranium?" asked Buck.

Johnny rolled his eyes. "That's fission, not fusion." He grabbed his boots off a shelf and started putting them on. "You're like those quacks down at the VA, using words you don't understand, wasting air. No point asking you anything. Let's roll. I need to poke around under the hood. Ain't met a machine yet I couldn't figure out once I got my hands into it."

Night was falling, leaving the sky gray and hazy when they got back to the flying saucer. The replica RV door had vanished, leaving an unbroken hull once more. Johnny practically ran to the saucer, moving with a speed he hadn't shown since he was a teenager. Johnny bent in close, squinting at the symbols. "Got a peek at these last time I was here. They look kind of like the petroglyphs at Judaculla Rock."

Buck didn't have a clue what a petroglyph was, but didn't want to give Johnny another excuse to call him a dummy. Determined not to get sidetracked, Buck nudged Johnny aside and placed his hands on the hull. "Don't be afraid," he whispered to the ship. "Johnny's here to help you feel better."

The hull rippled and flowed, forming a door once more.

"That's awesome," said Johnny. "And weird. Why does the door of a spaceship look like the door of an RV? Why would aliens who design their ships in circles use right angles for the hatch?"

"The hatch didn't look like this originally," said Buck. "I think it read my mind and found this shape."

"What did it look like originally?" asked Johnny.

"A vagina?" Buck said, not really intending for the answer to sound so much like a question.

Johnny smiled. "Maybe it read *my* mind! Tell it to change back to that!"

"I'd rather not," said Buck.

"Yeah, I guess it would be weird," said Johnny, sounding disappointed. Then his face brightened. "This is great! If the thing can read your mind, ask it what it uses for fuel."

"Maybe it can read *my* mind, but I can't read *its* mind. If it even has a mind." He scratched his head. "If I haven't lost my mind."

"Ain't nothing crazy about flying saucers," said Johnny. "Millions of civilizations gotta be out there, way more advanced than ours. There's hundreds of alien ships exploring our world on any given day. Thousands! You gotta expect a few will break down."

Without asking Buck's permission, Johnny opened the door and went inside, not bothering to remove his mud-caked boots. Buck followed. Now that it was dark outside, the room was lit by a gentle glow from the roof.

The table was still there, but it was no longer empty. Sitting on the table was a stomach. Buck had butchered enough animals in his day to recognize a stomach, even if this one was made entirely out of pearly ceramic. Instead of being covered with the little letter squiggles, this stomach replica had tiny veins and arteries crisscrossing the surface.

"That's new," said Buck.

Johnny walked over to the stomach. He pulled a hunting knife from his belt and grabbed the bit of replica intestine sticking out of the blob. Buck started to tell him that the knife was never going to cut the surface, but at the approach of the blade the stomach split, looking as if it was being sliced. Johnny peeled the flaps open. The stomach was full of metal, like scuffed up chrome. Before their eyes, the chrome turned gray, then black, giving off a faint smoke, smelling like batteries burning in a trash barrel.

Johnny scratched the black crust with a fingernail. His nail dug in easily, like he was scraping a bar of damp soap. Johnny yelped as the gunk beneath his fingernail gave off smoke. Johnny stuck his finger into his mouth, then instantly pulled it out. His nail was now actively on fire. He flicked his hand back and forth, splattering burning droplets all around, then squeezed his fingers into the palm of his other hand, snuffing out the flame.

"Guess we know what it eats!" Johnny said through clenched teeth.

"Your fingers?" asked Buck.

"No!" said Johnny. "You blind? Don't you recognize lithium when you see it? The stomach is full of lithium."

"So it eats lithium?"

"Christ, you got shit for brains," said Johnny.

"Shut your fuckin' mouth," Buck snapped, jabbing his finger into Johnny's chest. "I'm sick of you talking down to me! Can't you go two seconds without trying to show how fuckin' smart you are?"

Johnny stared at him, slack jawed. He looked like a dog caught sneaking scraps off a kitchen table.

"Sorry," said Buck, scratching the back of his head, not understanding why he'd boiled over. "I'm sorry."

Johnny shook his head. "Jesus man, how long have you been waiting to say that?"

"Since never," said Buck. "Johnny, you're a lunatic, but you're like a brother." He swallowed hard. "It's just... you wear me out sometimes. Sorry. I'm sorry."

"You got nothing to be sorry about," said Johnny. His shoulders sagged. "I'm an asshole. And I'm an asshole around you ten times over."

"Everyone needs an asshole to keep from being full of shit," said Buck.

"I'm the one full of shit," said Johnny. He wiped his eyes. "Jesus, how smart can I be? I live in a goddamned hole. Ain't no woman ever stuck around the second she saw my digs. You had Kate. You figured life out, man, the stuff that matters. I had my nose stuck in books while you were out there really living, you know?"

"You call what I do living?" Buck asked.

"The best kind of living," said Johnny. "You had a woman who took care of you."

"I had a woman I let down," said Buck, shaking his head. "Always told her I'd give her a better life, but year after year the farm kept losing money."

"You think Kate cared about money?"

"No," said Buck. "It's not that. It's... after our baby died...." He took a long, deep breath.

"Man, that was a long time ago," said Johnny.

Buck sighed. "One sorrow after another. I couldn't save her from all those troubles."

"But you could bear them with her," said Johnny. "Neither of you went through anything alone."

Johnny's words were like a knife in Buck's gut. Because, when it mattered most, when she'd pulled the covers over her on the night she'd died, Kate had been all alone.

Buck couldn't speak, but Johnny kept talking. "You got the important things in life figured out while I was busy rigging sump pumps to keep my bunker from flooding. Doesn't take a genius to see I'm jealous. I talk big because I feel small. I swear to God, I'll stop. I'll stop. I love you, man."

Buck furrowed his brow. "Does this conversation feel weird to you?"

"So weird," Johnny agreed. "Maybe we stepped through a vagina door after all."

"I think the saucer does something to my emotions," said Buck. "I just feel... stuff. Like, more than usual."

Johnny nodded. "I've noticed the hum since I got here. And the smells. For all we know it's using vibrations and pheromones to trigger glands and hormones. Trying to manipulate us into doing what it wants."

"Maybe," said Buck. "I don't think it's doing it for any bad reasons. I think it needs our help."

"And I want to help it," said Johnny. "The Navy never let me tinker on one of these things, so you better believe I want to get this ship back in the air. Let's focus on that instead of jawing about our feelings, what say?"

"Agreed," said Buck.

"Balloons," said Johnny, snapping his fingers.

Buck sighed. "That supposed to mean something?"

"We obviously need helium balloons."

"Obviously. We having a party?"

"No, you idio—" Johnny caught himself. "If this thing ate lithium, it wouldn't be hungry. It's got a belly full of the stuff! Lithium must be the waste product of its diet. Think about it: In a fusion reaction, what fuel would you need to create lithium?"

"Helium," said Buck, who didn't have a clue, but figured the balloons had gotten into the conversation somehow.

"*Ding ding ding*, you are correct," agreed Johnny. "Let's go."

"Go where?"

"There's a party supply store in Raleigh. They rent tanks of helium for balloons. You got a photo ID?"

"Of course I got a photo ID. Who doesn't?" Buck knew it was a stupid question the second he asked it.

Two hours later they were back with a truck bed full of helium tanks. Buck wondered how they were supposed to hook them up, but when they went inside there was a hose coming out of the middle of the table. The head looked ready to screw onto one of the tanks. Johnny did so, moving with the reckless confidence of a born mechanic, the kind of guy who fearlessly squirts starter fluid into a carburetor with a cigarette dangling from his lips.

After the first tank was drained, Buck realized he was craving steak. And Kate's collards. And her blackberry cobbler, with hand-churned ice cream melting on top of it.

"It wants another tank," said Buck.

Five tanks later, Buck's hunger lost its edge. The ship purred as it digested its gaseous meal. Buck looked up at the windows that encircled the room. Night had come on while they'd been inside. He could see the trees on the ridge backlit by the ceaseless glow of his unwanted neighbors.

Without warning, the room lurched. There was a rumble.

"What's happening?" asked Johnny, grabbing the edge of the table.

The hull of the saucer groaned like a barge rubbing against a dock, followed by a sound like gravel pouring out of a dump truck. Some of the windows had been completely black, covered in soil, but now all glowed with the encroaching photons of suburbia.

"We're flying!" Buck shouted. "We've pulled out of the hill!"

"Are you sure?" Johnny asked, craning his neck. "I can't see anything through these tiny windows."

In response, the windows flowed and merged, until they were as big as the windshield of an eighteen-wheeler. The lurching, shuddering motion of the craft pulling free of the hill gave way to perfect stability.

Buck pressed his forehead against the windshield, looking out over the countryside. They had to be half a mile in the air. They were high enough that he could see the lights of Raleigh in the distance. Beneath him, his farm was a dark patch of land, surrounded by acres of roofs and street lights. He gazed toward the ridge and the development beyond it. The headlights of cars rolled in and out of cul-de-sacs where Kate's farm once stood. The fathers and mothers and children sheltered beneath the countless roofs had no clue, no clue at all of the theft they participated in. The land had been purchased fairly, he supposed, and he supposed that people had the right to cover what they paid for with ugly houses, burying the past forever. But what gave them the right to the sky? Who permitted them to blot out stars and taint once black night a malignant gray?

As he'd felt the ship's hunger before, the ship now felt his loathing. The ship swooped toward the neighborhood, diving low, skimming along rooftops. As they passed, the streetlamps burst like fireworks. The headlamps of cars went dark. The vehicles slowed before drifting into ditches. As the saucer flew over the neighborhood, it left a wake of darkness a half mile wide, without a single light burning in any of the houses behind them.

"How's it doing that?" Buck asked.

"EMP?" said Johnny, though he didn't sound certain. "Power outages are a pretty common occurrence around flying saucers."

Buck felt a new type of hunger grow in his gut at Johnny's mention of other saucers.

"Oh Jesus," Buck said. "We gotta find it."

"Find what?" asked Johnny.

"The other saucer," said Buck. "This saucer didn't come here alone. It had a partner. That's why it feels so lonely."

"I've been telling you that there are other saucers for years," said Johnny.

Buck nodded. Johnny continued to talk, excitedly babbling about how the oceans were practically full of saucers. The navy eggheads had theorized that most alien life had evolved in alien oceans, so when alien craft came to Earth they came in ships capable of exploring our seas. The pearly surface of the saucer hinted at a civilization that had developed in a watery environment.

Buck only heard every other word Johnny said. He was too busy making sense of the memories flooding his brain, memories that weren't his. He remembered feeling tired and hungry after coming from… away. Far away. There hadn't been any food. Helium was the second most abundant element in the universe, but somehow he was on a planet where he couldn't find more than a few stray atoms to fill his empty belly. When his partner/mother/lover flew on to search for food, he'd rested in the field by the creek, too weak to fly away as the natives buried it. For centuries he'd slumbered beneath his blanket of earth, waiting for the return of the other part of himself.

"— just like the one at Seymore Johnson," said Johnny, coming to the end of a monologue that had been going for at least five minutes.

"What?" asked Buck, shaking free of the alien memories that had claimed him.

"I'm saying that this saucer is the spitting image of the one they've got at Seymore Johnson."

"Seymore Johnson? Ain't that down east?" asked Buck.

"The Air Force base," said Johnny, nodding. "It's one of the main sites where the government studies the alien ships they've retrieved. *Fortean Times* published pictures, and I swear this ship has a twin not even a hundred miles from here."

"That's a big coincidence, ain't it? We find a saucer and there's already another one like it so close?"

"Not coincidence," said Johnny, sounding excited. "If this thing ran out of helium, how far could the other one have gotten before it conked out? If they found it near here, it would be a lot easier to get it to Seymore Johnson than Area 51."

"And you know how to get there?" asked Buck.

"Maybe," said Johnny, scratching his chin. "Maybe not? I ain't driven on a main road in twenty years."

Right. Johnny had too many DUIs to ever get a driver's license again, and except for a single trip to the Outer Banks with Kate, Buck had never been more than forty miles from his house.

Buck felt a new hunger. A deep, gnawing need to learn the route to Seymore Johnson. Thanks to Johnny's paranoid warnings, Buck didn't have one of those phones with GPS.

"Do gas stations still sell maps?" Buck asked.

"I can't remember the last time I went to a gas station," said Johnny.

In his mind's eye, Buck could see a little display of maps next to the gum at the Circle K on Highway 70. The next thing he knew, the sky beyond the windshield blurred. When it snapped back into focus, they were over the parking lot of the Circle K. The lights in the parking lot flickered, then went out.

A hole opened in the floor beneath Buck's feet. He cried out as he found himself falling. No, not falling. Floating. He drifted to earth light as a feather.

When he went inside, a cashier pointed a flashlight toward him. "Can't sell you anything. Power's out." The guy seemed unaware that there was a UFO hovering over his store.

Buck saw the maps. He grabbed one labeled North Carolina. He went to the back of the store and grabbed a six-pack. Going back to the cashier, he placed a twenty on the counter. "Keep the change." He went back outside and looked up. In the dark sky, the saucer was nearly invisible. He gave a thumbs up. His boots lifted off the pavement as he returned to the belly of the saucer.

"Good to see you kept your priorities straight," said Johnny, taking the six-pack and tearing off a beer.

Buck also popped open a beer, feeling ungrounded after his levitation. He took a deep swig, then unfolded the map on the table, his eyes scanning the highways. It only took a few seconds to spot Seymore Johnson. He tapped the name with his finger.

The world beyond the windshield blurred again. When it came back into focus a second later, they were over what looked like an airport runway. Puffs of flame flashed beneath them as air defense systems kicked in, but if any missiles hit the hull, Buck never felt them. Helicopters rose into the air from a nearby field, but once they were a few hundred feet up, all their lights went dark. They spun back to earth like whirling maple seeds.

The saucer crept across the landscape until it hovered over the biggest Quonset hut Buck had ever seen. The corrugated tin of the roof crackled, then fell away in glowing flakes.

Waves of sorrow washed over Buck. He strained to see what was happening beneath him. The saucer formed a new window in the floor, so he could see the ground.

Below him was the second saucer, gutted. Most of the hull had been peeled off, revealing something like the ribs of an umbrella, jointed like bones, black as asphalt. Tight green beams flickered down from the bottom of his saucer onto an intact segment of the hull that sat nearby. Unearthly music filled the ship, a sound like a kettle drum covered in tinfoil accompanied by a single flute made of ice and sorrow. It was the loneliest music Buck had ever heard.

"The little indentations in the hull," said Johnny. "I think the lasers are reading them and turning them into noise. Like a record player with a needle of light."

"You read too much science fiction, Johnny," Buck whispered, but knew he was right. Buck dropped to his knees, feeling a crushing sense of loss.

"What's wrong?" Johnny said, kneeling beside him, putting a hand on his shoulder.

"It's dead," Buck said, his voice choking. "The other saucer's dead. The final message it made with its symbols was that it was sorry. So sorry it never returned to its lost half."

"How can you know this?" Johnny asked.

"Can't you hear the song?" Buck asked.

"This racket?" Johnny asked, plainly not hearing the same message Buck heard. Johnny had never had a second part of his soul to lose. There's a loneliness you can only feel when you're an isolated fragment of a greater whole. His loss of Kate was a gaping hole that opened his heart to the saucer. They were completely alone, together.

The floor dilated open again, but not beneath Buck. A beam of purple light lifted a small, fist-sized fragment of the broken hull slowly into the hold. The shard landed on the table then sank into it. The mournful music faded away.

There was another blurring of land and sky. This time, when the image sharpened, Buck found himself looking down at the Earth from a great distance, like he was seeing it from the moon.

"Great," said Johnny. "We're abducted. As often as I get probed, I shoulda seen this coming."

"We're not abducted," said Buck. He swallowed hard. Through the window in the floor, he could see the Milky Way. A shudder ran through him.

"Are you crying?" asked Johnny. "Getting probed ain't so bad."

Buck sniffled, wiping his cheeks. "The saucer's ready to go home. It's past time to go home, go home. It's saying goodbye. It can't take us with it. We wouldn't survive on its world."

"We barely get by on this one," said Johnny.

"Ain't it the truth," said Buck.

Buck felt drowsy. He closed his eyes for only a second. When he opened them, Buck was standing in his family's graveyard. What the hell was he doing here? Had he been sleepwalking? Was it dementia? To find oneself standing in a graveyard with no memory of walking there was a scary thing.

Only, he didn't feel scared. He'd been avoiding the graveyard for the better part of a year. The longer he'd stayed away, the harder it had become to visit. His presence here felt like some higher power had finally plucked him up and set him down exactly where he was supposed to be.

The sun was rising, painting the bare trees in yellow light. The wet grass was covered in dew. There were two dozen tombstones. He was standing in front of the newest one.

He knelt. He traced his fingers along the letters. The engravings beneath his fingertips felt familiar. Given the newness of the stone, the smooth polish, it reminded him of running his finger along the pearly interior of a shell.

He couldn't think of shells without thinking of the time he'd taken Kate to the Outer Banks, years and years ago. The weight of the memory was a heavy one. That trip to the beach... that had been where Kate got pregnant. That had led to a death neither of them had ever truly gotten over. Every good memory was negated by a bad one. But wasn't the reverse true as well?

"I'm sorry," he whispered. "I'm sorry I said what I said. I'm sorry I wasn't beside you." He stared at his hand on the stone, at his wedding band. In the ground beneath, the matching ring waited. "I cherished every second. Even the hard times. That's what I should have said. But you know me... shit for brains."

The ghost of a grin played across his lips. She'd known him. She'd known him, and loved him anyway, and forgiven him long before his final transgression. Deep down, he grasped that when she'd gone to bed the night she'd died, even though they'd slept under different roofs, she hadn't been alone.

The mute tombstone didn't dispute his conclusion.

Buck grit his teeth as he rose, bracing himself against Kate's stone. He trudged back toward his RV. A dozen feet away, he stopped and looked at his house. He climbed the porch steps. He sat in the rocking chair and took off his boots. He stared at them for a long time, trying to recall how he'd gotten them so muddy. He had a vague memory of digging something, but the last few hours were more or less a blank. He could smell beer on his breath, and beneath that, the faintest trace of moonshine. That probably explained a lot.

Setting his boots aside, Buck stood, rubbing his sore back. A night in a real bed would be the best medicine. He opened the door and walked into the kitchen. His eyes lingered on the cat jars, the curtains, and the mismatched, yard-sale plates and cups. In the living room, the fireplace mantel adorned with Kate's whatnots, the china birds, the framed photos, and the oyster shell she'd found on the beach. The two halves were rugged and rocky on the outside, misshapen, looking as if they'd never fit together. Inside, the shells were polished and pearled. The unlikely shapes locked together in a perfect match.

Buck belonged here, among these trinkets and touchstones, all the small accumulated treasures of their shared life. He walked into the bedroom and started to undress, home at last.

I Wear Devils

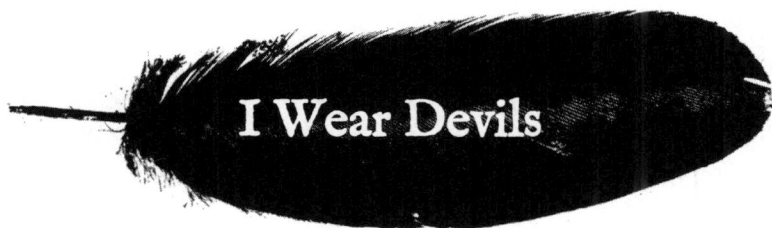

Getting into Hell is usually easy, but I'm doing it the hard way, working up a sweat on a freezing West Virginia mountain a little after midnight. I can't jab my shovel more than two inches into the churchyard without hitting a rock. I wish I'd worn different shoes. My black Keds were comfy for the long drive but crap for grave robbing.

Just so we're clear, I'm not trying to dig my way into Hell. Don't be silly. I'm exhuming the grave of a dairy farmer who choked to death drinking milk. People saw the hand of fate in his demise. Their belief imbues his bones with magic.

It smells like ripe cheese when I hack into the coffin. White bones sit atop a hardened puddle of ick. I twist the skull free and run back to the U-Haul. No time to close the grave. His relatives will probably think some depraved occultist stole his skull for some dark magic. They'll be right!

People like me are why I had Mom cremated.

I drive like a madwoman along one lane dirt roads. If I miss this hellmouth, I won't get another shot until the next full moon. That's a long time for someone to burn in a lake of brimstone because I couldn't say no to a donut. Once I reach the highway, I floor the accelerator and race toward my date with a devil.

How's that for a one sentence story of my life?

My name's Jaqueline Lantern. Really. Jacquie Lantern. It wasn't an easy name to grow up with. As you might guess from my skeleton tattoos, I've leaned into the year-round Halloween aesthetic. I'm not a witch! I hate when people assume that. I'm a necromantic chaos thaumaturge. If you need someone to explain the difference between a thaumaturge and a witch, honestly, I don't have the spoons.

An hour behind schedule, I screech to a halt in the IGA parking lot in Marlinton. Reverend Billy is shaking a cigarette free as he sits on the tailgate of his pickup. From the butts covering the ground, he's been waiting a while.

"Startin' to think you'd backed out," Billy says, cupping his hands around his lighter. The glow highlights the gray streaks in Billy's dark hair. Billy's native American, but doesn't know what tribe. He was abandoned in a rest stop, then raised by a pair of Bible-thumping snake-handlers. I've only worked with Billy once before. We didn't hit it off. He's a little Jesus heavy for my tastes. But, he's got the skills I need and lives nearby, so he'll do. If there's an app to rate preachers who cast out devils, I'd give him four stars.

"Sorry to cut things close," I say as I walk to the back of the van. "I detoured to grab a fresh skull."

"You've had a month to prepare," Billy grumbles.

"Shit happens. I picked up my doll from storage this morning and found out rats had gnawed the glyphs."

"Ain't you a little old to play with dolls?"

"I'll never be that old," I say. "But these days, I play with bigger dolls."

I open the U-Haul to reveal a mound of stone body parts. The statue toppling of recent years has been great for business. The doll has the torso of Thomas Jefferson, the legs of Robert E. Lee, and the massive, oversized arms of Bigfoot. I ran across the big guy in Olympia and had a chisel in my bag, as one does. The stone anatomy is linked with rods and gears I stole from a haunted clock tower in Dallas. That was an all-night job requiring numerous bribes and a smidgeon of arson.

I break out my Dremel and engrave a slapdash series of glyphs on the dairyman's brow. I'd hint at an interesting backstory for the Dremel, but some things are easier to order from Amazon. I frown as I finish the last glyph. Sloppy. Two stars, max. I'll be lucky if this skull doesn't crumble before dawn.

"Rise," I say, as I place the skull upon the doll's stone shoulders.

The doll rises, twanging and grinding to its full ten-foot height. I hand it a pickax and steer it to the "X" Billy has spray-painted on the asphalt. The parking lot feels like an oven. The hellmouth can't be more than a few feet below the surface. The other time Billy and I worked together, the hellmouth opened in an abandoned mineshaft, no digging required.

"Dig," I say to my doll.

Reverend Billy and I step back to avoid the flying chunks. "Fancy," he says as he watches the doll in motion. "You know I could have rented a backhoe."

"Whoever was operating the backhoe would get sucked down to Hell the second they broke through," I say. "The doll has no soul. Infernal gravity can't touch it. We're safe over here."

"We're breaking into Hell," says Billy. "Nothing about this is safe. If you'd gotten here on time, we could have done entwined warding spells. Sealed off the area in case anything nasty tries to sneak through."

"Don't sweat it. I do crazier shit than this all the time." I smile. He doesn't smile back.

Billy and I are never going to see eye to eye. Everything's serious with him. To me, nothing's serious. If I didn't embrace the crazy, I'd be a gibbering lunatic after all the things I've done. Not to mention the stuff done to me. Life's a joke, and I prefer being the one delivering the punchlines. Billy's in the trenches of a supernatural war fighting to save the world. I'm just in this for kicks. Plus, you know, the money. Usually. Tonight, we're working pro bono. I haven't mentioned that to Billy.

"We'll be fine," I say. Billy's frown is only getting deeper as glowing red light seeps up through cracks in the pavement. "The doll's working perfectly. How about you show me what you got under the tarp?"

Billy nods, flicking away his cigarette. He pulls the tarp free with a flourish, revealing a dog crate housing a runty pig.

"Old school," I say.

"Been casting out devils since I was twelve," says Billy. "Nothing beats jamming a devil into a pig."

"I'll escape this swine," the pig squeals, "then rip out your spine!"

"It rhymes!" I clap my hands with delight. Rhymers are top-shelf demons. Reverend Billy has gone above and beyond. "Awesome. Now help me into my straightjacket."

I wrestle my eveningwear from my bag. The pig watches closely as I pull the straightjacket on. The heavy jacket still reeks from the last time I used it. There's a dearth of YouTube hacks for getting the stench of brimstone out of cotton. Billy helps fasten the straps and buckles.

The pig furrows its brow, guessing what we're about to attempt. It grunts, "I shan't fear your cage of cloth! I'll shred it fast, then rip your heads off!"

"You brought the ether?" I ask Billy.

"Of course," he says.

"Wait, what?" the pig squeals, realizing the straightjacket is only part of the trap. "You snot!"

Billy cinches the last strap and asks, "Ready?"

"Ready," I say.

"Nickazeedle the Vile," Billy shouts at the pig. "Leave this vessel and assume your true form!"

"Shut your hole! I defy control!" Ol' Nick's defiance is an empty boast. The pig writhes and snorts as smoke pours from its nostrils. The smoke solidifies into a cliché from a medieval painting. He's got horns, red skin, a pointy tail, black wings, the whole package, including, you know, a huge, gnarly package.

Billy grabs me by the shoulders. He shoves his face right into mine and screams, "Jacqueline Lantern! Relinquish your mortal clay!"

The sensation of my soul peeling free of my flesh is literally unnerving. My spectral fingers slip out of gloves of skin and bone. The worst thing about it is the memory of the first time I found out this was possible.

My empty body falls limp. Tossing a soulless shell in front of a demon is like tossing a live mouse in front of a cat. Nickazeedle abandons his body to snatch mine. I slide into his devil-flesh before it can discorporate. As bad as it is pulling free of my body, slipping into a devil is a thousand times worse. Have you ever worn a tight corset? Like, steel ribs, laced until your eyes bulge? Imagine if that corset snapped shut on you all at once, and it wasn't just your torso compressed, but your arms and legs, fingers and toes, your tongue and ears and eyes. Then imagine that the corset is lined with razor blades. That's maybe a tenth of what I suffer when I take over a demon.

I gingerly try out my new fingers. The long black nails are sharp as daggers. I'm jealous. Grave robbing doesn't do my own nails any favors. I inhale, only to wind up coughing bile and blood. Devils are strong, but they aren't healthy. Every inch of my devil-flesh is covered with boils, blisters, and puss-weeping wounds. That's why devils jump into host bodies every chance they get.

I really, really wish Mom's nurse had never stopped at Krispy Kreme.

Nickazeedle has already dislocated the shoulders of my real body. He twists like a pretzel, trying to wrestle out of the straightjacket. Billy covers his mouth with the ether rag. Nickazeedle breathes out one last attempt at a rhyme, but his words are too muffled to make out what he's saying. His attempts at cursing only make him inhale the ether faster. He goes limp. I turn away, hating to see my body so vulnerable.

Just then, flames thirty stories tall shoot into the air. This is a welcome distraction from my body anxiety. The asphalt around the hellmouth starts to bubble. Billy carries my body to the passenger seat of the U-Haul. He's a good man, but of all the difficult things I'll do tonight, leaving my unconscious flesh in the hands of a man my father's age is the most difficult. Billy sees to it that my body is resting comfortably, then comes back around to the driver's side. He lights a cigarette before he climbs in.

"They'll charge me extra if you smoke in there," I say.

"The AC on my truck ain't worked in years," Billy says with a shrug. "Might as well stay comfortable until you're back. Who's the Court of Elders sending you after? Another girl with a rich daddy? Some tycoon's dearly departed mama?"

"Yeah," I say. "Somebody's mama."

I feel bad not telling him the truth. Now that he's invoked the Court of Elders there are probably a hundred crystal balls focused on him. The Elders won't be happy about our freelance incursion into the netherworld.

I flex my devil wings and fly into the flames, diving straight down. A veil of black smoke enwreathes me as I leave the living world and soar into the black sky under the asphalt.

Geologists will never admit it, but Hell is exactly where you learned it was in Sunday school. It's a lake of fire in the middle of the planet filled with damned souls screaming for eternity. The first time the Elders sent me here I was kind of disappointed at how unoriginal it was. Maybe it's boring by design. It might take the edge off the punishment if it was even slightly interesting.

In fact, the only interesting thing I've learned about Hell is that, for the most part, it's filled with good people. If you've been raised in Western vagueness about what happens to your soul after you die, you probably have some unconscious link to this place. If you die with any burden of guilt, you come to Hell to receive your punishment.

Of course, any decent person is going to feel guilty about something. Maybe they can't stop thinking about the time they got angry and slapped their kid. Maybe they fantasized a minute too long about betraying their spouse with some fresh, new face. Maybe they didn't fill in a grave they robbed because they have poor time management skills. It's small sins that fill Hell to overflowing.

Heaven is mostly populated with sociopaths incapable of shame. You can't throw a harp without hitting a senator or CEO. That makes it a second Hell. Neither is a great option. Fortunately, it's not a binary choice.

I land on a mound of smoldering brimstone on the shore of a flaming lake. Damned souls flail in the flames, wailing in agony. Any that get too close to the shore get jabbed by devils with pitchforks. Nickazeedle didn't have his pitchfork with him, so when a few devils look my way, I use my toe talons to gouge the eyes of some old man who's trying to crawl onto my rock. The devils turn back to pitchfork duty, deciding I belong here.

Maybe I do. I mean, I desecrate corpses for a living. I seldom make it through a week without committing at least one unspeakable atrocity. I can't even claim to use my talents for some greater good. The Court of Elders pays me a hefty fee to snatch souls out of Hell. Everyone I rescue has rich relatives who can afford the offerings the Elders require. Compared to the sketchiness of that, coming here to find my mother's soul is practically the work of a saint.

But I'm no saint. Neither was mom. Look, I don't talk much about my past. Most practitioners of the dark arts will broodingly regale you with tales of their tragic childhoods. I prefer to live in the here and now. From the moment I dug up my first corpse to practice on, I've controlled my own destiny. In the field of necromantic chaos thaumaturgy, I'm kind of a big deal.

Alas, explaining why I'm back in Hell requires at least a little autobiography.

Here goes. When I was fourteen, my father started lacing my meals with sleeping pills. He didn't want me to witness what he'd do next. Yet, witness it I did. You know how some people report that they float outside their body when they're sedated? I'm one of those people. My soul wanders free when my flesh gets shut down. I saw everything my father did. I told my mother, but my father denied everything. My mother convinced herself I was having nightmares. And it wasn't like I was going to convince some school counselor that I knew what I knew because I'd gained the power of astral projection.

I ran away from home, but not just to escape my father. The

science-based world taught in school couldn't explain my phantom journeys. I headed for New Orleans, seeking answers. I never looked back.

I survived on my own, a voluntary orphan, for over a decade. A few weeks ago, I noticed that the "lucky numbers" on a fortune cookie happened to be my parents' home phone. Against my better judgment, I dialed the number.

My mother answered. She wept when she heard my voice. I teared up myself. She told me my father had gone missing. He'd disappeared a few weeks back, right after Mom had told him her big news.

Mom was dying. Like, in a matter of days. Late-stage pancreatic cancer. She was all alone in the house, save for the hospice nurses. Five minutes after I hung up the phone, I'd bought a plane ticket back home.

Reaching my mom in Hell isn't as easy as booking a flight. I grab the guy whose eyes I gouged out before he sinks under. Necromancy has a lot of sub-disciplines, but the core skill is divination by studying the entrails of the dead. Human guts are a pre-modern Wikipedia. Any question you care to ask, the entrails can answer. Often, the answers are somewhat right.

I slice my writhing victim open and study the folds of his large intestine. They form a bloody, smelly roadmap. Since my mother is a recent arrival, she'll be near a shore. A malignant purple blotch shows me which bay I need to look in. I flap my wings and fly off to finish this.

My big mistake when I flew home to see my mother was wanting to start something. My dark magic couldn't heal her body. But I thought, perhaps, another sort of healing could begin. I thought we could finally talk openly. I thought we could work through why she'd let me down.

Now that my father was gone, would she confess to knowing what she must have known all along? My father was an unforgivable bastard. Had she been his victim as well, and I'd missed the clues because I was young and oblivious? For close to ten years, I'd convinced myself she hadn't failed me as much as, perhaps, I'd failed her. Couldn't I have done more to help her see through my father's lies? Had it been selfish of me to abandon her to the prison of her life, trapped behind bars with that monster?

She was asleep when I arrived. I sat by her bed for an hour. When she eventually woke I couldn't ask the questions I wanted to ask. We talked about my flight and the weather. She told me she liked my tattoos, then she started crying. I didn't ask her why. She knew she'd done wrong. She knew where she was going to spend eternity.

I decided that she'd suffered enough. Heaven and Hell aren't the only options when you die. I mean, you've heard of reincarnation. You know about spirits who wander the earth as ghosts. And the most merciful option of all is to come to a final end. Just as your body will decompose into soil, the last remnants of a soul can disperse into the ocean of mystic energy that roils beneath the material world.

As a necromantic chaos thaumaturge, I know how to disperse a soul at the moment of death. Unfortunately, I can't do it while the soul is clinging to a body. This is why I sat by my mother's bed, night and day, as she went into her final decline. I hadn't been able to rescue her from my father, but I could at least spare her an eternity in Hell.

I remember the last morning. I'd spent a long night watching her sleep, wondering again and again if she'd stopped breathing. Rays of sunlight pushed through the curtains as she opened her eyes only a little and whispered, "He was a good man."

"What?" I asked, leaning closer.

"Your father," she said, her voice weak and distant. "He tried... so hard. The way his father... hurt him. He fought every day... to be better."

"What are you saying?" I asked. "Are you saying his father sexually abused—"

"There are... all kinds of abuse," Mom whispered. "Your grandfather... never took care of his family. Any money he made...

he drank away. Your father grew up hungry... and swore it would never happen to us. He worked his fingers to the bone. He wasn't... a bad man."

"Mom," I said, squeezing her hand. "Mom, how can you say that? After what I've told you? Why didn't you—"

"I believed you," she said, squeezing my hand back. "He confessed... everything. S-swore it wouldn't... happen again."

"Again? What does that matter? If you knew he did it even once—"

"You can't give up on someone you love," she said, calmly, as if she wasn't stabbing me in the heart.

I pulled my hand from hers. I was trembling, ready to scream. At that moment, the morning nurse tapped on the bedroom door. I normally tried to keep the nurses out of the room, telling them I needed privacy. What I really needed was to make sure there were no witnesses when I cast my soul dispersal spell. Chanting and hand-waving in front of normies is awkward. Now, I welcomed the interruption.

The nurse said, "Becky tells me you've been up all night. If you need a break, I've got some donuts in the kitchen."

I brushed tears from my cheeks as I walked out. I had a donut, cold, oily and sickly sweet. In the upstairs bathroom, I threw up. I washed my face, staring in the mirror. Why had I returned? Why had I imagined I might save her? Why did I even want to?

But the face staring back at me from the mirror wasn't only my face. I have her eyes, her jaw, her lips. Perhaps it hadn't been her I'd come to save. Living like nothing matters is liberating until the day it becomes tedious.

I heard the nurse calling my name. I splashed a little more water on my face, toweled off, and went to face my mother's last moments.

But when I went downstairs, the nurse looked grave and apologetic. The nurse started to explain how quickly everything happened, but I didn't listen. My mother had said what she'd been hanging on to say. She'd had no reason to keep breathing after that.

I rushed into the room, praying I wasn't too late to cast the dispersal spell. Nothing answered my prayer. With my magically trained senses, the scent of brimstone was overwhelming.

The scent of brimstone is heavy again as I land on the shore of a bubbling caldera. I spot my mother, naked and frail, hip deep in flames. A trio of lesser demons lash her with whips.

Wearing a rhymer's skin, I'm bigger and higher ranking. I charge into the trio, slashing them with my claws. Two flee, but the last one tosses aside his whip. He's got a sword jammed straight through his ribcage that he draws out, hissing. He tries to stab me, but I poke him in the throat with my hooked tail, then twist the blade from his grasp. He turns, revealing a second face where his ass should be. I kick him in his lower nose and he races off across flames, using the faces of the damned as stepping stones.

"Jacquie!" my mother cries, stretching an arm toward me. "Help me!"

I'm not shocked that she recognizes me. The blood bond we share lets her see past my current skin. I don't call back to her. I don't intend to speak to her, or listen to anything she says. My plan is to drag her back to the material world as a spirit, disperse her, and be rid of my ghosts once and for all.

I fly toward her and grab her arm. I tug, but she doesn't budge. Something's holding her down. I beat my wings harder, lifting her. A second body emerges from the mire. It's a man, with his arms wrapped tightly around her.

It's my father. The top of his head is missing, the kind of wound you see when people blow their brains out. Now we know why he disappeared.

"Let go!" I cry, kicking him. The blow stuns him and his arms fall limp, but this doesn't free my mother. I see now that their bodies have melted together, joined at the hip.

"Save him!" my mother begs. "Save all of us!"

"Not part of the plan," I say, hacking at her hip with the sword, trying to cut her free from my father. But someone else's arm thrusts up from below their two bodies, grabbing the blade. Both bodies start to rise, and I see that my mother and father aren't alone in the pit.

My father's father emerges from the bubbling mire. His flesh is melted into my father's flesh. It's difficult to tell where one begins and the other ends. The bodies rise further, as people long submerged flex their dead muscles, moving as one mass. The faces of both my grandmothers rise up. I recognize a long-dead uncle, and there's my cousin who drowned, followed by face after face I've only seen in photo albums. Generations of relatives stretch boney fingers toward me, murmuring, "Save us! Save us!"

I grimace. I've seen this kind of interweaving before, but usually the joined souls aren't begging for more attention from a demon. My blood link to these people has changed the whole equation. Fortunately, this is exactly the sort of problem easily solved with cathartic violence.

I wrench my sword loose. I hack and bash my father's mangled body, a task made harder by the fact that other relatives keep trying to block my blows. Grunting, cursing, and chopping through bones in demonic fury, I finally get a clear shot at my father and decapitate the bastard. Watching his head tumble away isn't as satisfying as I'd imagined.

Now that my father's too mangled to fight, it's easier to chop at the junction of hips where my parents have grown together. I free my mother, but she twists, reaching out to grab my father's flailing hand as he falls away. Instantly, their flesh fuses.

"Are you kidding me?" I groan, straining to pull her away.

She weeps and blubbers. "I can't leave him! I can't!"

I ignore her, hacking to sever her hand, but now someone below her has grabbed her ankles. It's her mother, looking pitiable as she begs, "Save me! And my sister! And your grandfather!"

More bodies rise, hands grasping, the limbs tangling. My devil-heart hammers as I see how badly this has all come apart. No, not come apart. Merged together. Even in death, my mother's entwined with my father. Even in death, my father isn't sure where he starts and his father ends. How far down does this sick mess go? My family tree is nothing but a mass of tangled roots, feeding on pain and remorse. No one, no one ever tears free.

Including me.

Where I've grabbed my mother's hand, her flesh and my flesh have merged. Her skeletal fingers wriggle up the bones of my forearm, clawing deeper under the skin. I'm being pulled under by the writhing bodies who drag her down.

I swallow hard, knowing what I have to do.

"I love you," my mother pleads, as her fingers dig into the muscles of my upper arm.

"I love you too," I whisper, "but I have to let you go."

I place the tip of the sword in my own armpit, push, and twist. My severed limb falls free. I flap my wings and rise as my family cries out. Some curse me, some beg, and some can only bellow and grunt. Like some tumorous tentacle they rise in a swaying column, pursuing me. I turn my face toward the hellmouth and fly for all I'm worth.

Swirling between me and the hellmouth, the sky is black with wings. My family psychodrama has drawn attention. Demons swarm in from every direction.

It's me against all the legions of Hell. Which, again, is my life in a single sentence.

Luckily, I don't have "Necromantic Chaos Thaumaturge" embossed on my business cards for nothing. The necromancy is obvious; I steal power from death. Chaos means this power is unencumbered by the pointless rituals that encrust true magic like barnacles. And thaumaturgy? That's another word for miracle-working. I make stones stand up and walk. I know where the secret doorways to Hell stand open. I stroll through the fiery pits like a modern Virgil, as I wear devils like thrift-store sweaters.

I spent six months freezing my ass on Mt. Ararat to learn three of the fabled seventy-seven sacred names that devils dare not gaze upon. A jagged demon sword isn't as precise as a Dremel, but I take a stab at carving one of the names onto my sternum. I figure I've got it right as the nearest devil gunning for me shrieks before poofing into a sparkling cloud of glitter. I spiral upward, frying any devil close enough to gaze upon me as I strain for the surface. This buys me a few seconds before the remaining devils start plucking out their eyes and tossing them away.

They've got my scent and don't need eyes to track me. I've got maybe three minutes left before the hellmouth closes. If these demons follow me into the living world, once they tear me to ribbons, they'll start possessing the kind folks of West Virginia en masse.

The heroic sacrifice here would be to let the devils catch me, distracting them long enough for the hellmouth to close. But, seriously, you think I'm that noble?

I flap through smoke toward three faint rectangles of light. I emerge from the haze to read the letters I-G-A. My doll is standing next to the hellmouth, pickaxe in hand. I toss it the sword and shout, "Stab anything that comes out of this pit!"

I land in front of the U-Haul. "Billy!"

Billy opens the door to the cab. Next to him, my body is snarling and screaming. My hair is a mess and I'm dripping sweat. My cheeks look hollow, like I've lost ten pounds. The ether should have knocked me out for hours, but Nickazeedle has shifted my metabolism to high gear.

Billy looks at me, then at Nickazeedle, and shouts, "Both of you! Swap!"

This is easier than the journey in the other direction. I slide from the devil-flesh like it's greased. Slipping back into my own body is as easy as pulling on my favorite pair of jeans. Of course, now I'm trapped in a straightjacket, on the verge of a heart-attack. As I get full control back over my eyes, I see my doll hacking and slashing the demons boiling out of the pit. It's holding its own, but there are still dozens of hell spawn getting past.

Nickazeedle gazes at his severed stub of shoulder, then casts an evil gaze at me and Billy. He screams, "Heed my summons, hellish clan! Rip to shreds this whore and man!"

Too bad for him the demons are tracking me by scent. They fall upon Nickazeedle in a whirlwind of pitchforks. Blood spatters the hood of the van, eating through the paint. I'm never getting my deposit back.

Billy steps toward the demon tornado, Bible in hand. He's about to banish them when one of Nickazeedle's devil horns flies toward him and bashes him right between the eyes, knocking him to the pavement.

The demon horde finishes tearing apart Nickazeedle. There's at least twenty of them, tongues outstretched, tasting the air. They can't endure our world for more than a few minutes. They need to sniff out a host and I'm right under their noses. They charge toward the U-Haul. They press against the windows, licking the glass with purple tongues, nostrils flaring.

Then Billy rises, climbing onto the hood of the U-Haul. The demons try to grab him, but scream and pull away blistered fingers. Billy holds his Bible toward the sky and sings a hymn in a language I don't understand. Suddenly, the whole parking lot is awash in light. The devils wail in anguish as, in unison, they race back into the pit.

As if on cue, the flames and smoke get sucked down with them. The hellmouth closes, leaving my doll standing over the torn up asphalt, sword at the ready, but no one to attack.

Billy hops down from the hood. He opens my door and helps me stand. My legs are like rubber, but I manage to keep my feet under me as he starts unbuckling the straightjacket.

"You just earned your fifth star," I tell him.

He gives me a confused glance, then asks, "Find your mom?"

"You knew?"

"The Court of Elders filled me in before you even called me."

"So why'd you ask who I was saving?"

He shrugs. "The Elders said not to stop you, but I thought, maybe, if you said your plan out loud, you might hear the crazy."

"Why didn't the Elders want to stop me? I almost destroyed West Virginia!"

Billy shrugs. "Elder Nightmaw sank Atlantis. Folks gotta learn from their mistakes."

"Was it a mistake?" I ask. "I mean… was it wrong to want to save her?"

"If so, I'm in trouble. Saving people's the only reason I get out of bed."

"You know what I mean."

Billy nods. "Since you didn't bring her back, I can guess what happened down there. You did your best."

"Did I?" I shake my head. "I mean, seriously, I should have checked on my golem a week ago. We could have set up wards. I'm sloppy and careless and keep laughing it off, but what if the joke's on me? I'm so broken and damaged. I can't stop and think about what I'm doing, or why, or I couldn't do it. Sooner or later, my crazy is going to get a lot of people killed."

Billy shrugs. "You'll feel less crazy once we get you out of that straightjacket."

"It probably says a lot about me that I own my own straightjacket," I say, as he helps me pull my arms out of the long sleeves.

"Quit moaning," he says, and not in a joking tone. "The woman who gave birth to me tossed me into a trashcan. Big deal. Doesn't matter where you come from, only where you're going. You gotta trust in God's plan."

"I don't trust any God that would include my father in his blueprints."

"Okay. Leave Him out of it. You're all kinds of crazy, Jacquie. You're also a once in a generation thaumaturge. You'll change the world once you put your mind to it. Between you and me, I think you might change it for the better. You've seen enough evil to know the stakes. You're fighting on the side of light, even if you ain't seeing that light yet."

"You really think so?"

"Sure," he says. "And, if you turn toward darkness, don't sweat. I'll kill you before you do any permanent damage."

I grin as I brush my sweaty hair out of my eyes. "That's the nicest thing anyone has ever said to me."

Alas, there's no time to bask in the glow of his pep talk. Sirens are howling. Across the river, flashing blue lights speed toward the bridge.

Billy asks, "Can you drive?"

I nod.

"Take the doll. I'll handle the sheriff."

"How can you possibly explain this?" I ask, nodding toward the smoldering pit.

Billy smirks. "I've got a way with pigs."

I groan. The pits of Hell didn't stink as badly as that joke. I start up the van and shout for the doll to hop into the back. Once I feel its weight settle, I steer onto the highway. I keep my headlights off to help with the getaway. The clouds have mostly cleared. The asphalt glows in the moonlight.

I gun the motor and fly along the twisting road. My mind is churning. If the Elders want me to learn from my mistakes, I'm one step closer to being a genius. I didn't save Mom, and I sure didn't save myself. But maybe Billy's right; I'm good at this stuff for a reason.

I'm far enough out of town to turn on my headlights. I slow to a safer speed and turn onto a highway headed east. I'm balanced at the pivot point between laughing and crying. Whichever way I fall, it's going to be okay.

For the first time in a while, I'm grateful to be inside in my own skin, cruising down the highway, looking toward another sunrise.

And how's that for the one sentence story of my life?

Clockwork Melting

I **'m lost in concentration,** focused on my chisel and hammer, rough shaping the edge of the cog that towers over me. The work goes slowly. The ice is harder than iron. The rising wind and stinging snow fail to break into my awareness until the blizzard has reached full strength.

"Melvin!" I shout. "Melvin! Where are you?"

I go still, listening hard. The wind whipping through the sculptures whistles and groans, the dissonant notes forming an audio Rorschach test. For an instant, I'm certain I hear Melvin calling out, "Blake!"

"Melvin?"

Long seconds pass. Did I really hear his voice? Was it all in my head?

"Melvin! I thought there wasn't going to be a storm today!"

The wind is all that answers. Maybe he got the forecast wrong. Or maybe today is no longer today. Venus doesn't have sunrises or sunsets to mark the passage of time. It's eternal darkness, ceaseless cold, stark and vacant and timeless. My bodily modifications disconnect me from hunger or weariness. I've been so lost in my work, the blizzard Melvin told me was a hundred hours distant has probably arrived right on time.

The snow slashes like tiny knives against my bare hands as the world shrinks and vanishes. On Earth we'd have called this a whiteout, but Venusian snow is piss yellow. The phosphorescent cells of my brow grow brighter as I strain to see the cog I've been carving. All that's reflected is gold, gold, gold.

I slide my hammer and chisel back into my tool belt and hunker down, my back pressed against the companion gear I finished carving last month. Last year? Some previous decade? The parts all run together after a thousand years. The physical blueprints crumbled to dust centuries ago. The designs come to me only in fragments. I can no longer picture the final construction.

Not knowing which piece I'm sculpting is a sort of freedom. Each day, I wake with memories of the next sprocket or chain or escapement that must be carved. I trudge out across the ice to cut my memories into the material world. Once a part is complete, I forget all I knew about when and why I made it. I've become a robot built from nu-flesh and nu-bone, programmed by some stranger who bore my face long ago, on a different world.

My enhanced metabolism resists the cold, but if I can't see, I can't work. I fine tune my retinas into other spectrums, scanning through the ultraviolent, then down into the infrared. Nothing. I can't see my hands through the driving snow. Sculpting blind is a good way to ruin a cog. My chisel is sharp enough that even my nu-skin fingers might get lopped off. It can take weeks for them to grow back.

Maybe it's time to give up. Hunker in the bunker, wait for the storm to pass. When I first arrived on Venus, I sheltered from storms for weeks and months. That was when I still had a thousand frozen years before me. Now I have… thirty years? Twenty? That will pass in the blink of an eye.

The storms are growing worse each year as Venus gets closer to the Sagan Equilibrium. The phase two microbes have bound enough CO_2 into the rocks that it won't be long before the solar shields start letting daylight trickle in. Then phase three photosynthesizing microbes begin turning the remaining atmospheric CO_2 into oxygen. Little by little Venus will become a warm and pleasant place to live. Everything I've been working on will melt away into the new Venusian oceans.

I have to finish before that happens. It's the only way I'll find out what it is I've been making. In every creation there's a time where the initial dream has been lost and the final vision is blotted out by tedium and repetition. I've been trapped in this creative slog for centuries. The only way through it is to keep working. I need to find a different section to chisel out, something protected from the storm.

I stagger forward against the wind. I've worn paths into the ice over the years, forming a maze of alleys and trenches. I stumble through burning, stinking slush until I reach one of the deepest cuts. Sheltered by the walls, I shout, "Melvin!"

Nothing.

"Melvin!"

I wait for an answer, shivering, naked, my nu-skin itching as it repairs itself after my trek through acid slush. I draw deep breaths of the stinging atmosphere through my nose. My breath comes out in clouds that crackle as the vapor turns to snow. Melvin isn't coming. That damned monkey is useless anytime I really need him.

I scratch my bald scalp, pondering why Melvin doesn't answer me. The obvious answer is that he can't hear me over the wind. The more disturbing possibility is that Melvin doesn't exist. My head these days... I can't always trust myself to know what's real.

Lost within a deepening nightmare, I trudge blindly through the trenches. There are doors all along the path, but some instinct tells me not to take shelter within them. I stumble through snow drifts, past the tunnels that lead down into the geothermal steam works. It would be warm down there among the steam pipes, in the darkness where pistons thump like a heartbeat. I grit my teeth and flee the temptation.

I climb a crystalline staircase against a cliff on the lee side of the storm. I reach the dome atop the mountain and step inside.

I'm overwhelmed by *jamais vu*, the sensation that all this is something I've never seen before, although my hands must have carved every wondrous thing before me.

The dome overhead is a single crystal, grown over ages from atmospheric silica. With nothing but darkness beyond the dome, I stare up into a black mirror, gazing upon the distorted, inverse doppelganger of the clockwork city I've laid out gear by gear.

"You're late, Blake," says a familiar voice.

I turn. It's Melvin, in all his surreal glory. Melvin is a two-foot-tall monkey with purple fur, a green vest, and a propeller fez. He's five feet away, but I can smell his breath, rotten and fruity, like fermenting bananas.

"Where are your clothes?" Melvin asks, his brow knitting as he studies me.

"I've edited them out. What purpose did they serve? My cells can't freeze no matter how cold I feel. Who is there to be modest for?"

"The patrons, of course. Not to mention me."

"If you're real." I instantly regret saying this. If he *is* a figment of my imagination, it's probably a touchy subject.

Melvin shakes his head. "You haven't taken your meds."

"They mess with my mind."

"I've explained this a thousand times," says Melvin, sounding vexed. "When you go for weeks without eating and sleeping—"

"I don't need to eat or sleep."

"Yes, you do. Your body might be indestructible, but your brain can't handle the abuse. Your memory goes to shit. Not taking your meds makes it worse."

I shrug. "Without the drugs, I forget if *you're* real. With them, I forget if *I'm* real. They make me feel like a copy of a copy of a copy."

"I can't force you to take them," says Melvin. "But the patrons have waited a thousand years for you to finish your sculpture. It's going to be awkward explaining that you missed the deadline because you were too stubborn to take the same pills every other immortal relies on. I'm going to bookmark this conversation and add it to the project record."

"Oh no, not the record." Then I realize that, yes, I did agree to build something. For someone. And maybe that's important? "You said something about patrons?"

"You'd remember, if you took your pills."

I roll my eyes, waving him away. "You're wasting my time. I've got work to do."

I move toward a large table. There's a dismembered woman strewn across the surface. I gaze through her clear skin and down to the gears and rods and cables that will give her life. I pick up her detached face and stare at it for a long time.

"I know her," I say, in a doubtful tone.

"Was that a question or a statement?" asks Melvin.

I shake my head. "Does it matter? Is she anything more than another cog in this unfathomable machine I've built?"

"She'd be heartbroken to hear you say this."

"She's already heartbroken," I say, remembering why I stopped piecing her together the last time I was here. I put the face down and reach into the gaped rib cage, full of jumbled clockwork. I pick up the frozen heart. It's cracked down the middle. I see my own face in the glistening surface. *Jamais vu*. I should remember how I broke her heart, but I don't. Did I use too much force trying to fit her heart into the space I'd made for it? Did I get the shape of her heart all wrong?

I'll need to carve a new one. I smash the old one into tiny sharp shards with my hammer, then blow it away as glittering snow.

Measureless time passes. I'm placing the repaired ice woman on her pedestal. The click of the gears seating breaks the silence that fills the dome. I look up. The storm has passed. I can see the sharp arc of the stars emerging from the edge of the solar shield. When I first came here, starlight was an unthinkable dream. The deadly clouds that obscured Venus have been conquered by mankind's rapacious hunger for new lands. A race of immortals needs infinite space to make use of infinite ages. Yet somehow, with all of eternity before me, I'm running out of time.

Little by little, I grow aware of the sensors. They're flecks of sparkling dust, fine and clean-edged, nothing like the fat, ragged Venusian snowflakes. They settle over everything, including my skin.

"I think someone is watching me," I tell Melvin as I pour myself a cup of coffee in the bunker.

"The patrons are watching you. They feel what you feel, and taste what you taste. This was vital to your plans. Your sculpture will engage all nine senses."

"I'm part of the sculpture?"

"You're the primary focus. You've carved these icescapes to tell your story. You want others to understand what it's like to live inside your life."

I frown. "I'm not sure I understand what it's like to be inside my own life."

The years come faster and faster. The gears are polished and set into place. Cities of ice rise upon the turntables. The crystalline cast gets locked into their drive shafts one by one—babies, children, women, men, dogs and cats, birds in trees. Clockwork goldfish with frosted scales swim in ponds of antifreeze. One by one, gemlike flowers are set in place in a frozen park, roses, peonies, and ice-king daffodils. Among frozen grass set blade by blade, I place heads of budding clover with precision and care, recreating a lawn I must have once walked upon.

I rise after placing the last of the flowers. I rub my back. The work has been hard on me, but my body can renew itself. Nu-cell by nu-cell I'm replaced, again and again. I'm a walking, breathing ship of Theseus. Only the brain remains, fragmented, fractured, filled up.

"The clover was the last detail," says Melvin, who's perched on a bench next to the fountain.

"I know. Though I don't know how I know."

"You've forgotten everything by remembering it."

"I can never tell if you're trying to sound smart or stupid," I tell him.

"You knew this would happen. You studied the workings of the mind for so long. You understood the data limitations of a biological brain. You refused to go digital like everyone else."

I nod. There's a moment of clarity. "When we remember, we destroy the memory."

"Yes," says Melvin. "Bringing a memory to the front of the mind destroys the synaptic coding of the original memory. All that remains is a copy, the memory of remembering the memory."

I sit on the bench beside him, suddenly feeling a thousand years old, even though when I was that age, I was centuries younger than

I am now. But the ramification of what we're discussing weighs on me. "The things we remember most often, the things we remember best, are the memories we've most corrupted. What feels most real is almost certainly the most unreal."

"That's remarkably lucid," says Melvin.

"I did something to my brain, didn't I?" I run my fingers along the base of my skull. I don't feel a scar. But scars fade away on nu-skin. "I cut something. With a laser? A drug?"

Melvin nods his head. "A sonic knife."

"I've protected my memories by removing my power to bring them into my conscious mind. But my muscles still remember." I stare at my palms. "My hands know what I'm building. My back and my biceps know."

Melvin nods.

"Why would I do this to myself?"

"Because the brain isn't infinite. Once you commit to never dying, a biological clock starts to tick. At some point, you can't remember new things without losing old things—unless you go digital."

"Unless I destroy myself," I whisper.

"It's true that the original brain must be destroyed in the transference. But you gave up your old skin without complaint. You surrendered your eyes and teeth and testicles. What's so precious about that gray lump that you can't throw it away?"

I don't know the answer. I gaze across the park at the ice trees and the ice children and their dogs frozen in motion. A horse drawn carriage, halted in time, sits on a path of glitter not far distant. Seated in the carriage is the crystalline woman, the one whose heart I broke and remade.

"I used to sit beside her, didn't I?"

"And you will again. When you release the steam."

I go down an endless staircase in the darkness. I've worked in the cold so long I feel uneasy in the deepening heat. The atmosphere of Venus lost its hellish fire in mere centuries, but half a mile beneath the surface the planet is a furnace. The clockwork I've pieced together cog by cog can't be moved purely by springs and pendulums. Steam will bring my world to life. I strain to turn iron wheels. My muscles bulge beneath the weight. My nu-skin beads with sweat, forming salty rivulets as vapor roars through the pipes. Unseen pistons pulse and thrum. The ticking of cogs shake frost from the walls.

Eternity has stripped away all myths of an afterlife. We wearied of waiting for non-existent gods to bring us the rewards and punishments we justly deserve.

I turn the last wheel and look up the stairs I must ascend. It's time for me to put on my costume and take my place.

It's time to discover if I've built a heaven for myself, or a hell.

I enter a room built in ice to twice the normal scale. A giant man sits at a table, head bent, a magnifying glass before him. He's repairing a watch the size of a coffee saucer, a watch made of ice. My perceptions shift. The room is an ordinary size. I'm a child. The giant is my father.

He's an architect. He spends his days designing skyscrapers on a computer. He repairs antiques in the evening: pocket watches, grandfather clocks, and porcelain music boxes that play delicate melodies.

As my ice cogs engage, my father uses a pair of tweezers to lift the tiniest gear. He holds the wheel beneath his gooseneck lamp. The delicate teeth glint in the light. One tooth is missing. He sighs. It's an almost human sound, made by compressed air passing through reeds of ice. He swivels in his desk chair toward a cabinet with dozens of small drawers. He opens one filled with spare gears recovered from watches that couldn't be saved. He dumps them onto the table and starts sorting through them.

"It'll take forever to find a match," I say, leaning over the desk. I couldn't have been more than eight at the time. Nine, perhaps.

"If there *is* a match in here," he admits, in his musical reed voice.

"Let me have it." My eyes motion toward the gear. "I'll drop it in the scanner. The design engine will see the broken tooth and know how to replace it. We can print a new one in, like, five minutes."

He shakes his head. "If I wanted to do that, I wouldn't collect all these spare parts."

"But why do this the hard way?" I ask. "The printer is perfect for this."

"Then why stop at one gear? Someone somewhere has already uploaded scans of every part of this watch. I could download them and print a new watch that would look and work exactly like this one."

"Yeah. And Mom wouldn't complain about all the time you spend at junk stores."

"One person's junk is another person's priceless memory," he says. "A watch I print out of metallic resins has no value. If I can print it, anyone can print it. You could fill this room from floor to ceiling with identical copies of this watch. But this 'junk' watch was once rare. Only a few dozen were ever made. The materials were expensive. Only someone with decades of experience could piece it together. A printed copy is the real junk. The original meant something. It still means something."

"Does it?" I ask. "Hey, Melvin, what's the time?"

A disembodied voice from a hidden speaker says, "It's 8:02 pm."

"Why would anyone need a watch?" I ask.

As I speak these words, I know this scene has reached its end. The clockwork beneath the floor clicks and clacks and clangs as the ice walls sink away and my father unfolds, vanishing into the ground along with his desk and cabinet. I wobble a bit, spreading my hands for balance as the turntable I stand upon carries me to my next mechanical memory.

I know this room. It's the studio at my college. My father had hoped I'd become an architect like him, but AI was already designing houses and office buildings. Anyone could tell the program what they wanted, walk through a virtual model an hour later, edit it, approve it, and have it fully printed and ready for occupancy the following week.

Despite my youthful doubts about my father's hobbies, I'd inherited his love of working with my hands on actual matter. I drifted toward art classes that shunned monitors and digital tools. Sculpting was as obsolete as architecture, but I still liked the smell of damp clay, the way it felt beneath my fingers, the sense that the amorphous gray blob before me could be teased and tempted into revealing its true self.

In this version of the studio, I'm alone. I'm nineteen. Actual women are still a mystery to me. Despite this, or no doubt because of this, I see a woman in the clay, naked and shameless, her legs spread wide. With undeserved confidence I shape the clay, pulling my dream woman from the mire into the physical world.

I reach the stage where her body is formed and I'm left to work on finer details. Her spread legs reveal an unformed, empty gap. I touch it gently with my fingers and begin to shape her vulva.

A door opens and another student walks in, a woman. I should know her name. She's in several of my classes. Mary? Mandy? Maggie?

I swallow hard. I feel my cheeks burn as she fixes her gaze upon the nude woman I've sculpted. My fingernail rests at the end of the slit I've carved in an oval bulge. The student whose name I've lost looks at me with an amused smile.

"Don't mind me," she says, heading toward her own block of clay.

I hide my sculpture beneath a damp cloth and quickly exit the room.

The walls fall away. The gears click. The tables turn.

I'm in the reception hall of a large church for a wedding. Not *my* wedding. I'm in my late twenties. My sculpting talent hasn't landed me in galleries. Fortunately, wealthy brides and their mothers will still pay for "real" ice sculptures at wedding receptions. I did a few for friends right out of college. Now I do a dozen or more each month.

I'm setting up my work on the drink table. Across the room, caterers are carefully transferring an enormous wedding cake from a cart onto another table. There's a woman my age who seems to be in charge of the work. She glances my way. I look in her direction, staring, because she's familiar, and because the cake she's standing next to is amazing.

She walks toward me. "Hey," she says. "Did you go to State? Art major?"

"Oh wow. I do know you! You're Amanda, uh, Case?"

"Castle. My friends call me Mandy. You're Blake, right? You were an amazing sculptor!"

"Right. I mean, right, I'm Blake. Not that I'm an amazing sculptor. I make ice sculptures for weddings these days. It's not like you're ever going to find my work in museums."

"Oh my God, why not?" she says, looking admiringly at my sculpture. It's the bride and groom, holding hands. She gazes deeper into the ice. "This is amazing. Are those gears?"

"Yep. My dad used to work on music boxes in his spare time, so I'm incorporating some of what I learned from him. As the ice melts it will turn tiny water wheels. Little by little the bride and groom will shift to face one another. If the timing is right, at some point in the reception, they'll kiss, and the little ice chimes built into the base will play the wedding march."

"That's crazy," she says, in the enthusiastic, affirming sense of the word. "How do you even get ice to do that? Isn't it too brittle?"

"Pure water ice, sure. But I play around with various acids, minerals, and polymers to make the ice more resilient. By the end of the night, long after everyone's gone, this is going to be a big pile of smelly goo."

"Let's hope it doesn't melt early."

"No worries. This stuff's pretty rugged. I have a heater below the table I'll turn on about an hour before the reception."

"Wow." She looks impressed.

"I had the same reaction when I saw your cake."

She smirks. "I guess our work does have something in common. You work in ice, I work in icing, and we both get paid. And my aunt said I was throwing her money away getting my degree."

"Yeah, but back in college, I thought I'd be showing my sculptures in museums. Making this sentimental wedding stuff week after week is turning into drudgery."

"That's why I'm the boss of my own bakery now," she says. "I've got a team that handles the drudgework."

"But you still design the cakes?"

"Now and then. Half the time, the brides come to me with AI generated photos of what the cake has to look like. When I started, I was successful because I could bake great cakes and decorate them like a champ. But I've really built my little cake empire by leveraging my greatest talent, which is not strangling bridezillas."

I laugh. She laughs. Until this instant, though I can see right through Mandy's icy skin to the gears turning beneath, I've been lost in the illusion I'm talking to a real woman. But the sound slipping between her cold lips is more a honk than a laugh. The reeds are badly tuned.

I'm pulled back into the scene as her frozen eyes shift back toward my ice sculpture.

"Do you use dyes to make all the colors?"

I smile. "Nope. The ice is clear. But, when you work with ice, you're doing more than making shapes out of water. You're sculpting a vessel that holds light. I incorporate prisms and lenses to fill the ice with various hues. With each sculpture there's a moment when it's no longer an inanimate object. The light that fills it has brought it to life. I've created a vessel for souls."

She stares at me, looking uncertain if I'm serious.

I grin. "Just kidding, I'm not that pretentious. I throw around that 'vessel of souls' crap so that my clients don't faint when I show them my price sheets."

She laughs again, the same reedy honk, but now it sounds real. I didn't intend for this clockwork woman to make this sound. Art emerges from the imperfections. As lamps descend on the other side of the window to simulate the sunset, light fills her and I find myself gazing at a soul.

The days tick by with metronomic certainty and the mechanical display continues. Our courtship. Our own wedding day. I carry Mandy over the threshold of our first house. The birth of June, our daughter. I experience it all again, fresh, the memories blossoming anew in my long-fogged mind. What a wonderful life. How did I permit myself to forget a single moment?

I dance from turntable to turntable, carried to new memories. June's first Christmas, recreated in ice. The camping trip in Florida, where we watch the rockets launching hourly, carrying settlers and supplies to Crater City.

As each memory falls away, the joy becomes harder to bear. We live in an age of abundance and wonders. It's bittersweet as the cancers fall, one by one. My mother died only five years before a single intelligent pill could have saved her life. Every moment of sorrow and bliss spins away with the clicking of gears, carrying me into a future that was once my past. I meet Melvin in his newly printed purple body for the first time; he's June's companion, a gift for her seventh birthday.

The party contains hundreds of familiar faces, friends, and family, all carefully lit. I'm surrounded by souls.

Then the walls of June's birthday party fall away and the turntable carries me into a dark tunnel.

I don't actually see it happen. June is in the backyard, on the swing set. In the kitchen, I hear the squeaking of chains as she swings herself higher and higher. She laughs as she jumps at the top of her arc, the way she's done a hundred times before, flying through the air to land on her feet.

There is a soft thump, and the laughter stops.

I run toward the back door, but the walls are already sinking. The world turns beneath my feet. A church rises around me. There's a small coffin at the front of the room. The stained-glass windows filter in light. The frosty coffin is painted a thousand pastel hues of pink. But I don't see a soul within the ice. I don't listen as the ice-work priest intones his meaningless notes.

The clockwork carries me into a graveyard.

June is lowered into the ground.

All the memories before this one have seemed fresh and wonderful. But an old feeling settles into me now, the familiar chill. Ice always melts. Light always fades to darkness. The clockwork of eternity grinds all good things to nothingness.

The turntable carries me away. I pass through another tunnel of darkness.

"Melvin," I whisper.

"I'm here," he says. He walks toward me from the shadows.

"You should have watched out for her. You were programmed to keep her safe."

"It's impossible to avoid every risk. Every bite of food brings with it a small chance of choking. Would you have robbed her of the joy she felt leaping from the swing?"

I don't answer him. "This is hell," I say, at last. "Did I build this place to punish myself?"

"Is that a question you want me to answer?"

"No," I whisper. The clockwork raises a living room around me. "How long does this ride go on?"

"A long time. June's death is barely the beginning."

I ask no more questions. My legs move me forward, following stage directions only they remember. I find myself in a dimly lit warehouse. There's a block of coal-black ice in front of me the size of a semi-trailer. I look down and discover a hammer and chisel in my hands.

I set to work on the ice. My days of carving brides and grooms, unicorns, and roses are long behind me. Before June's death, I carved ice to hold souls. From that day on, my medium is darkness. I craft empty vessels for ghosts who never come home.

This new work has made me famous. The artistic respect I dreamt of long ago has finally come. The elites of the art world have an endless appetite for nihilism.

Mandy has entered the warehouse. I hear the click of her heels, ice against ice.

"Rayn called," she says. "The Louvre put in the winning bid."

I say nothing. I strike hammer against chisel against ice.

"That's kind of big news. Aren't you happy?"

I shake my head. "If I was happy, none of this could exist."

The tables carry me across years of frenzied creativity. I feed the world all my darkness, and in exchange I'm given respect and wealth. My works are displayed in capitols around the world. With every triumph I dig deeper into my misery, letting my work grow grimmer, darker. I feel an artistic duty to remind people that death will steal away all they've ever loved. I can barely stand to look at my own work. Why are others so eager to gaze upon it?

I go to an unveiling of my work in New York. I find myself in the park, the one where I carefully placed all the clover, and filled the fountain with spring-powered goldfish. The horse and carriage are in motion now. I climb into the cab, seating myself beside Mandy.

I recall her words before her musical voice whispers them to me in reedy notes.

"I've decided," she says. "I'm not getting the treatment."

My eyes go wide. "How can you say no?"

"You've spent the last fifty years reminding the world of the inevitability of death. Now, they can put you in a box for an hour, inject you full of goop, and what? You never die? Death's defeated?"

"Death's defeated. If the treatment had existed when June was born—"

"They don't use it on children," Mandy says. "It stops aging. At least of the body."

"Aging sucks. That's why mankind worked so hard to remedy it. When our grandparents were our age, they were frail and gray. If they could see us, they'd think we were thirty. Forty, maybe. Ninety-five is barely middle aged these days. Now that nu-cells have been perfected, immortality is possible, at least for those who can afford it."

"Which is a whole different debate," she says. Wrinkles form around her crystalline mouth. "Forget about the fairness of it. Forget about the ickiness that your skin isn't really your skin—"

"But it looks just like—"

"The flowers on my cakes looked like flowers," she says. "But real flowers wilt. Real flowers die."

"We're not talking about flowers."

"I'm not talking about flowers either. I'm talking about my cakes, which were made to be destroyed, carved up and eaten.

Watching my cakes get destroyed again and again wasn't some flaw in my process. It was where my art truly came to life. You understood that, once. Every beautiful bride you carved out of ice was fated to melt. If they'd never melted, there would have been no motion, and no music."

I shake my head. "My work was temporary because it had to be temporary. Now my work is displayed in subzero rooms in museums built to house them forever." I squeeze her hands. Her fingers are cold as ice. "What was once fleeting can endure. Eternity is a new medium to be mastered. I'm doing it. I'm getting the nu-cells."

She doesn't say anything. She looks into the distance.

"Think of the possibilities," I say, my voice rising. "I spent five years carving my last piece. Think of what could be made if I spent fifty years on a project. A century! They say now that the shields are up, Venus will start freezing in a few hundred years. The Colonial Authority will never let me do it, but I'm already dreaming about installing an ice sculpture on Venus on a scale that wouldn't be possible on Earth. I could carve a scene so grand it would sprawl across a continent. I'd need a thousand years to complete the work, but I could build cities! I could sculpt an entire life."

"Where do you see me in all this?" she asks. "You already vanish into your work for months with barely a word. I love you, Blake. But I don't know that my love can survive your absence for a thousand years."

"You could come with—"

"To a frozen world, locked in darkness, for a thousand years. That's certainly a winning proposition."

"You don't need to be nasty about it. And it's not like the Colonial Authority is ever going to agree to this."

"But you want to do it," she says. "It's where your head and heart are. I used to be the center of your world."

"You still are."

"No." Frost falls from her hair as she shakes her head. "These days, whenever you close your eyes... all you see is ice."

The memories continue to click by, but no matter what passes before my eyes, Mandy's words are all I hear. I went ahead and took the treatment, certain that she'd decide to join me in immortality. She held firm. I'd lived my life obsessed with death. She was the one with the courage to actually face it.

When Melvin brought me the news of her passing fifty years later, I hadn't seen her in fifteen years. There was an unbridgeable dividing line between immortals and the rest of humanity. There's a period of terror after the transformation, a feeling almost of regret, and the only way to move past it is to move on. The old life of days and weeks and years is like a childhood. The mind turns to the work of ages. People launch themselves to other worlds, prepared for ten thousand years of travel. The centuries required to turn lifeless worlds into Edens occupy a vanishing fraction of all the years before you.

The Colonial Authority hungered for art that reflected the possibilities of limitless time. I'm told the director's husbands were fans of my work and lobbied hard for the approval. Patrons were arranged to provide me with whatever resources I needed. I didn't go to Mandy's funeral; it was held on the day I finished working on my miniature version of the clockwork lifetime I would live on Venus.

The icy turntables continue to whirl and click, but I no longer follow my assigned role. I've gone rogue, wandering through the clockwork, retracing the dark tunnels, walking back to the day we met at a wedding. The music box of ice is still there, held in stasis by the Venusian atmosphere. The original melted away by the dawn following the reception, but this bride and groom of ice have been unchanged since I carved them centuries ago.

I find the stage lights I'd placed for the performance and light the sculpture once more. Colors fill the ice, but the souls are no longer there.

I bash the face of the groom with my fists until the body falls from the table. The groom's form cracks but fails to shatter. I kick it until the head breaks free, skittering across the ice. I stand there panting, staring at my bleeding hands. I'm keenly aware of the diamonds floating in the air around me, settling on my skin. I'm not the only one feeling my racing heart. The patrons are devouring my pain.

My jealousy is like a flame. This is *my* pain. This is *my* love, and *my* loss.

I'm a thief. I've stolen my own memories, and sold them to the highest bidders.

I sit on the park bench beside the frozen fountain for a very long time. I've become part of the landscape, another frozen figurine in this music box of memory and regret. None of the cogs of my mind turn any further. My emotions are as solid as the ice beneath my frost covered feet.

Melvin is sitting on the bench next to me. We're both half-hidden by snow. The wind is singing through the crystalline blades of grass.

"Atmospheric equilibrium has been reached," Melvin says, without prompting. "They'll open the shield now."

It happens all at once. The shield was never a solid structure. It's a trillion micro-satellites, not much bigger than a child's fingernail, aligned to capture light in every wavelength. They're mere atoms thick. When the magnetic engines turn them edgewise to the sun, they're invisible.

Sunlight pours through, and as the clouds above me break apart, the atmosphere fills with glowing phantasms.

The icescape surrounding me catches the light. I look toward the heavens, luxuriating in warmth upon my face as I gaze upon the sun for the first time in ten centuries.

Three days pass before I hear the first cracks. The ice is heating. Somewhere in the distance, there's a crash. Some structure I carved, a tree perhaps, has fallen. The blades of grass glisten as liquid coats their surface.

My eyes are clear, but the world looks as if I'm gazing upon it through tears. All the edges shimmer and blur. Water with the stink of rotten eggs runs in rivulets through the gutters of the park.

"It must be hard," says Melvin. "Watching the work of a lifetime melt away. In a few years, nothing recognizable will remain."

"I knew this day would come."

Melvin looks thoughtful. "But you worked so hard on this. You built all this to remember those you loved most."

"Perhaps I built it not to remember, but to forget. I have ten million years to love again. I've ten million more to lose love, and forget it all, again and again and again."

"You don't want to remember Mandy? You're willing to let go of June?"

"A frozen Venus is of no value to anyone," I tell him as the edge of the fountain gives way and a small wave of antifreeze washes across my bare feet. Transparent goldfish flop in the puddles, falling still as the tiny springs within them snap in the sunshine. "I never embraced ice as a medium because it would last forever. The art doesn't truly exist until I stop keeping it frozen. The beauty comes in watching it melt away."

Water gurgles down drains as I rise from the bench. When I walk, the frozen paving stones of the path crunch beneath my bare feet. For many hours I stroll through crumbling streets, across fallen walls, following the water down, down, toward a new sound, a distant rumble.

At last, I reach the shore of a massive lake. The surface churns as it's fed by a hundred newborn rivers. Icebergs the size of city blocks bob upon the waves.

I wade into the water and dive in. I remain beneath the acidic surface a long time, my eyes closed, adrift as the waters carry away all my yesterdays.

Eventually, inevitably, I emerge from my baptism, raw and red, gasping for air. I walk back to shore. My memories run off my flesh in dark rivulets.

Reborn and hollowed, I turn my face toward the sky, smiling, laughing, and hungry for tomorrows.

Mercy is for Morning

It was close to three a.m. when a woman came into the Borderlands diner. I slipped the book I was reading under the counter and said, "Morning."

She kept walking, her face mostly hidden by a hoodie, her hands jammed into her pockets. I couldn't tell how old she was. Her fashion skewed young, but all I could see of her face were gray lips against pale and waxy skin. Her frame was skeletal, her movements slow and shuffling. She made an odd, irregular clacking sound with each step. I peeked over the counter. She had a bundle of electrical cables hanging out of the back of her jacket dangling all the way down to the floor, tapping against the linoleum.

Her eyes darted around, hunting for something. Since she'd walked past the bathroom, I guessed what she was looking for. Sure enough, she took a seat at the far end of the counter by the wall next to an electrical socket. She needed to charge her phone, which meant she hadn't had access to a charger in the vehicle she'd arrived in, the eighteen wheeler that had pulled into the side lot a few minutes earlier. She was either a hitchhiker or a hooker. I know it's creepy to jump to conclusions, but I've worked third shift here long enough to know who stops in this time of night.

But she twisted my expectations. Instead of a phone charger, she pulled a plastic box the size of a brick out of her pocket and plugged it in. The lights flickered when she did this, and for a second I worried the fuses might blow. She plugged the wires she'd been trailing into the brick, and it lit up with multiple rows of LED lights, some green, some flashing red. The only clue as to what this device might be was a stylish lightning bolt "Z" on the front, the logo of the Zahn Corporation. Anton Zahn was one of the most famous inventors alive, though he was better known for his scandals than his technology. Still, there were millions of people walking around thanks to Zahn's artificial hearts. I never expected to see that kind of cutting-edge tech in a dive like Borderlands.

If you've ever driven on I-95, you've seen billboards for the place. Berto the Burro, a sombrero wearing donkey, encourages drivers to stop at Borderlands for gas, fireworks, and terrible Mexican food at the Burro-Ito Buffet. There's also a motel painted a radioactive shade of pink and a whole bunch of fiberglass dinosaurs.

And, of course, there's the diner, where I work the graveyard shift. It can get crazy on weekends, but weeknights are usually pretty dead. Nicer, less pothole-riddled truck stops down near Florence capture most of the truckers. The drivers we do get are either overly fond of racist mascots or don't want their buddies to see who else is in the cab with them.

Thirty seconds after the woman took a seat, the bell on the door jingled again and the Devourer of Souls strolled in. Devourer of Souls probably isn't his actual name. He drives a shiny black rig with red flame decals swirling over the cab. Even in summer he wears a black leather blazer. He sports a trim goatee, has a soft smile and smooth voice, and seems alright until you spot the big devil-head ring on his left hand and the 666 tattooed on his throat. He comes in a few times a month, always with a different woman in tow. His "girlfriends" usually look like they've got one foot in the grave, junkies with obvious needle tracks, or tweakers with missing teeth and empty eyes, showing a lot of skin regardless. Tonight's catch was a nun by comparison. That he brings them in for a meal could plausibly be interpreted as the act of a good Samaritan. Still, I can't help the uncomfortable feeling that the primary quality they share is that no one's going to look for them when they go missing.

"Coffee and the number three," said the Devourer, seating himself next to the woman. "Coffee for her too."

"Don't want anything," she said, so softly I could barely hear her. Her eyes looked anxious as she studied the LEDs on her power brick. Some of the red lights were now flashing yellow.

I took the coffee down to the Devourer. It had been a couple of hours since I made a fresh pot and evaporation had left the brew dark as motor oil, just the way he liked it. He took a long swig of the stuff without letting it cool. I took a closer glance at the woman. Her hands were smooth, youthful, but the same bloodless gray as her face. I didn't waste much time studying her. The Devourer normally reeks of cigarettes, but tonight there was a whiff of rotten meat around him that left me eager to retreat back to the grill.

On the flattop, I started working on the number three, a T-bone and eggs. I cooked it the way he liked it, which was hardly at all. The eggs received similar light treatment, sunny-side up, three of them. I ran his toast through the toaster twice, until it looked like charcoal. That's how he eats it. I wonder if he actually enjoys the food, or if he gets a kick out of dragging me in his over-the-top creepiness. After all, he likes to show off with half-dead dates.

He didn't look at me when I brought his plate to him. The woman had her hands jammed back into her pockets.

"Sure I can't get you anything?" I asked.

"I'm fine," she mumbled.

My nose wrinkled. The dead meat smell… it was her *breath*.

The stink didn't interfere with the Devourer's appetite. His plate was already a mess of blood and yolk. There was orange gore on his lips, speckled with black flecks of toast as he said, "Get her some pie."

"No pie," she whispered.

"Keep your strength up," he said. "Got a long night ahead of us."

"Our pecan pie is really good," I said.

"Not hungry," she said.

"No problem," I said, stepping away, wondering how long they would stick around. I hoped to get in a few more hours of reading before the breakfast crowd. I was currently slogging through *Les Misérables,* a book I'd somehow never read despite having an MFA in Writing. Yes, I'm aware I didn't need that degree to flip burgers on the graveyard shift. Why, yes, I have heard every joke you can make about my life choices. Truth was, right out of school, I had a good job offer to teach up in Ohio, but my girlfriend didn't want to move.

She and I had just recorded our first album together, because, sure, I'm not only a failed novelist, I'm also a failed songwriter. Our one video, "Mercy is for Morning," had, like, thirty thousand views on YouTube, which translated into about a hundred downloads on I-Tunes, which translates into less than I make in tips on a weeknight. Now my girlfriend's long gone, I live in a trailer with no hot water, and I pawned my guitar to buy a new alternator for my car. Once, I dreamed of fame, or at least of earning enough from my talents to pay a power bill. Alas, the only creativity that's paid anything is my exploration of the theme of eggs and bacon on the canvas of a flattop grill.

I scraped the grill as I contemplated my wasted life. The Devourer was almost done with his meal. The woman had her head bent down so that her chin touched her chest.

The Devourer said something to her in a low voice.

The woman shook her head.

"Come on," he said, a bit louder. "We had a deal."

"No," she said.

"This isn't a bargain you can back out of, sweetheart," said the Devourer, grabbing her arm.

"Ready for the check, sir?" I asked, hoping that reminding him I was here would interrupt whatever was unfolding.

"Yeah, we're done." He dragged the woman off her stool and tossed a fifty dollar bill on the counter. "Keep the change."

"I'm not going any further!" the woman said. "I'm done! I'm done!"

"You're done when I'm done with you," growled the Devourer of Souls.

"Stop!" she cried, as the power brick jerked from the socket.

"Hey!" I said. "Back off! The woman doesn't want to go!"

The Devourer of Souls glared at me. It was probably the reflection of the neon "open" sign, but I swear his eyes had fire in them.

"I've got the cops on speed dial," I said, keeping calm. You get used to dealing with belligerent drunks on the graveyard shift. Not that I thought he was drunk.

"Go on," he said, smiling. "Pick up the phone."

There was a *SNICK* sound and suddenly he had an open switchblade in his hand.

And I laughed. The gift shops at Borderlands are filled with the cheesiest crap you've ever seen, including fake plastic switchblades. I hadn't expected the Devourer of Souls to have a sense of humor.

His brow furrowed, like he didn't know why I was laughing.

Like his threat was real.

Like it was a real knife.

"Shit," I said, stopping in mid laugh.

"You done?" he asked.

"Please don't call the cops," the woman said. Her hoodie had been pushed back and I got a better look at her face. Halloween was two weeks away but it looked like she was wearing zombie makeup.

"You want to go with him?" I asked.

"No!" she cried. "But don't call the cops!"

"I won't," I said. Then I calmly reached under the counter and grabbed the .38 caliber revolver taped beneath the register. I aimed it at the Devourer of Souls. "Go," I said. "Leave her."

The Devourer of Souls closed the switchblade and said, calmly, "She begged for a ride. We made a fair deal. But, I guess this is as far as she wants to go."

"Just go," I said, keeping the gun aimed at him.

"Going," he said. He stopped at the door, looking back. "I'll be seeing you soon, William."

For half a second I freaked out that he knew my name, but, duh, I wear a nametag.

He left. The woman watched the door close. She looked like she might be on the verge of running out after him. Then she looked back at me and said, "Is that a real gun?"

"Nope." I held it up. "Plastic, weighted with putty. I'm told they sold these in the gift shops, like, twenty years ago. Never thought I'd actually point it at someone. Really didn't think he'd fall for it."

"Jimmy wasn't all that bright," she said, crossing her arms over her chest.

"Jimmy?"

"The guy you just chased out of here? You seemed to know him."

"I never knew his real name." I scratched my head. Jimmy? What a letdown.

"He's been listening to talk radio all the way since Richmond. Some crazy dude named Art Dunkle ranting about UFOs and the Illuminati. Only a moron believes that crap."

"You were hitchhiking?" I asked.

"I'm not a prostitute," she said.

"I didn't mean—"

"I never agreed to anything," she said. "What he thought, he thought, okay?"

"Okay," I said. "Is there, um, anyone I can call for you? Family?"

"I haven't had anyone I'm willing to call family in a long time," she said, sounding bitter. She raised her right hand to her lips and chewed on a nail. Her distress was plain, but I still wasn't getting a clear vibe just what was going on. She was probably in her early twenties, too old to be a runaway. Drugs? What drugs made you look like a walking corpse?

"I don't have any money," she said.

"I can call the motel across the road. The night clerk owes me a favor."

She shook her head. "I don't need to sleep. I should keep moving."

"To where?"

"The ocean?" she said, sounding uncertain.

"That's... a rather broad destination."

"Anywhere. It doesn't matter." She pulled up the sleeve on her left arm. She was wearing a ridiculously large watch, like a Fitbit on steroids, also bearing a Zahn logo. She grimaced as she looked at the watch and said, "Crap."

"What's wrong?"

"I'm barely out of the red zone," she said, moving back to the far end of the counter. "Look, pretend I'm not here for ten more minutes."

"I think I deserve to know what's going on," I said.

She shook her head as she plugged in the power brick. "You deserve to know nothing. It's safer."

"You think I care about safety? I pulled a fake gun on a dude with a real knife."

"You're a regular hero," she said.

"What the hell are you charging?" I asked.

She frowned. "Drop it."

"Whatever," I said, turning my back to her. The Devourer of Soul's big black rig was gone, but the fever-dream landscape of Borderlands, with its glowing neon and fake cactuses and life-sized dinosaurs had never looked creepier. If you a need a great place to piss off a devil-worshiping psychopath, seriously, you can't beat it.

Knowing I'd never be able to concentrate, I grabbed my book and took a seat at the counter.

"Is that *Les Misérables*?" the woman asked.

"Yeah," I said. "Read it?"

"I saw it on Broadway a few weeks ago. The same night I—" She looked at me for a few seconds, then shook her head. "Nothing."

I sighed, looking back at the book.

"I killed myself the same night I saw that show," she said.

"Now that's a bad review," I said. "But if Hugo goes on one more chapter with this Waterloo crap I might kill myself too."

"I'm not joking," she said. "Anton had stuck around the hotel lobby to talk to some investor he recognized. Told me to go up and get ready for bed. My heart was racing all the way to the penthouse. Anton rarely let me out of his sight. For about a minute, I really thought I had a chance to escape. I tried to stop the elevator at a lower floor, but the buttons wouldn't work."

I put the book down. It had to be a coincidence that she had gear with a Zahn logo and was talking about someone named Anton. "Anton was… a boyfriend?"

She shook her head. "I was his slave."

I furrowed my brow, unsure if this was melodrama or something more serious.

"When I got to the penthouse, running away felt impossible. So I took a knife from the kitchen. And I sliced open my wrists."

"Christ," I said. "I won't pretend to understand what you've gone through, but attempting suicide—"

"I didn't attempt," she said. "I died. I was dead for three days before they reanimated me. I'm still dead."

"Okay," I said, really sorry I'd asked any questions. Why had I assumed she'd be sane?

"I'm not crazy," she said. "It's all true. I've been the slave of Anton Zahn, the Ghoul of Silicon Valley."

"Right," I said, still thinking she was playing a game. On the other hand, if you going to name a famous billionaire most likely to have slaves, Zahn was a good choice. Zahn's interest in longevity didn't end at inventing artificial organs. He's, like, ninety, but looks thirty, and claims he owes his youthful vigor to a weekly infusion of fresh blood from youthful donors.

Sensing I still wasn't convinced, the woman stood, unzipping her hoodie and slipping it off, revealing her torso, pale green, the color of a hospital gown. Only it wasn't her skin, but some kind of rubbery-looking body paint. I couldn't help but stare at her breasts. Then I realized that the wires from the power brick were attached to a port below her left boob. She turned and moved aside her long blonde hair to show the shaved base of her skull, which had a stitched up bulge and a glowing red light faintly visible beneath her skin. This was either an amazing Halloween costume or I was looking at something I couldn't begin to understand.

"Anton is obsessed with immortality," she said. "He's worked on this for years. He replaced my old blood with some kind of high-tech substitute, and the bodysuit keeps me from rotting, though, if you've caught a whiff of my breath, it's not perfect."

The realization she could smell her own breath chilled me. Imagine living with that stink every waking second.

"Anton says that with fine tuning he can keep me reanimated a very long time. He's not doing this for my benefit. I'm a guinea pig for tech he intends to sell to his fellow billionaires."

I swallowed hard. I believed her. If you'd been there, watching her eyes, you'd have believed her too.

She pulled her hoodie back on, covering herself. Despite her deathly pallor, I could see she'd once been someone Zahn would have wanted around as a trophy.

"The private hospital room they kept me in had a window overlooking the roof of a lower floor," she said. "I smashed the window with an IV pole and bolted. Been hitchhiking since then. Jimmy's not the first asshole who expected something in return."

"Why haven't you called the cops?"

"Anton owns judges like he owns women," she said. "They'd throw me in jail for stealing his property." She jiggled the wires hanging from her. "Only, I won't stay in jail. They'll send me back to him. My only escape is death."

"If the suit's all that's keeping you alive, why not just unplug it?"

She shook her head. "Sure, I'll drop dead if the batteries run down. So what? Once he gets my corpse, he'll plug me in again."

"What if... I mean, with a real gun...?"

"Blow my brains out?" she asked. "What makes you think he'd give a shit? He didn't keep me around for conversation. A woman without a head would be his dream date."

I nodded. "That's why you're going to the ocean."

"If I went far out to sea and I weighed myself down... Anton has his own submarine, but the ocean's huge, right?"

"Pretty huge," I said. "I take my uncle's boat out to the Gulf Stream sometimes. Every time I go out, no land in sight, no other boats, I think, if I went overboard here, no one would ever find my body."

"You have a boat?"

"Um," I said.

"It's like I was meant to find you," she said.

"Look, I don't—"

"I gave you the option of not asking questions," she said.

"But—"

"What if this is your one chance?" she asked. "Your one chance to truly help someone who really needs it?"

I spend most of my life with my nose stuck inside a book. In every story, there's a moment when the character does something that alters the whole course of his life. This felt a lot like that moment.

I stood, tucking *Les Misérables* under my arm. "Are your batteries charged enough for a two-hour drive?"

"My God, you'll do it?"

"I've done crazier things." I hadn't. Turning down a good job to focus on writing songs for your girlfriend who's secretly sleeping with your drummer is technically more stupid than crazy.

She pulled the charger from the wall. "Won't you get in trouble walking out of here in the middle of a shift?"

"Oh no, I'll be fired," I said with mock distress, then shrugged. "A culinary artist with my spatula skills won't be unemployed for long."

As I said this, an SUV pulled into the lot. "Hurry," I said. "We'll slip out the back before anyone else sees you. Whoever's coming in can pour their own damned coffee."

She came around the counter and we darted through the back door. We stopped instantly when we found ourselves confronted by two large men in black suits getting out of an SUV parked next to my Honda.

"Hello, Mercy," said one of the men. He was bald, with a big gold ring in his left ear. In his suit, he looked like a blend of pirate, corporate attorney, and heavyweight boxer. His friend was even taller, with long dreadlocks, and, I swear, steel teeth. They looked ready to fight James Bond. I was a fry cook in a dirty apron who'd left his plastic gun sitting on the counter. My only weapon was my copy of *Les Misérables*. There were worse books to use in self-defense, but still.

"Fine," said the woman, Mercy, I guessed. "You've found me. I'm surprised it took you this long."

"You don't think the suit has GPS?" asked Pirate. "Or mics? We've heard every word you've said for the last eighteen hours.

Zahn said to wait and pick you up where it wouldn't cause a scene."

"You'd better believe there's going to be a scene," I yelled. "You aren't taking this woman anywhere. We've already called the cops!"

"Yeah, you haven't," said Pirate, grabbing Mercy by her arm. "Mics in the suit, remember?"

Dreadlocks reached into his jacket and pulled out a pistol. "Which is how we know you know too much to live."

I froze as he pointed the gun at me. He smiled as he saw fear flash across my face. I also got to see my terrified visage, since his steel teeth were like a row of tiny funhouse mirrors. I yelped as he pulled the trigger.

Les Misérables slammed into my chest like a fist, knocking the air out of me. I stumbled backward, looking down at my fallen book. It had a hole gouged out right where the "M" in *Misérables* should have been. I was suddenly grateful Hugo hadn't shut up about Waterloo.

Only, now I didn't have anything between me and the next bullet. But when Dreadlocks fired again, his arm jerked. The back of my neck was showered with hot gravel as the bullet gouged a crater out of the cinderblock wall. Dreadlocks' head tilted back, exposing his throat, and with a flash a slender knife blade sliced across his windpipe. Dreadlocks fell to his knees, clutching his throat, blood pouring between his fingers. Behind him stood the Devourer of Souls.

He smiled placidly as he said, "I hope I'm not interrupting something important."

Pirate pushed Mercy aside and reached into his jacket for his gun. The Devourer covered the ten foot gap between them in a heartbeat. He buried the switchblade to the hilt in the man's left eye. Pirate collapsed. The Devourer turned calmly toward me, licking the eye-gore off his blade with a grin.

"Don't know what that was about," he said, sounding amused. "But it wouldn't be very satisfying to let someone shoot you before I had the pleasure of carving you up."

As he stepped toward me, Mercy rose between us, fists clenched. "You sick bastard!" she screamed. "Don't take another step!"

As a reward for her bravery, the Devourer plunged the blade deep into her gut, lifting her from her feet. The motion brought her face only inches from his and he said, "What I'm gonna do to you, I couldn't care less if you're alive." With a grunt, he threw her aside, then looked back at me as she fell to the pavement.

He grabbed me by the collar of my shirt. He slowly, deliberately, brought the switchblade toward my face, resting the tip of the blade on my lower lip. My mind locked up. My arms refused to move at all.

"You sounded pretty brave in the diner, William," said the Devourer. "Seemed to find me pretty funny. Hmm? Why aren't you laughing now?"

"Maybe he doesn't get the joke," said Mercy, stepping up beside him, holding the pistol she'd grabbed from Pirate's corpse. She pressed the barrel against the Devourer's temple. "Drop the knife."

The Devourer didn't move a muscle for several seconds. Then he said, "I'm glad you're still standing. I enjoy a woman with a little fight in her."

"I said drop the knife!"

With manic speed, the Devourer spun, slapped Mercy's arm aside, then jammed the blade deep into her ribs. The impact knocked her sideways. As she stumbled to keep her footing, the knife twisted from his grasp. I jumped forward and wrapped my arms around him, knocking him to the ground. Unfortunately, he proved to be as adept at wrestling as he was at stabbing people. Two seconds later I was flat on my back and he was standing over me, the heel of his boot pressed against my windpipe, grinning like he was having the time of his life.

Three shots rang out. He finally stopped grinning. He dropped to his knees, mumbling, "The hell, man?" He pressed his hand over the bloody patch growing on his shirt. Finally, his eyes rolled up in his head and he went limp.

Mercy offered me her hand, helping me to my feet as she shoved the pistol into her pants. She lifted her arm, revealing the hilt of the switchblade jutting from her ribs. "Can you pull this out? It's stuck on something."

"Aren't you in pain?" I said, grabbing the blade.

"I barely feel anything," she said. "He might as well have stabbed a slab of beef."

I tugged on the blade. It came out with a sucking sound. Black gore thick as applesauce oozed from the hole before swiftly caking over. Unlike the rotten meat stink of her breath, the gore had a chemical stench, like Nyquil mixed with bleach.

"Thanks," said Mercy, kneeling to root through Pirate's pockets. She found a phone, then pressed his finger against the sensor, turning it on. She tapped the screen a few times then pointed the phone and the gun at me. "Hi!" she said. "My name is Mercy Gates. This is my confession. I'm kidnapping this guy. He just watched me kill a bunch of people, so I think he'll be cooperative. You going to be cooperative, Billy?"

"No one calls me Billy," I said. "What the hell are you doing?"

"Confessing," she said. "Now get into your damned car before I blow your brains out."

"But—"

"But nothing! Do it!" She shook the gun at me. I held up my hands as I walked toward the car, completely unclear why she was doing this.

She opened the passenger side door and got in. "Sorry about your car," she said. "I'm leaking from where he stabbed me in the gut. You might never get the smell out."

"It's okay," I said.

"I've stopped recording," she said. "You're a decent guy, who nobody calls Billy, even if you kind of look like a Billy."

"Will. I go by Will."

"I don't want you to get in trouble, Will. Tell the cops you were held at gunpoint the whole time. Maybe you won't even lose your job."

"Losing my job is probably what I need," I said. "I've been a little stuck."

"Take me to your uncle's boat," Mercy said. "We have two hours?"

"Probably less. No traffic." I tried to crank the engine, which was always a nail biter. I really needed a new starter. Luckily, the engine kicked in on the third try.

"Still plenty of time," she said, turning my radio to the AM band, going to the lower end of the spectrum until she heard a guy ranting about how Bigfoot was part of the gay agenda. "Excellent. His show's still on." She punched numbers into the phone as I took the onramp to the interstate.

"Hello Art Dunkle call screener," she said, in a forced, perky voice. "Look, you're going to want to put me on the air. Uh huh. Uh huh. I understand you've got a lot of callers already in line. For the last seven months I've been the slave of Anton Zahn. I'm ready to spill the beans on all sorts of filthy details about the secret sex cult run by the Ghoul of Silicon Valley. Can the lame weirdoes you've got on hold top that? I know! Right?"

Mercy put her hand over the phone and said, "I'm next."

She told her story for the whole drive. Every crazy thing, not just about Zahn, but a whole sex slave ring involving bankers and senators and an NPR news anchor, to the not trivial revelation about how she'd died three weeks ago and been brought back from the grave with tech that Zahn intended to lease to his fellow oligarchs. Her choice of forums meant that Zahn would likely be able to dismiss it all as nutty conspiracy talk, but what was she supposed to do? You really think the *New York Times* would have returned her calls? At least the truth was out there.

We arrived at the marina a little before sunrise. She started recording again as she explained her plan to steal the boat and throw herself overboard tied to the anchor. She emphasized that everything I'd done to help her had been because she had a gun, then she waved the gun in front of the phone camera before pointing it at me.

"Oh god, don't shoot me," I said, drawing on some of my earlier fear to sell the performance. I mean, we had fled from a crime scene leaving behind three corpses. This video might be all that stood between me and twenty-five years of federal-paid room and board.

"You should be okay now," she said, putting down the phone.

"I should be traumatized beyond all therapy," I said. "But, strangely, I'm okay with this."

"You're not going to give me some speech about how life is precious? Tell me I should cling to my second chance?"

I shook my head. "I won't pretend to know how you feel. Life *is* precious. But so are a lot of other things. I respect your choice."

She smiled, for the first time since I'd met her.

At that moment, the edge of the sun crept above the waves. The pink sky took on magnificent tones of gold. We were standing on a grassy strip near the water. The dew all around us sparkled like emeralds.

She looked at her feet and said, softly, *"Mercy is for morning, when dew is clean and bright."*

"What?" I said, my eyes going wide.

"A song. I used to listen to it all the time when I was, like, seventeen. Some band called Codex? You probably never heard of them. They did, like, one album, before splitting up. I bet I watched that video a thousand times."

"Yeah," I said, looking at the ground, shaking my head. "Never heard of them." I couldn't tell her I'd written the song. This moment wasn't about me.

"Good-bye," she said.

"Good-bye," I said.

"I feel like, I don't know, I should, like, hug you or something." She looked down at her gore-stained hoodie. "I'm kind of a mess."

"I'm kind of a mess myself," I said, stepping forward to embrace her, a motion that felt far more honest than any words I might have found as I sent her to complete her journey and she sent me back to start mine anew.

Suzie Durham, Reaper of Souls

Car lights rise across the darkened wall of my living room. The ghosts wail, "Repent, Suzie Durham! Doom is nigh!" I drape my arm across my eyes to block their phantom faces.

The doorbell rings. I don't move. I'm flat on my back on my floor. I started doing yoga nine years ago, when I was pregnant with Kayleigh. Ever since the glitch, my workout consists mostly of staring at the ceiling, waiting for doom.

The doorbell rings again. Probably a new guy. The regulars leave the groceries on the porch. Everything's paid on the app. I seldom let people see me. If I didn't have Kayleigh every other week, I'd have no face-to-face contact with anyone, except the ghosts.

Right after the glitch, I tried to be normal. I went to therapy, shopping, and PTA. I'd do morning runs. But, dogs would go crazy the second they caught wind of me. In stores and schools, little kids ran when they spotted me. At the support groups, my fellow glitchers wouldn't stop staring. It's like they'd never seen a seven-foot-tall, bald, musclebound woman with absurd breasts. Plus, you know, my retinue of wailing ghosts.

Again, the bell. I grab my phone and launch the app for my doorbell. "Leave the groceries," I say through the speaker. Then I glance at the screen. A four-foot-tall blue rabbit is standing on my welcome mat.

"Jason?"

"Sorry, Suzie," he says. If it's possible for a rabbit to sound sheepish, he nails it. "I work for GroceryGrabber now. Took this order without noticing the address. Since I'm here, I figured I'd say hello."

"Hold on." The ghosts warn of doom as I drag myself to my feet. I grab my robe, a 4x from the big and tall store.

I open the door and look down at Jason. He gazes at me with softball-sized eyes. They'd be cute in a cartoon. In real life, they're unnerving. "You expect me to believe this is a coincidence? I don't need you to check up on me."

"Right," says Jason. "I hustle through twenty deliveries a day on the off chance I might run into my ex-wife. You've seen through my fiendish plan."

"Why do you even need this job? You qualify for disability."

"Maybe I can't be a cop anymore, but I'm not disabled. I can walk, and I still have opposable thumbs." He holds up his hand, showing his bulbous fingers. "I'm just trying to get by as best I can."

"How noble of you."

"I'm not trying to be noble."

"No. You're humblebragging about how you're better at coping than I am."

"How is this about you?" he asks. "I'm just—"

"You're implying I should get on with my life even if I am a glitched-out freak."

"I know you get sick of people staring. I'm a cartoon rabbit; I get it. But, lots of glitchers have gone back to work. Maybe, when you have your surgery—"

I rub my eyes, trapped inside an argument we've had a hundred times. Jason believes my problems will be fixed with a boob job, like if I could fit into a b-cup again everything will go back to normal.

"You know the waiting list is, like, five years," I say. "There are glitchers waiting for mouths; I'm not a priority. Plus, there are things surgery can't fix."

"Doom is nigh! Repent! Repent!" the ghosts cry, proving my point.

Jason pretends not to notice. He changes tactics, telling me about Kayleigh's homework. He then asks about the house, whether anything needs fixing. I regret opening the door. I shut down his attempts at small talk. He's not here for small talk. He wants to talk about big things. He wants to tell me we're still a family. His optimism attracted me when I met him. Now, his positivity is poison. He acts like I'm the reason our lives were torn apart, acts like everything would be peachy if I showed a little grit.

Jason doesn't get it. Doom isn't nigh. Doom came and tore our world in two. Happy thoughts will never be enough to glue it back together.

After Jason leaves, I groan as I lower myself onto my yoga mat. My glitch body is inhumanly strong, but no match for my boobs. Even with my custom bras, my lower back feels full of broken glass. It doesn't help that I'm always hunched over to avoid hitting door frames.

I was logged into *Dragon Apocalypse* when the glitch hit. I was leveling up Rekka, a busty, half-naked Reaper of Souls. You might assume that Rekka was designed by some sexist male nerd with zero understanding of female anatomy, but, nope, Rekka's all mine. Years before the glitch, I did concept art for Greatshadow Games for their upcoming MMORPG. They wanted a body-builders-of-the-wasteland vibe and I was hungry for the paycheck. I was breastfeeding Kayleigh while I was drawing all these exaggerated physiques. Maybe a psychiatrist could explain why I made Rekka so busty. I never gave a second thought that her top-heavy torso would result in her lower vertebrae grinding into sand.

When the game went live after years of delays, I got a kick out of exploring the world I'd helped bring to life. Rekka was battling basilisks when the glitch happened. Everyone playing video games at 3:33 that afternoon physically transformed into their characters. Millions died in the days that followed. Some players glitched into monsters or aliens and were gunned down by cops. Even some glitchers who'd been playing humans, like soldiers or superheroes, wound up killing themselves. Life stops making sense when a stranger's face stares back from every mirror.

Was the glitch proof we lived in a simulation? Was it aliens softening us up for invasion? Had a Russian particle accelerator altered the laws of physics? No one knew. We still don't know.

"Repent, Suzie Durham!" the ghosts cry, breaking me out of my memories.

And I would repent, I would, if I still believed there was anyone to repent to.

It's Monday, and my week for Kayleigh. I'm strapped into my back brace and an industrial-strength bra. I lurch around the house vacuuming while I wait for the oven timer to chime. My kitchen might be the best smelling spot on the planet. I've been baking since dawn.

When Kayleigh's with her dad, I mope around in my robe and live on cold cereal. When Kayleigh's here I make an effort to eat real food. I dress in baggy sweaters and long, colorful skirts I make myself. I've picked up a slew of homemaking skills during my solitary confinement. If you'd told me when I was a purple-haired geek with three roommates that one day I'd be a suburban mom who collects cookbooks instead of comic books, I'd have laughed at you.

It wasn't easy training my oversized fingers to do even simple crafts like knitting. When I was an artist, I made a living with fine motor skills, but I can't make my hands do the intricate line work I used to be known for. After the glitch, Jason would buy me drawing pads and my favorite pencils, seemingly oblivious that any pencil I picked up snapped in two. I don't know. Maybe I should try drawing again. When I first glitched, I couldn't pick up eggs without crushing them. Now, I'm the queen of cakes and cookies.

Drawing was the talent of a Suzie Durham that glitched out of this world. It would feel like a betrayal to tread on her territory. Besides, my baking mania does help others. There's a glitcher shelter downtown. I ship them boxes of baked goodies every other week. My uncle swears he'd front me money to start my own bakeshop. He means well, but it would never work. People feel guilty enough about carbs without anguished ghosts scolding them with each bite.

The bus drops off Kayleigh as I pull the last cake from the oven. She'll be bummed that I don't have any cookies waiting for her, but her birthday is next month and I'm trying to level up my cake decoration. This batch of cakes used up the last of my flour. I've already ordered a twenty pound sack online, but it won't get here until Wednesday. Sorry, Kayleigh.

The second Kayleigh comes through the door, I stop stressing about a lack of cookies. The lights glow brighter when she's in the room. Her voice drowns out the ghostly murmurs. Kayleigh never pays any attention to my choir of the damned. As for my grotesque body, well, her dad's a rabbit. One of the kids in her class is an anime girl with a giant head. I can't decide if it's merciful or terrifying that she accepts all this as normal.

At 8:30 she starts getting ready for bed. A little while later, I've got her tucked in. I'm about to switch off the lights when she says, "Mom! I forgot! I need cookies tomorrow."

"What?"

"For the bake sale. There's a note from my teacher."

"Bake sale?"

"Check my book bag," she says. "I forgot to give you the note. Sorry. Love you!"

Back in the kitchen, I find the note, dated a full month before.

"Doom is nigh!" my ghosts inform me.

I glance at the clock. It's after nine, too late for a delivery. Should I call Jason? Asking him for anything gives him false hope.

Maybe I can slice up the cakes and send those? The teacher's note specifically says how much everyone loves my chocolate chip cookies.

The grocery store is a quarter mile away. I can get what I need and be back in thirty minutes.

Or…

I study my retinue of ghosts.

Jesus, I shouldn't try this. It probably won't work. Maybe it will. I mean, Rekka's whole gimmick is materializing ghosts to do her bidding. Why couldn't I send one to the store? In the early post-glitch, Jason begged me to test if my game powers worked in real life. He thought I might like having the ghosts wash dishes or fold laundry. I dug in hard against the idea. Conceding any upside to the glitch gave Jason ammunition for his weaponized pep talks.

Now, doom is nigh, and I'm desperate.

"Garnax!" I say. "I summon thee!"

The ghosts go silent. They're as shocked as I am. A shadowy fog takes substance before me. It's Garnax. He's a cult leader you fight in one of the first quests in *Dragon Apocalypse*, when you learn that children are disappearing from the village of Tondor. Garnax has no special powers, only a sacrificial dagger. After the dagger drinks the blood of a thousand innocents, it summons Horgoth the Sky Ripper. You capture the dagger after it's been used 999 times. If you're dumb enough to make the thousandth kill, summoning Horgoth is instant suicide. However, if you wait until level 40 and have a good enough team, you can battle Horgoth and capture his Crown of Wishes. It's a prize that justifies the dagger eating up an inventory slot.

Garnax is a pot-bellied loser. He's dressed in ragged, blood-soiled robes. I order him to wait, then run upstairs to grab some of my pre-glitch sweats.

Once I get him dressed, I hand him a five dollar bill and send him on his way. Right after the glitch, I'd make myself go shopping. Garnax has watched me walk to the store and buy stuff a dozen times. Maybe this is going to work.

Back in the kitchen, I measure the other ingredients. When Garnax gets back, I can throw it all together. The dough will need time to rest. I can set my alarm for 5 a.m., pop the cookies in the oven and get them bagged before Kayleigh's bus gets here. That's how you level up as a mom.

I set up the mixer and glance at the clock. I start to second guess myself. I mean, how can I even know if Garnax made it to the store? What if he fades out of existence once he's out of my sight? With my luck, right now there's a crumpled sweat suit outside the backdoor of my garage.

I go to the garage and look into the backyard. I don't see any abandoned sweats.

Then my heart skips a beat. There's a ladder leaning against the house at Kayleigh's window! I turn and see that the ladder in the garage is missing.

I race upstairs. I'm being crazy. The guy I hire to do the yard also cleans the gutters. He probably forgot to put the ladder back.

I open Kayleigh's door. Her bed is empty. The window is wide open.

"Oh no," I say.

My ghosts moan, "Repen—"

"Shut up!" They shut up. This is only going to buy me about two minutes of quiet.

I run back to the garage. I've got a gun safe there, bolted to the floor. It's not for guns. When I glitched, everything Rekka wore came over to the real world. She had a Scythe of Sorrows, a Sleep Wand, and Dragon Bone Armor. Leaving that stuff where Kayleigh could get at it would have been a major parenting fail.

The safe is wide open. Garnax was floating over my shoulder every time I've dialed the combination. My Sleep Wand is missing. So's the Dagger of Horgoth.

Doom is nigh.

Through the open door of the garage, I hear sirens. The sky over the nearby shopping center tints with flashing blue.

Stupid, stupid, stupid! When I sent Garnax to the store, I didn't specifically forbid stealing back his dagger or kidnapping a victim. His first goal will always be summoning Horgoth. So why didn't he stab Kayleigh in her room?

Horgoth is going to be hungry. Garnax needs a lot of warm bodies around for Horgoth to devour. Walking through a grocery store waving a dagger will draw a crowd of cops pretty fast.

I call 911, wasting precious minutes trying to explain what's happening to the dispatcher. I tell her that the cops need to pull back. Bullets can't hurt Garnax. Materialized ghosts can only be damaged by enchanted weapons. I sound deranged. The dispatcher keeps going, "Ma'am, slow down!"

I hang up. No one's going to believe me.

Except Jason. I call him as I pull the Dragon Bone Armor out of the locker.

"What's up?" he says, sounding wary.

"I summoned Garnax!"

"You what?"

I blurt out all I know and trust him to keep up. I tell him to use any contacts he still has on the force to get the cops to pull back. Kayleigh's in enough danger without adding stray bullets to the mix. I put Kayleigh in this mess. I'll get her out of it.

I finish buckling on the Dragon Bone Armor. Luckily, it fits okay over my clothes. Two boney dragon claws hold up Rekka's naked boobs in the game, but my heavy-duty bra shields me at least a little from their perma-grope. It's not the most dignified look, but the armor is enchanted to boost my strength and toughness. The second the claws grab hold, my back pain vanishes as magic floods through me.

I grab the Scythe of Sorrows and run out into the yard. I leap into the sky. The armor's wings of flame erupt from my shoulder blades. I soar over the rooftops, leaving a trail of sparks.

Flying over the grocery store, I look down onto a lot full of flashing lights. Every cop in the county has been called out for this, plus a couple of ambulances. Has Garnax killed anyone? Is Kayleigh still alive?

I see a cluster of unmarked vehicles with flashing lights. An older guy in a windbreaker is shouting orders to officers. He's who I need to speak to.

I land behind the cops, scythe in hand. I'm a menacing giant with demon wings. The cops open fire immediately. Luckily, with my magic armor, their bullets feel like marshmallows thrown by toddlers.

The guy in the windbreaker shouts, "Hold your fire!" He steps toward me. He looks familiar. This is the jerk who fired Jason! Jason glitched while playing *Critter Crossroads*. Officially, he didn't lose his job for being a giant rabbit, but because he'd been playing video games on his phone while on duty.

"Suzie? Suzie Durham?" the man says. My mind fumbles for his name. Captain Asshole is what Jason usually called him. Anderson!

"I'm glad you recognize me, Captain Anderson," I say. "The guy inside the store is bulletproof. I'm the only one who can stop him."

Anderson nods. "I just got off the phone with your husband."

I reflexively start to say ex-husband, but hold my tongue.

Anderson shakes his head, looking weary. "The world hasn't made a lick of sense since the glitch."

"Can you see Garnax?" I ask, noticing how many officers have scopes pointed at the store.

"The knife guy?" asks Anderson. "Yeah, he's not really hiding. He's holding a little girl hostage. Says he'll kill her if the clerks inside don't obey him."

"The little girl is my daughter, Kayleigh," I say.

"We've got a SWAT team positioned outside the stockroom," says Anderson. "Can Garnax be hurt by teargas?"

"Kayleigh can! Don't gas my daughter!"

"You got a better plan?"

"I can dematerialize Garnax if I get close enough to give the command."

"I can't let a civilian inside," says Anderson.

"I can't imagine how you'll stop me." I flap my wings and launch into the air. I zoom toward the front doors. They slide open as I swing my legs forward to land. I fold my wings back into the armor so I don't set the place on fire.

I hear Garnax shouting. It takes only a few seconds to make it to the baking aisle. He's had cashiers stack bags of flour into a sacrificial altar. Kayleigh is on the altar, sound asleep.

Garnax holds his dagger high over his head. In his other hand, he's carrying a bag of flour and the five dollars I gave him.

"Garnax!" I shout.

He looks at me with wide eyes. His ghostly face grows whiter.

"Return!"

Instantly, he poofs into fog, howling as he rejoins my ghostly retinue. The dagger and flour hang in midair above Kayleigh. They drop.

The bag of flour smacks Kayleigh on the thigh. She jerks from the impact, as the dagger falls half an inch from the side of her cheek. The sharp tip punches into the makeshift altar without ever touching her. I let out a long, slow breath.

Kayleigh sits up, looking confused. "Ooow," she groans, half asleep as she rubs her thigh.

"Kayleigh!" I cry, running toward her.

"Mom?" she asks, sounding baffled. She tries to stand, placing her hand on the altar to steady herself. She cries out and jerks her hand up. The side of her palm is bleeding. She's run it along the edge of the dagger.

The Dagger of Horgoth has tasted the blood of a thousand innocents.

"Doom!" my ghostly chorus screams. "*Doom is now!*"

A shaft of white light shoots up from the hilt of the dagger, burning a twenty-foot hole in the roof. I grab Kayleigh, holding her tightly as hurricane winds sweep through the store. Bags of flour burst and I'm engulfed in a blizzard, completely blinded.

I stagger through the aisles, sneezing and coughing. All around me, people are screaming. There's a crash as parts of the roof collapse. Outside, a war zone erupts as terrified cops open fire at the sky.

I stumble through the sliding doors, wiping my cheeks. My tears have covered my face in batter. I crouch behind a row of shopping carts, clutching Kayleigh to shield her from stray bullets.

"Mom!" Kayleigh screams. "What's happening?"

I know what's happening. Horgoth is coming. Oh God. What am I going to do? What can I do? There's no way I can ever let go of Kayleigh. If the world ends, it will end with her in my arms.

Then a blue, furry, three-fingered hand grabs my shoulder. I look up into Jason's enormous eyes. His whiskers twitch as he says, "I've got her! I've got her!"

"You shouldn't be here!" I scream at him. "I don't need you to save me!"

"I'm not here to save you! I'm here to protect Kayleigh while you save us! Fix this!"

"Are you crazy?"

"Trusting you is the opposite of crazy," Jason says. "You designed Horgoth. I'm guessing you designed a way to stop him!"

Jason never understood my job. All I did was concept art. Anytime I played the game, I had to figure out stuff like any other player.

On the other hand, I was the one who drew Horgoth with a crown, and jotted in the margins, "Crown of Wishes," not knowing the developers would actually use it in the game.

Jason peels Kayleigh from my arms. Lightning strikes the parking lot all around us. One second, there are cops standing behind a nearby car, then, *boom*, a bolt, and nothing but a crater.

Jason looks at me, worried but hopeful. I see myself reflected in his gaze, bristling with muscles and magic. He says, "You can do this!"

I draw back my shoulders, fists clenched. He's right. I'm Suzie Durham, Reaper of Souls. I can fix this!

I unfold my wings and soar out over the parking lot, spiraling up. Above the shopping center, the sky is torn in an endless gash across the stars. Through the gash I catch glimpses of a hellscape, lakes of lava and rivers of blood, not my most original work when I first sketched this exact scene. Still, all that red looks pretty good framing the black form of Horgoth. He's a dragon with wings about two miles across. He's covered with iron scales that crackle with lightning. His claws glow with eldritch energy as he tears the rip in the sky ever wider, trying to wriggle through. His head and neck are already on our side of the rift. I drew him using the skull of a prehistoric rhinoceros for reference. With the world on the verge of annihilation, am I a terrible person for noticing how awesome my creation looks in real life?

Here are my options. I can engage in battle with Horgoth and try to kill him fighting solo, which is crazy. Or I can skip the fight and go straight for the Crown of Wishes.

I command my ghosts to whirl right at Horgoth's face. While they distract him, I fly in a wide arc, coming in from the side. I rise through the rip in the sky hoping to get a clear shot at the back of Horgoth's head.

My breath catches as I pass through the rift.

I look back into the world and see... *everything*.

James Maxey

Literally everything, past, present, and fragments of futures. I'm in the Realm of Dark Gods. From here, I have the perspective of a god. So many of the invisible patterns that guide a person's destiny stand revealed. I see every moment that brought me to my present crisis. I finally understand what caused the glitch.

Horgoth wasn't created as part of a game. Horgoth has always existed. He moves from world to world, cracking open skies and feasting on the ripe planets below. To reach a new world, he needs a sucker to open a mystic portal.

While he couldn't enter our world physically without a portal, he could extend enough of his godly intelligence to plant visions of himself in receptive, creative minds. Our game became an entry way for people to believe in Horgoth and his magic. Once he had this toehold in our world, he used his Crown of Wishes to bring the game magic into the real world, and the wish slopped over into other digital realms, causing the glitch.

Horgoth did all this knowing it would lead to this moment, when he'd rip our sky in twain and devour billions of souls beneath it.

Since Horgoth used the Crown of Wishes to trigger the glitch, I can use the crown to undo it! I race down, leaving a trail of smoke. Horgoth unleashes a barrage of lightning from his scales. Despite my armor, the bolts knock me around. In my mind's eye, my life meter plunges from green to red. Then I notice the bolts are targeting the Scythe of Sorrows. I'm flying around with a lightning rod! I toss the scythe away and laugh as the lightning keeps striking it while I fly on unmolested.

I reach Horgoth's head and grab the crown, which is big enough that my whole house could fit inside. I'm grateful for my excessive muscles as I yank it free. Horgoth howls in protest. I soar away as the crown shrinks, exactly like it does in the game. I put it on.

The Crown of Wishes gives a wearer +50 insight. This means I'm crushed by +50 despair. My plan won't work. Horgoth is a god; his wishes can't be undone by mere mortals. My plan of undoing the glitch crumbles.

But as my magic insight fails, a lifetime of gaming kicks in. A mortal mind can't use the full power of the Crown of Wishes, but that's also true inside the game. No programmer could possibly code unbounded wishes; in gameplay, the wishes are a menu of specific options. Most often, players use the crown to unlock unique magic items. Another option is to wish yourself through time. You can send your character back to redo your completed quests, this time with the full powers and experience of your higher level self.

As I think through these possibilities, future timelines twist and tangle before me. I have a vision where I wish for a scythe that can kill Horgoth, but when his corpse falls from the sky it flattens the city. I think about going back in time and simply never drawing Horgoth. In that alternate reality, Horgoth simply appears in the dreams of another artist. The glitch still happens. I never switch bodies, but Horgoth makes it through anyway. What if I only jump back about an hour? Horgoth is still trapped in the Realm of Dark Gods, waiting for Garnax to summon him.

If I stay in the god realm long enough, maybe I'll see a better future. With each second, lightning decimates the world below. Half my neighborhood is a smoldering crater. The dead must number in the hundreds, maybe the thousands. Horgoth's maw opens wide to gulp down their souls. *I'm out of time!*

"I wish I'd never summoned Garnax!"

I blink. I'm back in my kitchen, holding Kayleigh's note about the bake sale. I'm no longer wearing my armor. My back is killing me.

I look in the garage. The ladder is still there. The gun safe is locked. I go upstairs and crack open Kayleigh's door. She's sound asleep. I gently close the door.

"Repent," moan the ghosts. "Doom is nigh!"

I roll my eyes. "You guys need some new material."

I grab my phone. A second later, Jason picks up.

"Something wrong?"

"I need to run to the store. I know it's a pain, but could you come over so that Kayleigh's not alone?"

"What do you need? I can get it for you."

"I think…." I pause, taking a deep breath. Jason ran to my side when the sky was literally being torn in two. He'd do anything for me, but there are things I've got to do for myself. "It's simpler if I go. I know what I need. I can't stay inside forever."

"Good for you," he says. This morning, I would have found his cheerleading condescending. I don't know. Maybe a little positive reinforcement isn't the worst thing.

As I hang up, I worry about what I've done. Maybe Jason thinks I'm inviting him back into my life. Maybe he thinks this is the first step toward being a family again. He's probably already daydreaming about us running a little Mom-and-Pop bakery together. He might be thinking of how good it would be for Kayleigh not to uproot her life every single week. More than anything, he wants our lives to go back to normal.

It won't happen. We can never be the people we once were. But maybe the people we've become should be allowed a chance at happiness.

I go to the gun safe. I contemplate it for a long minute, then dial the combination. The dagger is still there. I've watched a million YouTube videos on cake decoration. I wonder if there's a tutorial for melting down a dagger? That will have to wait until I've finished my cookie quest.

I strip down to my tights, put my magic armor on, then pull my sweater and skirt over the bones. I look ridiculous. My shoulder spikes poke through the wool. Luckily, late-night grocery store dress codes are notoriously lax.

I walk out to the front yard to wait for Jason. I stretch my arms overhead, a movement that normally brings me to the edge of tears. There's no pain at all. I wind up in tears anyway. My laughter drowns out my ghosts as I gaze into the untorn sky.

Angst of an Atomic Ant

Dr. Mayhem loomed over me as he adjusted the dials on an enormous machine. A beam of pulsing radiation inched closer and closer to me. Of course, at that moment, I didn't know his name, or even what a name was. Nor did I know what a dial was, or a machine, or radiation. How could I? I was only a tiny ant, with an infinitesimal brain, so small that Dr. Mayhem had required an electron microscope to cut open my carapace and implant almost invisible specks of metal and silicon into my rudimentary nervous system.

Then, *ZZZAP!* The radiation beam focused on me. The chemicals surrounding me in the petri dish vaporized. My carapace burned as the quantum computing microchips grafted onto my nerve cells soaked up all the energy being fed to them.

For a few minutes, everything was confusion. For reasons I couldn't yet comprehend, I was suddenly imbued with the knowledge of what words like "infinitesimal" and "rudimentary" meant. Worse, my point of view shifted, leaving me dizzy and discombobulated as all the objects around me became smaller and smaller.

Dr. Mayhem, who'd towered over me like a titan mere seconds before, shrank until he was only twice my size, then exactly my size, then half my size. When the shrinking stopped, *I* was towering over *him*, with my head pressed against the metal roof of the abandoned warehouse where he'd built his laboratory. It was then I understood that Dr. Mayhem and his equipment hadn't gotten smaller; I'd gotten bigger. Enormous! Colossal! Gargantuan!

Monstrous.

The realization of what I'd become flooded into me as I grappled with self-awareness for the first time. Dr. Mayhem had transformed me into a creature thirty feet tall and at least a hundred feet long. The quantum microchips grafted to my nervous system boosted my intelligence a million times over.

Despite the insights provided by my newborn intellect, I couldn't guess why Dr. Mayhem had not only turned me into a monster, but also made me a genius.

Though I had no vocal cords, I instinctively rubbed my middle leg against my abdomen, creating vibrations to produce sound. The torrent of new vocabulary gushing into my enhanced brain told me this process was called "striation." It took me only a few seconds to fine tune the vibrations until they formed the word, "Why?"

"Why?" Dr. Mayhem asked, his eyes narrowing as his lips curled into an evil grin. "For revenge, of course! Revenge against all those who mocked my genius! Revenge, most of all, against Mother Justice and the Virtue Battalion for daring to imprison me! All because I robbed a bank or two in order to fund my vital research! My embiggening ray could have changed the world! You, my greatest creation, shall make them pay for their insolence!"

I striated my abdomen once more. "I mean, why did you make me intelligent? Knowing what I've become is pure agony. Only a few hours ago, I was a worker in a colony, laboring alongside half a million brothers, faithfully serving our queen. Now, I'm alone, the first and last of my kind. You created me as an instrument for mindless destruction, then gave me a mind that comprehends my isolation? Was it mere cruelty that you inflicted me with this accursed knowledge?"

Dr. Mayhem shook his fist at me. "I certainly didn't give you intelligence so that you could ask foolish questions! By now, your quantum brain should have deduced the truth! Cease your prattling! It's time for you to trample my enemies into the dust!"

I tilted my head, gazing upon my creator through faceted eyes. There was something odd about my eyes, beyond the fact they were now several yards across. Each facet of my eye was seeing the world in different spectrums of energy. I could see the electrochemical impulses flowing in Dr. Mayhem's brain. My bio-electric intellect quickly deciphered these signals, decoding them by performing a quintillion equations in zeptoseconds. In enlarging my body, Dr. Mayhem had burdened me with so much mass I shouldn't have been able to stand under my own weight. He'd enhanced my brain to trigger latent psychokinetic powers. My power of mind-over-matter gave me unfathomable strength to crush Dr. Mayhem's foes. My self-awareness and alienated angst over what I'd become were merely unwanted side effects.

With my newfound intelligence being only a few minutes old, I had no emotional tools to handle the rage growing within me. I hated what I'd become, and hated the world that made my existence possible. Dr. Mayhem wished for me to destroy things? Well, why not? My mere existence was proof that there was no justice in the universe. Trampling a city into dust wouldn't solve my existential crisis, but it might provide welcome catharsis!

Before I could unleash my wrath upon my first and most obvious target, there was a bright flash, followed by a thunderous *BOOM!* My fore-legs were the size of tree trunks but still not wide enough to shield my eyes from the glare as the white hot molten remains of the roof fell into the room. The flaming slag splattered on my chitinous thorax. I reared onto my hind-limbs in pain, which tore away even more of the warehouse roof.

In the sky above me were three humans, a tall woman with her eyes covered by a blindfold, a burly man with a jetpack and camouflage fatigues who carried what looked like a cannon, and a slender girl with neon blue hair who flitted about the sky, her blurred limbs emitting a loud buzz.

"It's over, Dr. Mayhem!" the blindfolded woman called out. "Hummingbird, grab the doctor! Thundergun, keep his monster busy!"

Before I could rub my abdomen to form the word "wait," the man with the huge gun took aim and pulled the trigger. There was another blinding flash and a deafening clap of noise. Something slammed into my thorax, knocking me backward. I flailed about, completely blind and deaf. Ants don't have ears; we sense sounds by feeling vibrations in our legs. Right now my entire exoskeleton was ringing like a bell. I writhed on my back in helpless confusion.

Fortunately, my discombobulation lasted only a fraction of a second. The quantum circuits grafted to my nerves processed information at the speed of light. I swiftly remembered that the entire purpose of this circuitry was to empower me with telekinesis. With a thought, I silenced my ringing carapace and floated into the air, righting myself. By willpower alone, I reset the photoreceptors in my light-blasted eyes to restore my vision.

Thundergun took aim at me once more, plainly consternated that his first shot hadn't finished me off. This time, before he could pull the trigger, it was a simple matter to pulverize every bone in his fingers with but a thought. With a tiny bit more concentration his entire gun fell apart into a pile of fragmented metal.

"A little help here!" Thundergun screamed, holding his injured hand. He looked at the blindfolded woman floating overhead; Mother Justice, I presumed. "This monster is tougher than it looks!"

"Tougher, smarter, and even more enraged than I was before you showed up," I shouted as I rose higher. I no longer even needed to rub my abdomen to make sound. I could simply vibrate the air with my mind to give voice to my agonized thoughts. "You attacked without provocation! You fear what you don't understand!"

"We understand you're a mutant abomination created by a madman to destroy everything in its path!" shouted Thundergun.

"Hmm," I said. "I suppose humans can also fear what they *do* understand. And rightly so! I'll destroy you all… once I've killed the monster that created me!"

With a speed that no doubt surprised my attackers, I flew toward Dr. Mayhem, my mandibles opening wide, intending to snap him in half. The blue-haired girl, Hummingbird, buzzed in from the side and grabbed the deranged scientist, zipping him clear of my snapping bite.

Fast as she was, Hummingbird could never fly faster than the speed of thought. With my faceted, multi-spectrum vision, I could see her muscles and skeleton moving in concert to create her rapid flight. With no effort at all, I willed the tendons of her left rotator cuff to rip.

Hummingbird cried in pain as she plummeted. Inches from the floor, Thundergun zoomed in with his jetpack and caught her and Dr. Mayhem. Annoyed, I ruptured the fuel line of Thundergun's jetpack. Flames flew back along his legs as the three of them corkscrewed into a high speed spin before smashing through the far wall of the warehouse. Thundergun twisted his body at the last second, either by chance or design, to take the brunt of the impact.

From the tangle of bodies that now lay beyond the wall, Dr. Mayhem rose on trembling legs. I floated toward him, watching his eyes go wide with terror.

Mother Justice drifted down from the heavens, placing herself between me and my accursed creator.

"That's enough," she said, holding her upraised palm toward me. "I can't let you kill Dr. Mayhem."

"Why not?" I demanded. "He's your enemy! You should be glad I'm doing your job for you!"

"Our job isn't to kill him. It's not even our job to punish him. We only want to arrest him, to turn him over to the proper authorities so that he can't hurt anyone else."

"He's already hurt me! I demand vengeance!"

"I can't permit vengeance," she said. "I can only promise you justice."

"Justice?" I said, as my computer brain fed me waves of wireless information. I instantly comprehended the American judicial system, and its pathetic inadequacies. "You think throwing him into a prison cell can ever fix the harm he's done to me?"

"No," said Mother Justice. "But letting victims seek their own revenge is a path to anarchy. We do what we must to preserve the common good."

"What does the common good of mankind matter to me?"

"You're an ant," said Mother Justice. "Of all the species on earth, yours should grasp the importance of selflessly acting for the good of all, rather than selfishly seeking to serve yourself. Humans and ants aren't all that different. We do our best when we work together."

"If I were still an ant, I might believe this," I said, feeling a wave of sorrow building beneath my still boiling rage. "But I'm a monster now, all alone, never to be reunited with my brothers. There can be no justice for me. Revenge is all that remains! Stand aside, or I'll scatter your molecules into the stratosphere!"

"Do what you must," said Mother Justice. "I won't stand aside."

I glowered at her, my anger building. Yet... there was something in her face. A look of calm resolution that unnerved me. Did she have some trick, some hidden power I was unaware of that might be capable of inflicting harm upon me?

To my surprise, she answered my unspoken question.

"I don't have the strength to harm you. If you choose to kill me to reach Dr. Mayhem, I can't stop you."

"You... you're telepathic," I said. "You're reading my thoughts."

"Yes," she said.

"I'm wondering why you aren't fleeing in terror, if you can see the rage within me."

"I see the pain within you," she said. "A pain that comes from loneliness. Just like in all the others."

"The others?" I asked.

"You aren't the first giant insect that Dr. Mayhem has brought into the world," said Mother Justice. "Or the first we've stopped from murdering him."

"By stopped, you mean you killed the other monsters," I said. While she could see into my thoughts, her thoughts were hidden from me. "You can't let something like me simply wander free in the world."

"We can," she said. "Admittedly, it's a somewhat small part of the world. There's an island in the Pacific that the United Nations has transformed into a preserve where creatures like you can live in peace, far removed from mankind."

"A prison," I said.

"A home," she said. "Not all of Dr. Mayhem's creations have been as intelligent as you are. With the right leadership, the island might be transformed into a paradise."

"Now that you've told me of such a place, I can find it without your help," I said. "There's no reason I shouldn't go ahead and crush Dr. Mayhem's skull like a melon!"

"Please don't crush my skull like a melon," Dr. Mayhem whimpered.

Addressing him directly, I snarled, "You made me a monster! Now you beg me for mercy?"

Dr. Mayhem dropped to his knees, lifting his hands toward me. "Begging! Yes! I'm begging you!"

"I'm not begging," said Mother Justice. "I'm only clarifying your options. You can kill him and forever be the monster he wanted you to be. You can let him live and define your own identity. Dr. Mayhem might have created you, but only you can choose what to do with your life."

I contemplated my choices, searching through the collected online libraries of mankind, absorbing every digitized line of literature and philosophy in the time it took a tear to trace its way down Dr. Mayhem's cheek.

As I analyzed the wisdom of ages, I saw the uncomfortable truth. The fact that I'd been born meant I was now fated to die. Dr. Mayhem, too, would die, as would Mother Justice, as would the very planet I stood upon, one day, when a swollen sun consumed it in its final dying throws. In the Ozymandian vastness of time, whether I killed Dr. Mayhem mattered nothing at all.

"Are we truly born only to die?" I groaned.

"Welcome to the human condition, Bub," said Thundergun who was back on his feet, clutching his ribs. "Or the inhuman condition, in your case."

"Our time upon this world is finite," said Mother Justice. "Which means we must make the most of each moment granted to us. Do you want to live the remaining span of your life as a killer, or as a being capable of wisdom and mercy?"

I nodded slowly, weighing both paths.

"I shall spare him," I said to Mother Justice.

"I knew you would. As for getting you to the island, we can arrange——"

"There's no need," I said, rising into the air. "Your thoughts are hidden, but your companions are open books. I see the location of the island in their minds. I can travel there under my own power."

I glanced at Thundergun and Hummingbird, both of them battered and bloodied. I saw their broken bones and internal injuries caused by my attack. With all the medical knowledge of humanity flowing into me, I used my telekinesis to knit their bones, muscles and blood vessels back into proper order.

"Safe journey," said Mother Justice. "I hope you'll no longer feel alone once you reach the island!"

"Loneliness is my destiny," I said to her as I hovered over the destroyed roof. "But, with my fellow atomic insects, perhaps there will be comfort in being alone, together."

I turned my faceted eyes toward the west, seeing the distant Pacific in my mind's eye. The wind roared across my carapace as I soared toward infinite possible futures.

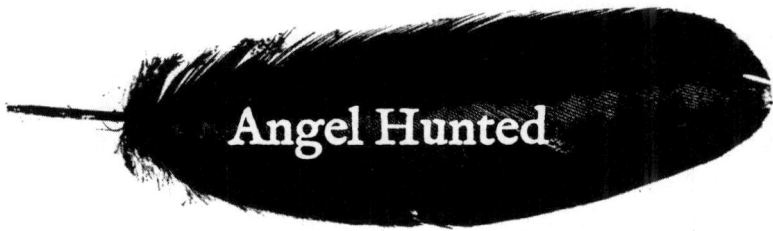

Angel Hunted

1. Scientist

Albert was afraid to open his eyes. Something very bad had happened—he couldn't recall exactly what. His body remembered what his mind couldn't. His heart raced, ready to burst. His fingers were thrust firmly in his ears. His jaw clenched, his teeth aching, as he waited for the next awful shock.

Flat on his back, holding his breath, Albert waited for an endless, horrible moment. Then, somehow, the endless moment gave way and time returned. Nothing had happened. What exactly was he afraid of? Why couldn't he remember?

Albert gingerly pulled his fingers from his ears. The world didn't sound terribly frightening. Birds were singing, a nearby brook was gurgling, a light breeze stirred the leaves of trees. He hadn't heard a bird in years. And trees? After the bombs, there shouldn't be any trees. The bombs? The bombs. The bombs were part of the horrible thing he couldn't remember.

In addition to the birds and the trees, the other novel sensation was sunlight on Albert's skin. It warmed his body and made his eyelids glow, tempting him to peek. He still couldn't find the courage. Still, it felt pleasant, all over his chest and legs.

Wait. Was he naked? Why would he be naked? He reached down and touched his body, quickly pulling his hand away. He was, in fact, naked. And plainly outdoors. In what certainly sounded like some sort of park. His terror dimmed, replaced with a growing embarrassment. He wasn't sure what to do with his hands. If people were watching, was it more embarrassing to cover his genitals with his hands, or keep his hands as far from his genitals as possible? He decided to stretch his arms far out to the sides of his body, his palms outstretched, facing up.

He flinched as something hard fell into his open palm. What was it? Something warm, round, firm yet soft, its surface covered in a fuzz of fine hair. It felt almost like a tiny baby's severed head. The bombs! The dead were falling from the sky!

But when he found the stem, he decided the object in his hand felt more like a large peach than a baby's head. But why should peaches be falling from the sky?

Albert opened his eyes. Albert's curiosity always won out over his fears. He risked gazing upon a post-bomb world of horrors simply to discover that the object in his hand was, after all, a peach. He sat up. For as far as he could see, the world was made of food. Apple orchards grew next to orange groves beyond which were bananas and plums, all tangled with grapevines and raspberries. Did even the tropics have such a mix of fruit?

The climate didn't remind him of the tropics. The rolling land and gentle air reminded him of the Swiss hills he'd roamed in his youth. Absent-mindedly, he bit into the peach. Its juices were sweet, its aroma heavenly. Why had he awakened in such terror? Had he been having a nightmare? Or perhaps it was more likely that he was still asleep, and this was all a dream?

No. This was actually happening. Perhaps his eyes could be deceived, but his nose? His tongue? His fully exposed and well-warmed skin? Just where had his clothes gotten too anyway?

Suddenly, he remembered. His clothes had burned away. He'd been on fire, the air itself had burned. He remembered the air raid sirens, and the stale taste of his own breath in the gas mask as he lifted the little girl who had fallen on the rubble-strewn street. He had turned back to the shelter, the weight of the child tearing open the half-healed wound in his leg and then... and then he had gone deaf, and his clothes were on fire, and the child's hands were pulling at his hair and... beyond that his memory failed. His memory was always failing these days, though not as much as he wished. There was so much he wanted to forget.

Perhaps he'd died on that war shattered street. Perhaps the bomb he'd help create was finally used. He was dead, and this was... Heaven?

Albert didn't believe in Heaven. And if one should exist, he, of all people, would be the last person to deserve an eternal reward. Albert shook his head. A rabbi could pursue this line of thought, but he didn't trust it. There must be another answer. Others found his thinking almost mystical, taking place in some abstract world beyond sight and sound and touch. Nothing was further from the truth. As a scientist, Albert possessed a zealous love of reality, and the first source for discerning reality must be the senses. The peach-juice still on his lips, the sun on his back, the prickly green grass beneath his legs—all real. He had to accept this.

He cleared his throat.

"My name is Albert Einstein," he said. It sounded right. He could accept this as fact. So he moved on to a more challenging assertion: "I'm not dead."

"Are you sure of that?" asked a voice behind him, a strong, deep voice that resonated with the beauty of warm brass.

Albert turned. Behind him stood a man, taller than average, his skin like molten copper, his long hair flowing like spun gold. He wore white robes that seemed woven from clouds, and from his back grew silver wings that stretched out to twice the length of his body.

"Ah," said Albert. "You never know."

2. Angel

"An angel!" said Albert, in a voice half giggle, half sob. "I bet my soul your kind didn't exist. A poor bet, it seems. Ah, but you never know. You never know."

"But you *will* know. You, alone, will truly know," the stranger said. "None of the others I've brought here could ever hope to understand what was happening. Of all the humans ever born, you alone possess the genius to truly understand your fate."

"Genius?" said Albert, amused by the word in this context. "Do you know the original meaning of the word? A spirit! A watching angel! I'm no genius. Though you, perhaps, are the genuine article?"

"The genuine genius," the angel agreed. "A watching spirit. I've had my eye on you for quite some time."

"I see," Albert said. "So. This is Heaven?" The word sounded strange coming from his mouth.

The angel chuckled mirthlessly. "You think you'd be permitted even a glimpse of Heaven."

"No. But where else could we be? Certainly Hell couldn't be such a paradise?"

"This is the Garden of Eden. It's more suitable to my purposes than Heaven. Hazraphet, the angel who guarded the gate, didn't have any objection to my using it. At least, none he mentioned while I was carving his heart out with his own flaming sword."

"Ah. Then you are no angel," said Albert. "Which makes you... a devil?"

"Neither," the stranger said. "I'm an archangel. *The* archangel, now. The others are long since dead."

"Ah. I see," said Albert. "And would you have a name?"

"Of course," the archangel said. "And to know an angel's name gives you great power. Fortunately, my name is a string of seven heavenly syllables that cannot be uttered by any human tongue."

Albert thought this was a strange thing to feel fortunate about. The archangel paused, as if to allow the drama of the moment to sink in. Then he said, "If you insist upon naming me, in many human cultures, I was known as Gabriel."

Albert started to say, "Pleased to meet you," but he wasn't, so he didn't. Instead he said, "You said I alone would understand my fate? I fear I shall disappoint you. I don't understand what's happening at all."

"Let's run over the highlights. First, I've brought you here to kill you."

"Ah," said Albert. "Then I'm not dead."

"That's... relative," said Gabriel. "If there were such a thing as absolute time, then yes, you died several millennia ago. The whole Earth is dead, in fact. It never recovered from the unity bomb."

"The... unity bomb. The Nazis built one?" Albert asked.

"Three. Only one was used. No one was alive to trigger the final bombs."

Despite the bright sun, all the warmth in Albert's body vanished. His worst fears had been realized.

"*Mein Gott,*" he said, his voice choked. "*Mein Gott.*"

"God's gone," said Gabriel. "He hadn't really been interested in the Earth since the trilobites died, and had no interest in starting creation again after all his old work had been destroyed."

Albert wiped his cheeks, his tears glistening in the fine hairs on the back of his hand. He noticed how young his skin looked. He clung, once more, to the last, desperate hope that this was, after all, a dream. He should just ignore Gabriel, this strange figment of his demented mind, and try to sleep again. Alas, already his curiosity was three steps ahead of his better judgment. "Trilobites? Why would God have cared about Trilobites?"

"He was one," said Gabriel. "Four-hundred miles long, with a shell like black pearl. Gazing into the surface of God was like looking into an eternal void, a blackness that devoured all. He was a majestic creature, all wrath and glory. To see him in the ocean depths, churning the primordial muck, giving birth to countless new life forms from little squiggles of clay... I miss Him, truth be told. It's your fault he's gone."

"My fault?" said Albert.

"The Unity Theory was quite a nice bit of work, for a human. The angels never dabbled much with math. God was delighted by your insight into the structure of reality. Your unification of quantum mechanics and relativity revealed possibilities God had never contemplated—time-travel, alternate histories, other universes. God left for a world where he'd never lost his temper and wiped out the trilobites. I assume he's happy."

"God... found delight in my theory?" said Albert, wiping his eyes. "This is curiously satisfying. The thirst for knowledge, the quest to understand creation. In my heart I've known these things to be... holy. I've often wondered if, should there be a God, curiosity was his gift to mankind."

"God gave you nothing," said Gabriel. "After God lost interest in the Earth, we angels dabbled for a while with our pet projects. Metatron, the angel of the dinosaurs, was rather successful for a while. Then came the age of mammals, and Metatron's star faded. Michael was the angel who most liked to mess with you monkeys. He's the one who built this Garden, a laboratory for perfecting the human diet. Perhaps God approved of our tinkering, but who knows? Angels could no more understand God than you monkeys could understand the minds of angels."

"Ah," said Albert.

"You say that a lot," said Gabriel. "Ah."

"And is it for this you are going to kill me?"

"Don't be absurd. I'm going to kill you for sport."

3. Sport

"You'll kill me for sport?" Albert said. "Because… because of what I did? To help create the bombs that destroyed the world? This is my punishment."

Gabriel laughed. "Oh, what an ego you have. You think you matter enough to be punished? Don't be absurd. I'm going to kill you simply because I enjoy killing things. After God left, we angels no longer had any sense of purpose. We had to find new ways to amuse ourselves. Hunting fills my days nicely. You humans are turning out to be fine prey. I overlooked your species for a long time, only partially because you were extinct. I never imagined you'd be better prey than my angelic kin. But when I beheaded Asrafel of the Seraphim, I recalled that he once lost a fist-fight with one of your kind, a strange little monkey named Jacob."

"I know that story," said Albert. "Jacob wrestled the angel, and the angel was overcome."

"Yes, but the story leaves out the fact that Asrafel was drunk off his ass. I wasn't sure if Jacob really beat him, or if Asrafel had choked on his own vomit and passed out. Anyway, using the time warp equations present in your unification theory, I plucked Jacob out of the time curve and brought him here. Jacob was quite entertaining. Not any real challenge, of course, but he fought dirty, in ways angels would never dream of. He gouged out one of my eyes with his thumb! He bit off part of my nose! Invigorating!"

"You seem to have recovered."

"In seconds," Gabriel said, smiling broadly. "But it was his spirit that counted. The angels always knew that they weren't my equal. Jacob actually thought he had a chance, up till the moment I plucked his arms from their sockets. Killing his hope, watching his pride drain from him as he staggered about unable to wipe the tears from his eyes, provided me with immense satisfaction."

Albert sighed. "I fear I must disappoint you." He raised his open palms. "I'm a pacifist. I won't fight you out of principle."

"Principle!" Gabriel laughed, a harsh sound like clashing cymbals. "You still believe you hold some moral high ground? You killed everyone on Earth with your beloved principles. You solved the Unification Equation. It occurred to you before you ever published your work that the most direct way to test your theory would be to build a bomb. You published anyway, believing that anyone with the intelligence to understand your theory would also possess the wisdom not to build such a device. This, even though you'd already been forced to flee Germany to avoid the atrocities of the Nazis. You knew the evil that lurked within men. Publishing your equation was like giving toddlers a box full of hand grenades. What did you think would happen?"

"Enough," said Albert. "I know my mistakes better than you. The Nazi's saw Jews as animals, and I thought much the same of them. I thought all true scientists would flee their regime."

"You never believed anyone who could embrace the Nazi philosophies would have the intelligence to grasp your equation. Your reputation was great enough that you were able to convince the Americans not to pursue their own bomb program."

"What would it have availed? My estimation of Nazi intelligence have proven correct," Albert said. "The Unity bombs must have destroyed so great a portion of the Earth's atmosphere as to make it uninhabitable. With their own stupidity, the Nazis destroyed themselves along with everyone else."

"Yes. They killed themselves. You were right about human stupidity. Does that give you satisfaction?"

"None. Which is all the more reason I will not fight you. Do you imagine I don't understand my guilt? Kill me now. Make is as painful and degrading as you desire. If you like, I will scratch you a little, if that will give you any amusement. At least my life will have done some small good for someone."

Gabriel grinned. "You shall not disappoint me, Albert Einstein. You're correct. It wouldn't be any fun to kill you now, when you desire death. Which is why you're in the Garden of Eden. It's very difficult to not enjoy life while you're here."

"Ah. You may underestimate my capacity for thwarting my own happiness."

"We'll see. I've plucked your body from Switzerland, on the day of your twenty-third birthday, at the peak of your physical prowess. I've plucked your mind from forty-three years later, as the burning atmosphere ate through your flesh. Only then could I be assured you'd gained wisdom to match your formidable intellect. Now, you're at the peak of your mental and physical prowess, surrounded by a paradise designed for your comfort and pleasure. You shall enjoy your time here, I promise you."

"Perhaps you should have consulted my ex-wives. They would have been glad to inform you that any happiness I lay my hands upon is swiftly dissected, drowned in formaldehyde and placed upon slides for microscopic analysis. On a subatomic scale, I've found the universe to be built of fundamental particles of misery."

"You think yourself cynical," said Gabriel.

"Am I not?"

"Your cynicism is a disguise. A mask that fools even you, perhaps. But behind that mask is a man who takes joy from his understanding of creation. That is the man I want to hunt."

"Ah. I'll be whoever you wish," said Albert. "Let's finish this."

"I will not kill you today, Albert Einstein. You may again be an old man before I come for you. But when I come, you will fight me, with a thirst for life you've never before known. When I come, you will die in ways you can't imagine."

With those words, Gabriel was gone. Albert looked around. Gabriel had simply vanished between blinks. Only the bent blades of grass where the angel had stood gave evidence to his presence. Albert wished he could dismiss the episode as a hallucination, but the evidence of reality was too strong. He was young again. He rubbed his bare legs. His muscles were hard as metal cable beneath the skin. These were the legs that had propelled his bicycle across countless miles of mountainous roads. His legs felt good. He felt healthy, at least physically, better than he had in decades.

He was trapped in the Garden of Eden, he'd just had a conversation with a sadistic angel, the world had been destroyed, it was all his fault, and he felt amazing.

"Ah. I'm mad, of course," he said, but he didn't believe it. He collapsed onto the warm grass, and laughed until his face hurt.

4. Curvature

"Gabriel must believe I'm an idiot," Albert said, shaking his head and turning away. Not that he turned away too quickly. The young woman stretched out sleeping by the pond was comely, long and lithe, with dark hair and well-rounded breasts. An obvious temptation for a lesser man, but if Gabriel had been around, Albert would gladly have lectured him on the folly of his ways. Never again would he be tempted by a woman. His marriages had been miserable. Women simply never fit comfortably into his life. The moments when he'd been most deeply in thought, contemplating the mathematics of space and time, would always be the moments when his first wife would decide it was absolutely vital to discuss why he hadn't picked up his socks from beside the bed. By the time of his second marriage, to simplify his life, he stopped wearing socks. To simplify his life further, after his second wife left, he'd decided never to again to waste his energies on trying to understand a woman. The curvature of space-time, yes, this he could fathom. The twists and turns of a woman's mind? Impossible! Fortunately, the garden was vast. With proper precautions, he need never cross paths with the woman again. He walked away, feeling some slight satisfaction that he could so easily best Gabriel's manipulations.

A hundred feet on his journey away from the woman, he stopped. Gabriel had indicated that he hunted and killed men. Could he have hunted women as well? If the angel enjoyed a dirty fight, it seemed almost inevitable. He'd assumed the woman by the lake was sleeping. What if she was dead? Had his heart grown so cold that he would deny her a burial?

"Hush," he said to the voice within him. "Don't fall for his trickery. Keep moving."

But what if she were wounded? What if Gabriel hadn't finished her off? Perhaps she was suffering, dying by inches?

"Ah. Don't be a fool," he said.

But he *was* a fool. No matter what course of action he decided on live, again and again, his chosen paths always led to disaster. Walk away, or return to bury her, ruin faced him either way.

"Shut up," he said. "See if she is alive. If so, walk away."

Albert sighed. Why could he never win an argument with himself?

As he approached the woman, he grew more certain she was dead. She hadn't moved even slightly, and looked far too pale. Even a few yards away, he couldn't see her breathing. Of course, his innate decency kept him from staring at her torso too closely. Since he was still naked himself, he hoped, if she did awaken, she would return the courtesy. Still, he had to at least observe her closely for wounds.

With analytical eyes, he surveyed her body. If not for the hairiness in appropriate places, she might almost have been a marble statue, crafted by some soulful sculptor. What a pity that even one of such physical beauty wasn't immune to Gabriel's evil.

More certain than ever she was dead, Albert knelt next to her. He placed his hand upon her neck to check for a pulse. Instantly, her skin warmed, and her color darkened. Her eyes opened.

"Heeyah!" she cried. Her fist shot forward, striking Albert hard on the nose. He fell on his butt as she leapt to her feet.

"Keep your hands off me you son of a bitch!" she snarled, placing her legs far apart and waving her hands before her in a snaky, sinuous motion. "Heeyah! Yah!"

"Ah. I knew this was a bad idea," said Albert, carefully prodding his bleeding nose with his fingers.

"Damn straight, it was a bad idea," she said. "Give me back my clothes before I kick in your teeth!"

"Madam," he said, holding up his open palms. "There has been a misunderstanding—"

"Heeyah!" she cried, and kicked out. Fortunately, his teeth proved sturdier than either of them imagined. He was only knocked flat on his back by the blow.

She loomed over him. "Ain't nothing to understand, Buster. All I know is I wake up with a naked man crouching over me and my clothes are gone and I'm God knows where!"

Albert rolled on his back in the grass, trying to sit up. He failed miserably.

The woman circled around him, swaying like a dancer. He'd heard of the martial arts, kung fu and judo, but had never before seen them practiced. How could something that looked so silly be so effective? He wiped the blood that trickled from his mouth with his forearm.

"There's more where that came from," she said. "So talk. Where the hell am I? How long was I out?"

"We're in the Garden of Eden."

"Right," she said, then danced forward and delivered a solid kick to his ribs. "You want to give me the straight answer?"

"Madam," Albert gasped. "The only thing I want is for you to stop kicking me!"

"So, talk. How long was I out? Where am I?"

Holding up his open palms once more, Albert said, "I may be able to answer you, but first, what is your last memory?"

The woman continued to lunge and sway in orbit around him. He could see in her eyes that she was actually thinking over his question.

"Are you a spy?" she growled.

"No."

Her movements slowed. Her brow furrowed. She appeared to be distracted by her memories as they returned. Albert thought of making a run for it.

She said, "Okay. I was... I was in Canada? When the Nazis started coming over the North Pole, Truman opened up the forces to any able bodied person and I volunteered. Three months later, I was working with a surgical crew fifty miles from the Canadian front line. I was in a truck with the rest of my unit when... maybe we hit a mine? There was fire. I couldn't breathe. The next thing I know, I'm here, wherever here is. Is this Florida? California? It was snowing in Canada."

"I don't think it ever snows here," said Albert. "If I told you again that we are in Eden, would you kick me?"

"Yes."

"Then you are in California."

5. The Whole Naked Thing

"You're lying," she said, bouncing around with fresh energy, looking like she was trying to figure out which part of his body she wanted to kick next.

"Ah. You have good instincts," said Albert, sitting up. "The fact that you can tell when I'm lying should let you trust me when I'm telling the truth, yes?"

"Trusting you is the last thing I got planned. Even overlooking the fact you were about to rape me!"

"I swear I was merely checking your pulse."

"Yeah, and there's a bridge in Brooklyn I'd like to sell you. You think I don't notice your accent? You're a Hun!"

"Please," said Albert.

"Don't deny it."

"I'm a Jew," said Albert. "I renounced my German citizenship decades ago."

The woman narrowed her eyes and looked him over. She folded her arms across her breasts.

"Yeah," she said. "You kind of look Jewish. Honestly, you kind of look like a young version of that old guy in the newsreels. The bastard who said we should stay out of the war. What's his name? Einstein."

"Would you kick me if I told you my name was Einstein?"

"Definitely."

"Ah. Then my name is Al."

"Okay, Al. Care to take a stab at explaining where my clothes are?"

"Well," he said. "Ah."

Albert stroked his jaw. Should he go with the truth, getting kicked again and again until she listened? Truth had always been his one, true religion. Now, he found himself embracing the religion of not getting kicked again.

"I'm waiting," she said.

"You were, ah, quite injured by the... by the mine," Albert said, watching her closely for any sudden movement. "You have, ah, you've been in a coma. The army brought you here. To Florida. Obviously. To this special hospital. They have this therapy here, you see, where they.... where they treat coma patients with direct sunlight. This is why they needed to undress you."

She frowned, but didn't look ready to strike. "You don't sound too convincing."

"Ah. There's a simple explanation," said Albert. He looked down at the grass, gathering his thoughts. Blood dripped from his nose, flecking the deep green grass with red. "I'm a patient also. Yes. I've only recently revived. I'm still suffering disorientation. From a head injury. I may lapse back into my coma if you strike me again."

The woman lowered her arms.

"Really?" she asked.

Albert stood up, with a fresh ruefulness of his lack of clothing. If he'd had a shirt, he could have sopped up the blood on his face.

"Maybe I should go get you a doctor," she said.

"The doctors are all on vacation."

"Then a nurse—"

"You said you were a nurse," Albert said.

"I never said I was a nurse," she answered, sounding suspicious.

"You're a woman, assigned to a medical unit—"

"How do you know I ain't a doctor?"

"Are you a doctor?"

"No. You're right. I'm a nurse. Just don't go assuming things about me."

Albert rubbed his temples. "Conversations like this are why I stopped wearing socks."

"What?"

"It's not important," Albert said. "But since you're a nurse, perhaps you can care for my bleeding nose?"

"I ain't got any supplies," she said, rolling her eyes. "I'd need some cotton for your nose, and some alcohol for your split lip. For the time being, tilt your head back and pinch your nose."

Albert did so.

"I know what's going on here," she said.

"Elaborate," he said.

"You're embarrassed. You don't want to go get a doctor because you'd have to tell them you were beaten up by a woman."

"That is the least of my worries."

"Then I'll be right back." She looked around, at the tree covered hills, then asked, "Which way to the hospital?"

"Back," said Albert.

"Back?"

"Back in time a few thousand years."

"You feeling confused again, Al?"

"What's your name?" he asked.

"Zoe. Zoe Monroe."

"A lovely name. Zoe, are you sorry you hit me?"

"A little, maybe. I was just surprised and, you know. There's the whole naked thing."

"So you won't hit me again, even if you don't like some of the things I say?"

"I can't promise that."

"Ah. How about this? Give me five minutes to say whatever crazy thing I want. Promise you won't hit me during those five minutes."

"Five minutes." Zoe nodded.

"Good," Albert said. He noticed how stupid his voice sounded with his nose pinched. He decided he preferred the bleeding, and let go. "You and I are the only two people alive."

Zoe shook her head. "Now we really need a doctor. I done kicked the sense out of you."

"Zoe, there are no doctors any more. Well, technically, I'm a doctor, but not a medical doctor. I *am* Albert Einstein, from the newsreels. This is the Garden of Eden. We are only alive because an angel named Gabriel is bored. Remember I have at least four minutes before you kick me again."

Zoe frowned. "I can't tell if you're bonkers, or just trying to be funny. And failing, if you are."

"Ah. I don't see why it couldn't be both. Alas, I fear, it's neither. Everything I've said is serious."

"Just wait here," Zoe said, her voice suddenly gentle. "I think you might have a major brain injury. Let me get a doctor. And find us both some clothes, for Christ sake."

Zoe ran towards the highest hill, occasionally looking back, perhaps to see if he was chasing her. Albert stumbled toward the pond, dropping to his knees. He splashed cool water onto his bloodied face.

"Keep running, Zoe," he said, though she couldn't hear him. "There's a madman on the loose." The surface of the pond returned to mirror stillness as the last of the water dripped from his face. "Ah. There he is now."

6. Hoo Boy

After Zoe vanished over the hill, Albert walked in the opposite direction. He'd been here almost a day now, and had already discovered that the Garden covered a vast area. With luck, he could avoid Zoe and her kicks for quite a long time. She was obviously able-bodied, and seemed reasonably intelligent. If she'd served in the army, she was probably better trained at surviving in the wilderness than he was. She'd do fine without him.

He wondered exactly how big the Garden was. He had time on his hands. Mapping his surroundings would make a good project. Gabriel had said it might be a long time before he returned. Perhaps some sort of shelter should be constructed. Clothing, too, might be made somehow. He couldn't quite see himself dressed in animal pelts, but no doubt in all this botanical diversity there were hemp or cotton plants. He didn't know how to spin such fibers into thread, but how hard could it be to figure out? Then again, clothes had always been such a nuisance. In his final years, he'd simplified his wardrobe down to a single suit, two shirts, and a week's worth of underwear. Perhaps nudity was the simplest path, especially in Eden, where the bugs never bit and the plants had no thorns.

So, forget the clothes. How about fire? As plentiful as the fruits and vegetables were, he would eventually hunger for meat. The ponds were full of fish and the fields abundant with rabbits and quail, all moving sluggishly. No need to eat them raw, if he could find some flint and... *hmm*. He had no iron to strike the flint against. Could he make iron, if he found the proper ore? But to smelt the ore, he'd need flame. And to light the flame he'd need steel.

"Hoo, boy," he said, running his fingers through his hair. "For this I completed university?"

That night, he sat under a tree, rubbing sticks together, when he realized he wasn't alone. In the moonlight, Zoe emerged from the shadows of the surrounding trees, ghostlike, her arms drawn tightly across her breasts. The bravado that had lit her eyes earlier had vanished.

"How did you find me?" he asked.

"I went back to the pond," Zoe said. "I followed the blood on the grass until it got dark."

"I stopped bleeding hours ago," he said.

"I kept going the same direction," she said. "Found places where you'd been, apple cores where you'd stopped for a snack, some footsteps in the creek mud where you stopped to drink. Eventually, I heard you cussing."

"Ah. I showed the world how to release the energy contained in the fabric of space-time itself, but I'll be damned if I can get fire out of these sticks!"

"Where are we? What's going on?" Her voice was quiet, childlike.

"I told you," he said.

"You believe what you told me, don't you? You talk like you do."

"My curse in life," he said, "Is that I always find it easy to believe the truth."

"Are we... are we dead? Everything here's so perfect it's terrifying. There's fruit on every tree, all ripe at the same time. There's a breeze, but it doesn't give me chills, and me in my birthday suit. I've never walked barefoot this far without stepping on at least one sharp rock. It's like... like Heaven."

"We aren't dead."

"So what's happened?"

"I doubt I can explain it to you."

"I ain't dumb, mister. Tell it to me straight."

"Ah. It's not that I think you can't understand, it's just... let me have a little time to think things over. I don't know that I fully understand what's happening, but once I do, I promise to explain it."

"Promise?"

"Trust me," he said, looking away from her face towards the sticks in his hands.

"You'll never start a fire like that," she said.

"You know a better way?"

"In the army they trained us to start a fire with flint and steel."

"No steel."

"I also know how to make a bow from a branch and some shoestring, then spin wood in—"

"No shoestring either."

"We can cut off some of my hair, and braid it into string."

"Ah," said Albert. It took him almost a full ten seconds to realize, "No scissors. Not even any sharp rocks, as you observed."

She grinned. "You got teeth, don't you?"

7. Ember

"I do still have teeth, despite your best efforts to remove them," Albert said, rubbing his swollen lips. "What of it?"

"Look, I'm spooked, and would really like a fire," she said, teasing out a lock of hair as thick as a pencil. She got on her knees and leaned her head towards him. "Just bite off this bit as close to my scalp as you can."

"Perhaps I could just pull it?"

"That would hurt."

"You complain to me about getting hurt?"

"Yank or bite, just do it."

Albert took the strand of hair and wrapped it around his fist. He tensed his arm to pull hard, but something stopped him. It wasn't her fault she'd struck him when she was confused and scared. No reason both of them should suffer.

He leaned forward, his nose close to her scalp. He could smell her, the real her. All women in his experience smelled of perfume and shampoo. Zoe was sweaty, with nothing to disguise it. The odor was curiously beautiful. He pulled her hair over his swollen lip, between his front teeth, and bit. Her hair was salty and tough. He chewed, and she held still and kept silent, but he still had the feeling he was actually pulling more hair from the roots than he was successfully cutting.

"Ah. There," he said at last, when the final strand snapped free.

"Give me that," she said, taking the hair from him. "I'll braid it. You go hunt down the right sticks. I'll need a slightly curved one for the bow, about as thick as your little finger and as long as your forearm. Then we need a straight stick, bone dry and real hard, about this thick and this long," she said, holding her fingers and her hands apart. "And a bigger chunk of wood. The log you're sitting on will probably do, if it's dead enough. Get going, Al."

"And so it is the woman who will sit home and weave while the man goes forth to hunt," Albert said.

"Don't give me no lip," Zoe said. "Even if I've given you some to spare."

Albert chuckled and ventured forth from beneath the tree into the not-so-darkness. The moon glowed brightly overhead, and the stars were the same stars he'd seen all his life. Eden, it seemed, was on Earth.

The needed sticks were absurdly simple to find. He wondered if all basic human needs could be found so close at hand. He turned over a few stones, but found no matches.

When he returned, she had finished her braiding, and now held a thin, tight string. She bent the curved, green branch against the ground and tied the string to the ends. She then looped the string around the dead branch, shielded her palm with a concave stone, and began to twirl the stick against the log, pulling the bow back and forth in a sawing motion. She never asked for his help, and he never thought to offer it.

"If we get the fire—"

"When," she interrupted.

"When we get the fire, we should keep it going. That will save us future trouble."

"At least we've proved we ain't dead," she said, grunting with the effort of the bow. "Heaven would have electricity."

"What if we didn't earn a place in Heaven?"

"Hell's already got fire."

"Ah. I cannot argue with this logic."

Albert waited. Zoe panted as she picked up the pace. Finally, she pulled the stick away to reveal a tiny, glowing ember. Two dried blades of dead grass were quickly placed against the ember. A gentle puff of her breath stirred a tiny flame to life. She added a twig, then another.

"Don't tell me you forgot to bring the wieners," she said, as she nurtured the flame into a respectable campfire.

"You ask this of a naked man?"

"Hah. I didn't mean for it to be that kind of joke."

"I was thinking earlier that clothes could be fashioned if I could find some cotton."

"Maybe," she said. "Be a lot of work."

"You seem capable," said Albert.

"I never learned to sew, really. I didn't get good with a needle until I learned to stitch up wounds. Besides, don't go presuming that I'll do things for you. I take care of myself and expect a man to do the same."

"Ah. A charming attitude. You must have many suitors."

"Don't want 'em. Don't need 'em. I've been alone since I was six. Lost both my folks to the flu. My grandpa raised me, but he was lame from polio and half blind, so I spent as much time caring for him as he did for me."

"I'm sorry," Albert said.

"Why?" she asked.

Albert frowned. "It's what I have been conditioned to say in polite society."

"You can forget that stuff," she said, a smirk on her face. "I ain't polite."

8. Philosophy

"Very well. Since society is no more, we're free to set our own rules," said Albert.

"Always have lived by my own code," said Zoe.

"Ah. And what is your code?"

"Things break, you fix 'em. You lose ground, run faster. Keep going until something kills you."

"A remarkably concise philosophy."

"It keeps me going," she said, adding more sticks to the fire. "You got a philosophy, Al?"

"You never know."

"That's why I'm asking you."

"No, no. That's my philosophy. 'You never know.' I picked it up from my uncle, a devout atheist for as long as I can remember. Then, one Sabbath, he comes downstairs dressed in his finest, heading to temple. 'What brings this on?' I asked. 'You never know,' he answered. I've come to find wisdom in the words. Being certain of things is a trap of the mind. One's only hope of understanding comes from a stance of acknowledged ignorance."

"If you think you're Einstein, didn't he know just about everything?"

Albert rubbed his hands over the fire, fighting a chill, even though the night was quite warm. "That man knew only enough to destroy everyone and everything."

"You're talking like you ain't him. Like he's dead."

"You never know."

"What's that supposed to mean?"

"You'll never have any way of knowing for certain if I am telling you the truth. Even I can never know. Am I really Albert Einstein? Or am I only his memory? Nowhere in my 'theory of everything' did I incorporate Eden, or angels. To say I knew 'everything!' What arrogance!"

"But you do believe everyone's dead, except me and you?"

"Yes."

"You believe this is Eden?"

"Yes."

Zoe sat for a long time, quietly feeding sticks into the fire. Then she sat back, watching the flames for a while. After a long time, she said, "Here's what I believe: I'm dog-tired and could use some sleep."

Albert nodded. "We have a belief in common."

"We can both sleep here, next to the fire. But don't get any bright idea that I'm sleeping with you, understand? I'm a light sleeper, and I don't have to be standing to get in a good kick, you got me?"

"I promise to be the perfect gentleman. Sleep well."

Albert settled down into the soft grass beyond the circle of stones she had gathered round the fire. A thick pad of moss proved soft enough to rest his head upon. Zoe surprised him by moving around the fire and lying down right next to him, almost on top of him. She rested her head upon his shoulder, her eyes never meeting his.

"Everyone dead," she whispered. "Christ sake."

"Don't think of it," Albert said, smoothing down her hair where it rose in a small peak, cowlicked by his spit. "Don't think of it," he whispered, not for her benefit, but for his.

The enormity of what he'd done struck him. Everyone dead. Billions. Not only people. Beyond Eden, there were no more dogs, or cats, or birds, or kangaroos, no elephants, no mice. And no trees, grass, flowers, bushes, or mushrooms, save for here, in this, strange, angel-sheltered petri dish. Everything gone, and it all his fault. Getting kicked in the ribs was far more pleasant than the cold spear of guilt that pinned him to the ground, all but breathless.

Ah, but he wasn't breathless. And as he breathed, he could smell Zoe, a slightly sour, slightly sweet aroma that seemed the most natural thing in all the world to be smelling. The warmth of her skin distracted him, and slowly pulled him from the maw of guilt that threatened to devour him. Her warmth was pleasant, her skin soft against his. He looked down at his naked body, his eyes drawn by a sensation he hadn't felt in years. He raised his leg, to hide what might be an unwelcome sight if Zoe were to open her eyes. Perhaps he still held more interest in women than he suspected. He wiggled his injured nose and winced from the pain. It proved a therapeutic distraction. As his head cleared, Albert resolved be kind to Zoe, but only as a fellow traveler. He would never fall in love.

"You never know," she mumbled, in response to some private thought of her own. And then she grew softer, if such a thing could be imagined, for her skin was already softer and smoother than the satin gowns his second wife had worn to bed. She was sleeping, snoring softly. *Wonderful, she snores,* he thought. The discovery of this flaw was all that was needed to silence his own mind. Sleep claimed him.

9. Boundaries

In the morning, he woke hungry. Zoe was already awake, crouched by the fire, with a carp about a foot long laying on a flat stone. She didn't say a word as he moved to her side. He found that she'd already gutted and scaled the fish, using the broken shell of a stream mussel as a knife. How resourceful.

To show that he could be of some use, he wordlessly took the stone with the fish and set it down in the coals at the margin of the fire. The fish soon started to sizzle.

After a few minutes, Zoe finally decided to speak. "If this is the Garden of Eden, and I ain't saying it is, then there must be a gate."

"Why?" Albert said, as he gingerly nudged the edges of the stone to push the cooking fish towards more vibrant coals.

"I mean, I wasn't the most attentive kid in Sunday school, but at least a little Bible stuck with me. When God kicked Adam and

Eve out of the Garden he put an angel at the gate to make sure they didn't come back."

"Ah. Gabriel did mention such an angel. Apparently, that angel was one of Gabriel's victims. So if there is a gate, it's unguarded."

"If we find the gate, we can leave," she said.

"If there is anywhere to go."

"If we find it, at least we'll know," she said.

"I had planned to map the surroundings. Explore the boundaries of Eden. Perhaps we'll find this gate."

"Is it burning?" She eyed the fish. "Smells like its burning."

Albert gingerly nudged the fish to an even hotter part of the fire. "Some fish have worms. Better overcooked than undercooked."

"I get the feeling you're a fussy eater," she said.

"Not especially."

"Well, I'm ready for my half. Even if it's raw it ain't gonna kill me. I got tough guts."

She leaned over the coals with her makeshift mussel shell knife and chopped the fish in half. She pushed her half onto one of the flat, round rocks she'd washed to serve as plates.

"It's done," she said, talking as she chewed. "Yow! It's hot! But good."

"So it sounds as if we have a plan," he said, scooping his half of the fish onto his plate.

"Map the place. Find the gate."

"If there is a gate."

After breakfast, they began to walk. Zoe kept a very crude map on the back of one of the plate-rocks, marking it with the end of a charred stick. Albert didn't pay much attention to her efforts, keeping his own map in his head. Memory had never been the strongest of his mental abilities, but when needed he could press it into heroic service. He was good at counting, and while living in Switzerland, out of simple curiosity, he'd calculated the length of his average stride in meters. Two thousand four-hundred fifty-six steps (or 5.65 kilometers) after leaving their campsite, they found the wall.

They could see the wall for several minutes before actually arriving at it. Zoe mistook their reflections for other humans and ran forward, though only for a moment. Albert soon caught up with her, as his mirror counterpart reached the other Zoe. Together they walked forward, until Albert could reach out and touch his reflection, or at least attempt it.

The mirror-wall proved impossible to actually touch. Albert pressed his fingers forward, meeting unseen resistance centimeters before he could touch his reflection's fingertips. The pressure reminded him of the force one felt trying to press together the positive ends of two magnets. It was like an invisible, textureless cushion. Albert wondered if the force that pushed him back was the same force bouncing back the light. He noted the wall didn't have the same distortions an ordinary mirror would, nor did it have any glare. The perfect reflection gave the illusion that the land continued on, infinite.

"What is it?" Zoe asked.

Albert thought he detected a touch of fear in her voice, but he had never been good at reading emotions. Fear was uncalled for. He hoped.

"It's real," he said.

"I know it's real. I can see it's real! What the hell is it?"

"Stay calm. It's only a barrier."

"But what's it made of?" she asked, reaching out to touch it. "Is this some kind of, I don't know, witchcraft, maybe?"

"Hah!" Albert said, surprised by her superstition. "Witchcraft? Dismiss it. If this is real, it cannot be supernatural. If a thing exists, it is natural. We can eventually solve its riddles."

"I ain't never seen nothing like it."

"A hundred years ago, who knew about radio waves? Human senses are not designed to see or hear them. Now the devices needed to detect radio waves can be found everywhere, probably your own home. Or did you think that the music coming from your radio is played by fairies?"

"Al," said Zoe. "I ain't stupid. Don't talk down to me."

"Witchcraft, indeed," he muttered, shaking his head.

10. Reflections

"Fine," Zoe said, sounding like she was getting angry. "I ain't heard your explanation, genius."

"Because I don't yet have an explanation," Albert said, "I don't know what we've found. If we had iron, I could test to see if the barrier had any magnetic properties. If we had a Geiger counter, or even just a radio, there are other tests I could devise. But simply because we lack the tools to analyze what we've found is no reason to regard this barrier as existing beyond the known laws of physics. Light can be bent. Light also has pressure, a measurable force. And space-time itself can be curved. This barrier is likely an artifact of advanced technology."

"You sure seem confident in science for a guy who says with a straight face that he's spoken directly with an angel."

"I knew my answer wouldn't satisfy you."

"No," Zoe said. "Actually, it's kind of helpful. Maybe we can figure all this out, with enough time and the right tools. I'm just spooked, is all."

"I understand. But, we should be joyous in this discovery! Now that we've found a wall, our odds of finding a door are vastly improved."

"There's that," she said, and smiled. "So, right or left?"

"I miss money," said Albert.

"Ain't nothing to buy here."

"This is a choice easily made with a coin flip."

"Left," she said.

They walked, keeping their reflection to their right. Albert watched the wall as they walked, at first trying to penetrate its mystery, eventually only to watch himself. He had seldom seen himself naked in a mirror able to reflect his entire body. He'd never seen himself in one able to reflect his movements as he walked for any length of time. Fascinating, the way the muscles of the legs expanded and contracted beneath his skin.

It had been a long time since he had worn this body. Twenty-three, Gabriel had said. This was how he looked in 1902. It had been a long, long time since he felt this strong. If the bomb hadn't fallen, if his life hadn't taken such a strange detour, he'd still be... what? Sixty-six? With his otherwise firm grasp of numbers, he'd always had to search the most cobwebbed sections of his mind to recall his exact age.

He'd never cared much about his appearance. There were many days where he hadn't bothered to comb his hair. But the man in the mirror-wall was quite the dashing rogue, with his head full of dark hair and not an ounce of fat on his bones. Al had never really missed his youth, but he wasn't unhappy to see it returned.

And then, the guilt struck home once more. Not unhappy? Who was he to enjoy anything? All through the war years, as Hitler made ever greater advances, he'd been haunted by what ifs. What if he hadn't persuaded Roosevelt to stay out of the war all those years? What if the Americans had entered the war to defend Britain or Russia, instead of sitting on the sidelines until the Nazis were pouring into Canada? Could things have been different? Could all his grief had been averted?

In the final years of his life, his only reason for carrying on to the next day was his violin, which he played for hours each evening. The slow, mournful cries the instrument produced gave voice to emotions he could never speak. He would end his evenings with his aged fingers aching from pressing the strings. His cheeks would be wet with tears as he closed the instrument in its case.

How distant that seemed. Walking in the sunlight, breathing the clean air, his mind busily contemplating the mysteries of the mirror wall, he was not merely not unhappy, he was, in unguarded moments, possibly enjoying himself. Gabriel's inclusion of a beautiful woman had proved to be unnecessary. True happiness would probably always elude him, given the magnitude of his sins, but a thirst for life was returning. He desired to unravel Eden's mysteries. That's what Gabriel wanted. To kill a man who cherished life.

"But I'll die a pacifist," he said, his voice firm with conviction. "I shall deny him the satisfaction of a struggle."

"What?" Zoe asked.

"Ah, my apologies. I'm thinking aloud."

"Ah," she said. "I see." She frowned. "You've got me saying 'ah.'"

"Ah," he said. "It's not the worst sin." His shoulders sagged. He knew a thing or two about worse sins.

"Let's rest by that stream," she said. "We can rustle up some lunch."

While he had watched the muscles in his legs as they walked, it was only when he sat that he truly felt how hot and tired he was becoming. 9.52 kilometers now, and Zoe hadn't complained once. Gabriel had been clever not to bring his first wife, Maria, back to life. If Maria had walked half as far, her grumbles would have driven him to jump from a high cliff. Not that they'd found any high cliffs.

"Penny for your thoughts," said Zoe. "You can use it for decision making."

"I'm still thinking about the wall. What holds it in place? What power keeps it from dissipating?"

"Witchcraft is still all I got," said Zoe.

11. Terrarium

"I thought we were done with the nonsense of witchcraft," said Albert.

Zoe shrugged. "My Aunt Jo claimed to be a witch." She stopped, looking as if she was lost in memories. "Mostly what she was, though, was dirty. I think she took up being a witch because it kept Uncle Bo from complaining when she let the dishes pile up in the sink."

"And what did your uncle think about this?"

"Folks say that Bo cussed Jo out once, not long after they shacked up. He got awful sick soon after. Couldn't walk for a week," Zoe said. "After that, he kept his mouth shut."

Albert scratched his chin, with its day old, sandpapery stubble. Neither of his wives had ever tried to poison him. Perhaps he was a more tolerable husband than they'd led him to believe.

Day stretched into evening, and they made camp beneath the shelter of a rock ledge. Albert grumbled as he tried his skill with the fire bow. Zoe busied herself cleaning a rabbit she'd killed with a well-thrown stone.

The night was awash with stars by the time the fire was ready.

"Wish I could tan the hide of this rabbit properly," Zoe said. "I could make a sort of bag out of it. We're starting to have more than we can carry just with our hands."

Zoe's industriousness was becoming a burden. In addition to the fire-bow, she insisted they carry the plate-stones, as well as the mussel knife, plus the map and charcoal pencil. Still, Albert knew that it was safer to carry these things than to assume they could be easily acquired again.

"We could leave the map behind," Albert said. "I doubt that it will be needed. While it's difficult to measure precisely, the wall is curving in a consistent arc. Unless it deviates soon, it's going to eventually form a large circle, approximately twenty kilometers in diameter."

"Twenty kilometers... that's what, about twelve miles?"

"You know the metric system?"

"I served in Canada, remember?"

Albert nodded. "My best hypothesis is that Eden is some sort of terrarium."

"That's a five-dollar word."

"Like an aquarium, only with land," he said.

"We're in some kind of fishbowl?"

"That theory fits the observable facts better than anything else. Tell me, have you ever heard of evolution?"

"Of course. Al, I ain't completely ignorant. I did have nurse training in the army, and I spent a lot of time talking to doctors. I might never have been to college, but I pick up things fast."

"I don't doubt it. It's just that evolution is still a widely resisted theory. People who believe the Bible is infallible seem to regard it as a threat."

"I don't believe the Bible is infallible," said Zoe.

"I never said you did."

"You said it like you did."

"I didn't."

"I don't take nothing at face value," Zoe said. "Grandpa always said, 'If you swallow anything whole, you'll choke on it. Use your teeth.' Not that he had any teeth."

"I think, Zoe, he meant it metaphorically."

"I know that! Jeez! You always act like I ain't smart enough to get what you're talking about. 'Oh, you know metric, oh, you've heard of evolution.'"

"Zoe, I didn't mean—"

"Just because I got a hillbilly accent don't make me dumb. I talk like I talk. Everyone I grew up with talked this way, Al, the same reason you have a German accent. So just talk to me normal without asking if I know everything. Anything I don't follow you on I'll be sure and ask about, okay?"

"Ah. Of course. I apologize. I meant no offense."

"Whatever. Just don't think I'm some kind of hick."

Albert started to explain that he didn't think of her as a hick, then held his tongue. Every argument he'd ever had with a woman was a circuitous affair leading nowhere. Best to drop the matter. But what if she was right? He hadn't been thinking of her as an equal. He'd regarded what intelligence she possessed as purely utilitarian, good for making fires and catching dinner, but hardly up to grasping the riddle of their present circumstances, let alone solving it.

"What were you going to say about evolution?" she asked.

"Only that natural selection is not the only evolutionary force. Artificial selection has crafted new strains of dogs, cattle, plants, and even bees. Gabriel said the angel Michael made Eden. Perhaps Eden is a laboratory. A controlled environment where mankind could undergo experiments."

"What kind of experiments?"

"I can't even speculate."

"Get back to me when you've got an actual idea, Al," Zoe said, sounding weary.

Albert shrugged.

She shook her head. "Sorry. Say whatever you think. Your ideas beat anything I've come up with," Zoe admitted. "You've got a good head on your shoulders. No wonder you've convinced yourself you're Einstein."

Albert sighed.

12. Silver-Tongued Devil

The fire calmed into coals good for cooking. Zoe placed the wooden spit holding the rabbit over the coals and said, "There. It can't get done soon enough for me."

"If I haven't said it, I'm grateful that you've proven such a skillful hunter," said Albert.

"No big thing," she said. "It's not like there was a grocery store in the holler I grew up in."

"Where did you grow up?"

"About thirty miles outside of Bluefield, West Virginia," she said. "Where I lived wasn't exactly a town. Just a gullied side road with about thirty shacks along it, up the hill from a rail depot where coal cars got swapped out. Pa would hitch a ride into Bluefield once or twice a year for things like sugar and flour. Everything else we either grew or caught. If we find clay and I can make a cooking pot, I got to fix you up some possum stew. I promise you ain't never tasted nothing like it"

"I can confirm that."

"The key ingredient is hard work, like all these miles we've been putting in. When you're starving after a day's work, even tree bark tastes good," she said.

"If you say so," he said, hoping she wouldn't try to feed him bark.

"There was a little one room school house over in the next holler," Zoe said. "A tiny library. One cookbook, with pictures. Used to look at things fancy people ate like lobsters and oysters and think, hell no! Then I remembered that the eggs I ate for breakfast came out of our chickens' butts and figured that there ain't no rhyme or reason to what tastes good in this world."

Albert chuckled.

Zoe poked the rabbit with a stick. "This might take a while. While we wait, I'm gonna go for a swim. I stink something fierce."

"I'll come with you," he said. "It has been many years since I've worked up such a sweat."

They didn't have to walk far to reach the nearest pond. Eden abounded with ponds and streams, none large enough to pose any real obstacle while walking. Zoe dived in, and Albert held back for a moment, struck by the notion that he was going skinny dipping with a woman for the first time in his life. It was a silly thing to be aware of. The last twenty-four hours had been one unending stream of firsts with a naked woman, from building a fire to skinning a rabbit. But as he watched her slim body slice gracefully through the water, he realized he was staring at the curve of her buttocks. He found their mathematical perfection mesmerizing.

"Come on in," she called, as she turned to float on her back at the center of the pond, revealing her firm breasts, glistening with beads of water in the moonlight. "The water ain't cold at all."

Albert ran into the pond, afraid of diving into strange waters, but anxious to have the water hide his growing erection. He didn't know what she would say if she saw it. She was right, unfortunately. The water wasn't cold. His erection persisted.

"Something the matter?" Zoe asked, swimming towards him. "You look worried."

"Ah. I'm fine."

"God, my hair's going to be all tangled after this," Zoe said. "I need to make some kind of comb."

"I've no doubt that it will be a fine comb."

"Al, it's okay."

"What?"

"Let's just say I saw what you're trying to hide. Ain't the first I've seen, not in my line of duty."

"I wasn't hiding it," he said.

"I know you're a gentleman," Zoe said. "You've been real nice to me. Not many men would have kept their hands off me, let alone their eyes."

"Ah. There are so many other interesting things to look at here."

Zoe's face fell. "You saying I ain't worth looking at?"

"No! No, just, but... the whole garden, such a mystery—"

"You seen one apple tree you seen 'em all."

"Zoe, you are a beautiful woman. I promise I would look, indeed, stare at you under different circumstances."

"You're a silver tongued devil, Al," Zoe said, and splashed water into his face. When he opened his eyes, she was swimming back towards shore.

13. Hillbilly Waltz

They ate the rabbit in silence. The meat was tough and stringy, and in desperate need of salt and pepper. Would he know a pepper plant if he saw it, he wondered? Were the tiny black corns in a pepper mill found on bushes or on trees?

Zoe didn't curl up next to him. She stretched out on the other side of the fire, lying perfectly still, but he could sense she wasn't sleeping. He listened to the chirp of crickets, the croaking of frogs, and the songs of night birds. He'd slept in cities far quieter than Eden.

"Jesus," Zoe said, tossing and turning in the dark. "I wish we had a radio."

"Music would be nice," he said.

"I was thinking of a show, a cop show or something. Ever listen to the *Adventures of Superman?*"

"Never. I've found it odd that so many American's wish to fight Nazi's while openly celebrating the adventures of a fascist *ubermensch.*"

"That ain't exactly what the show's about," Zoe said.

Albert shrugged. "Ah, but who am I to judge? Despite his overt antisemitism, I confess I find beauty in the operas of Wagner."

"Opera? Like the stuff sung by fat ladies who break glass?"

"That's... not a completely inaccurate summary of the art form."

She nodded. "You and I probably have different tastes. I'm more into bluegrass. Didn't need a radio for that. My family always made its own music."

"Oh?"

"Guitar, fiddle, dulcimer. Even a mouth harp. I played 'em all."

"Fiddle? You play the violin?"

"Like the devil himself!"

Without warning, she rose to her feet, and held her hands up. She began to play a ghost violin, her fingers moving with such precision, her bow arm flying with such rhythm he could almost hear the music. The tune was so different from the ones he played, fast and full of life. She swayed her hips and burst into song:

Boil them cabbage down
Turn them hoe cakes round
The only song that I know
Is boil them cabbage down!

"Except it ain't the only song I know," she said, halting her performance. "I know hundreds of songs. Thousands, maybe. Plus, I just make up stuff when the spirit moves me. Don't know how to read or write music, but that ain't never slowed me down. I can give Bill Monroe a run for his money!"

Albert realized his mouth was hanging open.

"Too hillbilly for you, huh?" she said, self-consciously.

"That was wonderful," he said. And it had been. Not the lyrics, perhaps, but her voice, her energy. How had he forgotten the joy of music? How had he ever come to regard music only as an expression of his pain?

He rose to his feet, holding is hand toward her.

"Shall we dance?"

"Sure. What kind?"

"A waltz," he said, stepping to her and taking her in his arms. Her breasts pressed against his chest as he began to hum the *Blue Danube*.

"I don't know how to waltz," she whispered.

"You'll pick it up easily enough," he said, and began to lead her.

She was awkward at first, out of step. He began to sing the notes aloud, *"La da da dee dee, dee dee, dee dee."*

"I think I've heard this song," she said, relaxing into his lead. Soon she anticipated his steps, and began to hum along. "Are there words?"

"Words are superfluous," he answered.

"My, how you talk," she giggled.

They danced for long hours, stepping to the music of their voices, and the orchestra of crickets.

Albert realized Gabriel had beaten him. With Zoe's arm around his back, her hand in his hand, her body close, Albert was happy. Though he knew it was a trap, he wished he could live in this moment forever.

14. Beyond

The next day, they found the gate. The daylight was already waning, though they hadn't traveled far. They'd passed the greater part of the day lying about in the shade of the rock shelter, eating the rest of the rabbit, and talking. Zoe had countless stories. Only twenty-two, she had lived more in those two decades than most people did in seven. Albert explained in detail his own story, including more details of his conversation with Gabriel.

She smiled. "Al, you sure got a great imagination."

It bothered him that, with all the evidence before her, she still couldn't accept that they were merely pawns in the game of a deranged angel. What would it take to convince her? On the other hand, what was the point of convincing her? He'd concluded their talk with a shrug, and suggested they keep moving.

They had barely walked over two hills before Zoe had spotted the dark area in the wall.

They ran towards the opening, a rectangular hole in the strange barrier, large enough to pass a plane through. They stopped abruptly when they saw what lay beyond.

"Jesus," said Zoe.

Albert walked forward, squinting. The gate shimmered slightly, and the view beyond was difficult to bring into clear focus. Outside, the sky was black, like night, only the sun was still in the sky. The ground outside the gate was covered in snow and ice, the terrain flat and featureless. Or almost featureless.

Albert drew closer for a better look at what he saw. Even a meter from the gate, no cold or wind from the frozen desolation beyond passed through to Eden. The grass grew lushly to the very edge of the gate, then gave way to a half-meter thick strip of raw rock, beyond which lay snow a meter deep. No doubt the gate was as impenetrable as the wall.

He reached his hand forward, expecting resistance, but it passed through as if nothing was there. He withdrew his hand suddenly. His fingers ached from their brief exposure to the icy air beyond.

Wind came, silently swirling the snow beyond, rearranging the landscape a flake at a time. In the center of it all was the sword.

The sword jutted up from the snow like a cross. It lay a few dozen meters outside the gate. The snow around it was pink, with strange brown lumps all around it. The wind shifted, and the golden feathers that covered one of the lumps ruffled and caught the sunlight.

"What's happening?" Zoe asked. "Why are the stars and the sun out at the same time?"

"I'm uncertain," he said. "If Earth's atmosphere were gone, it might look like this. But there is wind. Curious, yes? Still, if all the water vapor has frozen from the air, the sky might no longer scatter light."

"So we're trapped here," Zoe said. "We can't go out into that."

"Not for long, no," he said. "But if there is wind, there must be some air pressure. A man could survive, if only for a minute. I need to go out and see what Eden looks like from the other side. And, if I can reach the sword, it might prove useful."

"The sword?" Zoe squinted. "Is that what that is?"

"Looks like it, no?"

"What's around it?"

"Confirmation that I did, indeed, speak with an angel."

The wind shifted again, sending the feathers on the severed angel-wing dancing.

Zoe stepped back. She began to tremble.

"It's true," Zoe said, choking. "Oh God, I didn't want to believe you, but it's true. We're angel hunted. Gabriel's going to kill us."

"Don't think about it," Albert said. "That could be a long way off. For now, we must live as well as we can. The sword will make a handy tool, yes?"

Zoe looked as if the sword were the last thing on her mind. At last, she nodded.

"Just be careful," she said.

"I promise," Albert said.

Albert had spent many a winter in Switzerland. He was no stranger to cold. Even the chilliest wind could be endured, especially for the short time it would take him to retrieve the sword.

He stepped onto the strip of rock. His feet tingled, as if static electricity were jumping from his toes. He gritted his teeth and scrambled up the bank of snow.

"Of course, in Switzerland I had clothes," he said through chattering teeth as he struggled to stand. The surface was packed hard, polished by the wind. The ice crystals were like tiny shards of glass. He inhaled, the air as sharp as if he were swallowing razors. He fought the urge to turn back.

"Focus," he said. "Grab the sword, then go back."

He staggered forward against the wind. The heavens were arrayed with a clarity he'd never imagined, but he had no time to gaze upon the stars. If he tarried, he'd lose fingers and toes to frostbite. He kept his eyes fixed on the sword.

He stumbled over something round and hard, like a bowling ball beneath the snow. He fell. The sword was almost in reach of his sprawled arms. He crawled forward, closing his fingers around the hilt. Oddly, the metal didn't seem as cold as the air surrounding it. The snow around the blade had melted, and refrozen into ice. He'd never be able to pull it out.

"Don't give up," he growled to himself, and yanked the blade. To his astonishment, the blade pulled free of the ice effortlessly.

As he struggled to his feet and turned back towards Eden, he noticed what he'd tripped over. The severed head of a man lay half buried in the snow, his eyes open with surprise, his mouth frozen in a scream. Something moved within Albert, a realization that this was his fate. He could bear it, but for the thought of Zoe weeping over his body. Or would Gabriel kill her first? Was he that much of a monster?

Albert wrapped his numb fingers in the dead angel's silver hair and pulled the head free. He would carry it back to Eden for a burial, a burial his own corpse was unlikely to receive.

He looked up, ready to return to Eden while he still had the last bit of sensation in his limbs. Eden was gone. Nothing lay before him but blank, endless snow. Had he gotten spun around? He turned around. Nothing but snow in every direction.

Which way had he come? The snow was too hard. He'd left no footprints.

"Zoe!" he called out. "Zoe!"

But when he'd still been inside Eden, he couldn't hear the roar of the wind. No doubt his voice never reached her. He was going to freeze to death. That was one option to thwart Gabriel's plan, he supposed.

15. Unreal Sky

Albert swallowed, his mind racing. Looking around, he found the hole the sword had rested in. Beyond it was the indentation left by the half buried head. He'd walked in a straight line to get here. Following the line formed by these two small marks would put him on the right path to Eden. If Eden was still there. What if he'd travelled through some one-way space warp? A wormhole that his mass had collapse the second he traveled through it?

"Noooo!" he howled, willing his feet to move, inching himself forward. He no longer felt any pain from the snow crystals. He no longer felt the ground at all. He seemed to be gliding across some abstract painting, a plane of unbroken white paper beneath a sky of black ink. If he spread his arms, he might change into a kite in such an unreal sky.

He fell. It felt as if he were rubbing his face along a cheese grater as he slid. But at least he could feel it, feel something besides the cold. He needed only a minute to rest, to get his head clear. He could spare a few seconds to close his eyes and think.

So he closed his eyes. His head was full of thoughts.

He thought about bicycles and violins and of a glass of milk on his mother's table.

"Cabbage?" his mother asked.

The smell of her cooking filled the house. Americans thought boiling cabbage smelled bad. Americans were imbeciles.

Then he wasn't at his mother's table, but in her bed. Her bed was comfortable and warm. He was almost feverish beneath the down blankets.

Then his mother snatched the blankets away and the cold air rushed in.

"No!" he screamed. "I don't want to get up."

"Al!" his mother shouted, shaking his shoulders.

Only, his mother never called him Al. Whose voice had said that name?

His face was rubbed raw across sheets rougher than burlap as his mother grabbed him by the ankles and dragged him out of bed. He kicked, or tried too. He had somehow misplaced his legs. Probably in his coat pocket, with his reading glasses. He clutched the pillow with his right hand and the bedpost with his left. They were dragged forward as well. The bed went on forever, acres of burlap to be scraped across, until suddenly the bed wasn't beneath him anymore, and he tumbled to the grass.

"I don't want to go to school," he mumbled. "Everyone tells me I'm stupid."

"Al, I can't understand you. Wake up! Speak English, not German."

Albert opened his frost coated eyelids. Zoe knelt above him, rubbing his cheeks, his fingers, his chest, even his toes, all at once somehow, as if she were Kali, with a dozen frantic hands.

"You heard me call to you," he whispered. "You came for me."

"You were stumbling around like a drunk hobo. I saw you fall. I wasn't going to let you freeze to death. You're the only waltzing partner I got!"

"You could have died as well," he said.

"Shucks," she said. "You weren't all that far from the gate. Only, when I grabbed you and turned around, I couldn't see the gate."

"But you found it," he said.

"You left little blood specks in the snow when you first climbed out. You must have cut your feet. The snow was sharp as needles."

"The sword—"

"Don't worry about the sword."

"But, the angel head—"

"I saw it," said Zoe. "You had its hair tangled around your fingers. You had your other hand closed tight around the sword. You didn't let go of 'em till I pulled you down the snowbank."

Albert turned his head towards the gate. The head and the sword lay on the thin strip of stone that separated Eden from the hell beyond.

"You're still so cold," Zoe said. "I wish we had a blanket I could put over you while I build a fire."

"I'll be fine," Albert said, though he couldn't feel his arms or his legs.

"If I have anything to say about it, you will be," she said, crawling over him. "Tell me if you have trouble breathing."

She stretched herself out upon him, her chest on his, her legs resting upon his own. He could feel her weight, but her warmth eluded him.

"I can breathe fine," he wheezed.

Her face was inches from his own.

"Your lips are blue," she said.

She brought her hands to his cheeks and kissed him.

Albert somehow found the strength to close his arms around her.

"I feel warmer," he said as she pulled away from the kiss and looked into his eyes.

She kissed him again.

The heat flowed into his body, tingling in his hands and feet and other extremities.

That night, they built no fire, but he was very warm indeed.

16. Hexing Hoodoo Mojo Magic

In the morning, Albert carefully slipped from Zoe's arms, trying not to wake her.

"Where ya going?" she mumbled.

"Shush, my love," he whispered. "I'm not going far."

He rose to his unsteady legs. He still felt weak, and the tips of three of his toes had turned black. It looked like he'd keep all his fingers, fortunately. Until Gabriel pulled them off his hands, at least. He walked to the thin strip of stone that held the sword he'd almost died for. The angel's eyes watched him as he bent to grasp the blade.

"Be careful," the severed angel head said.

"Of course," Albert said, lifting the long, gleaming blade. The second the sword hit Eden's air, it burst into flame.

"Yaah!" yelped Albert, dropping the weapon. He stepped back from the dancing flame.

"Told you," said the head.

The truth of who was speaking suddenly lodged in his brain. He turned to the severed head.

"You're... still alive?"

"I wouldn't call this living."

"Ah," said Albert.

"Sort of an awkward moment, huh?" the head asked.

"You're Hazraphet, aren't you? Gabriel said he'd killed you with your own sword."

"Gabriel? Is that what he's calling himself these days?"

"Yes. What else would he be called?"

"I can tell you a little secret that will make your life much easier."

"Al?" It was Zoe. She had fully awakened and now stood behind Albert.

"It's okay, sweetie," Hazraphet said. "I bite, but that's all I do now. Judging from those bruises on your neck you're into that sort of thing."

Zoe touched one of the round, purple patches on her neck and blushed. "Ain't you the fresh one," she said. Then she frowned. She looked at Albert. "How is a severed head talking to us? How is that sword on fire if this isn't witchcraft?"

"Witchcraft?" asked Hazraphet.

"Hexing. Hoodoo. Mojo. Magic! Whatever it is, it ain't right!"

"I won't argue with you there," said Hazraphet. "And it would take far longer than a mortal lifespan for me to explain the works of angels."

"Try me," said Albert.

"Hey," said Hazraphet. "I know you. You're Albert Einstein! I didn't recognize you at first, since you're so young. I guess Gabriel's been mucking around with time again."

"Using my time curve equations, apparently," said Albert. "So, if angels have things to learn from me, you should trust that I can learn from you."

"Maybe," said Hazraphet. "I mean, you might get the big picture, if not all the details. Basically, all of reality is nothing but information. Numbers all the way down."

"The mathematical foundations of reality are hardly a secret to me," said Albert.

"Yeah, but there's mortal math, and there's angelic math. We were made to be editors of reality, adding a little here, subtracting a little there, keeping the whole thing in balance. We aren't physical beings in any way you'd understand."

"I've stubbed my toe on your forehead. You seem physical enough."

"You're experiencing four of the seventeen dimensions that compose my form. I'm completely, truly dead in about twelve of those dimensions. Lucky for you, Gabriel is sloppy."

"I don't know that I'll consider it lucky if I wind up seventy percent dead," said Albert.

"With humans it's more of fifty-fifty situation. You're dead or you're not. And I can tell you a secret that will keep you on the right side of that equation."

"What secret?" asked Albert.

"All in good time," Hazraphet said. "First, let's see about getting me a little more comfortable. My nose needs scratching like you wouldn't believe. I'd rather be sitting on a nice fluffy pillow than this hard rock. And bring my sword. It'll come in handy. Be careful to only hold it by the hilt. You won't even feel the flames."

Zoe stepped carefully into the circle of burnt grass that held the sword and lifted it while Albert picked up Hazraphet.

"Well," she said. "I guess we ain't gotta worry 'bout building fires no more."

17. Twelve Years of Hard Labor

Albert rested in the shade of the same tree he and Zoe had slept under that first night. From across the fields he heard the door to the house slam. That would be Joseph, bringing his lunch. He'd lectured the boy a dozen times about the proper way to close a door, but somehow it wasn't taking. No doubt he'd picked up his hardheadedness from his mother's side.

Albert untied the shirt he wore to let the breeze better dry his sweat. He missed his early nudity in Eden. He almost regretted sowing the cotton and building the loom, but Zoe had insisted on clothes once their family was on the way. Albert didn't see the logic behind it, but knew better than to argue. Besides, clothes did have one advantage. It was always so sweet to slip Zoe's clothes from her shoulders. After four children she was more beautiful than the day he'd first met her.

Not that he was doing so badly himself. Twelve years of hard labor in the clean air and gentle sun had transformed him. His body ached more now, but it ached in muscles he didn't know he had when he first came here.

His eldest son arrived, carrying a pail that contained a little clay pot of stewed possum and cabbage, and two biscuits as fluffy as clouds.

"Ah," said Albert. "Your mother has outdone herself."

"The house stinks like cabbage," Joseph said, wrinkling his nose.

"You are the young American, yes?"

"What's an American?"

"Another time, I will explain this to you. Now, share lunch with me."

"Not the cabbage."

"Yes, the cabbage. It's good for you. You'll grow up strong."

"I'm not hungry," said Joseph. Which was probably true. It was difficult to teach children to enjoy their vegetables when they need only lean out their bedroom window to pluck ever-ripened apples, grapes, and cherries.

"One day, you'll learn to appreciate your mother's cooking. You're too young to appreciate the finer things in life."

He forked the cabbage into his mouth and hummed with pleasure.

"But *you* appreciate them," someone said behind him, as a winged shadow fell across the grass. "The finer things. Your life has never been better."

"Joseph—"

"Who's that?" Joseph asked, looking over Albert's shoulder.

"Son, run and tell your mother he's come."

"Who's come?"

"Run!"

Joseph ran, across the field back towards the log house.

"You should run as well," said the voice behind him. "I'll give you a head start. You've had your fun. Time for me to have mine."

"No," Albert said, standing and turning to face his visitor.

Gabriel smiled, a smile as cold as the snows beyond the gate. "Don't tell me you won't struggle to hold onto this life. You've never been happier than now. A woman you love, and four healthy children. Your life's become precious. Can you really surrender all this without a fight?"

"I'm not a creature such as yourself," Albert said. "I've no love of violence."

"Then we'll sweeten the stakes a little. For every minute you fight, I'll add a minute before I seek out that lovely wife of yours, and those healthy little children, and pluck their eyes from their heads and eat them like grapes."

"I've no love of violence, but I did not say I wouldn't fight. I said I wouldn't run. You shall never lay a finger on my family."

"Brave words. You're looking fit these days, Albert Einstein. You think your new body is a match for an angel?"

"My mind is," said Albert. "Hazraphet has told me much about the ways of angels. The form that stands before me, for instance, is but a fraction of your true self. Angels are more conceptual beings than physical creatures. Destroying your body will not destroy you."

Gabriel grinned. "I never said this would be a fair fight."

"But it will be. Because Hazraphet also told me the rules. An angel must always obey commands given by those who speak their true names. And he has told me your true name."

Gabriel rolled his eyes contemptuously. "What good does that do you? Only Hazraphet could say it, and the name gives no power to other angels. You've always had a head full of useless knowledge, Albert Einstein"

Albert stuck out his tongue.

Gabriel turned pale. He lunged forward, fear in his eyes, his long, metallic nails reaching for Albert's throat.

18. Use Your Teeth

Albert said the name, the way Hazraphet had taught him, the high screeching vowels that made his teeth ache, the twisted consonants he'd learned to make only after he'd slit his tongue in three places. He said the name, and then he said, "Stop!"

Gabriel put his hands over his ears and fell to his knees.

"No," Gabriel growled. "I won't allow this!"

"You have no choice in the matter. You will do as I bind you."

Gabriel ground his teeth, his head twisting on his neck as if trying to escape his body. Then he spat, and said, "I will do as you bid... master."

"That had to be painful," Albert said. "Humiliating, yes? You aren't accustomed to defeat."

"This is no defeat," said Gabriel. "This is but a momentary turn in a game I have all eternity to win. Certainly Hazraphet explained that an angel cannot be commanded to harm himself. I need merely wait a blink of an eye, and you will die of old age. Then I can pluck you once more from the time curve, before you've altered your tongue."

"That is a good strategy, if one is patient. My patience is at an end. Stand up."

Gabriel stood.

Albert said, "I bind you to fight me."

"What?"

"Fight me as you imagine a man must fight, using no weapons but your limbs. Make your strength no greater than mine. Feel pain as a man feels it."

Gabriel's eyes opened wide. He tilted his head back and laughed. "What? Are you mad? This is your binding? This is what I wanted in the first place. Prepare to die, Albert Einstein."

Gabriel charged at Albert, his eyes wide with excitement.

"Heeyah!" Albert cried, kicking upwards, placing his foot in the center of the Gabriel's face. Gabriel spun backwards, tripping over his own wings, landing on his hands and knees, laughing.

"I'd hoped she'd teach you how to fight," he said. "I'm very pleased. Very pleased indeed."

Like lightning, Gabriel twirled and lunged, aiming for Albert's legs.

Albert jumped clear, but as he landed the angel's hand closed around his ankle. He hit the ground hard, unable to roll with the impact the way Zoe had taught him.

Gabriel rose to his knees and yanked Albert closer, striking a vicious blow to his stomach. The cabbage Albert had swallowed moments before made a sudden return to the world.

He struggled for breath as Gabriel regained his feet.

"I like fighting like a man," Gabriel said, giggling. "I like kicking!" The angel's foot exploded against Albert's kidneys.

"I like pulling hair," Gabriel said, bending over Albert and grasping a handful of hair. He lifted Albert, bending his head back until he looked up into Gabriel's eyes.

"And I do so love scratching eyes," Gabriel said, bringing his steel-nailed fingers inches from Albert's face.

Albert's fingers closed around a fistful of the sandy soil he'd spent the morning tilling. As Gabriel's fingers descended, he threw the dirt, catching Gabriel in the eyes.

Gabriel let go of Albert's hair and staggered backwards. "Tricky son of an ape," he cursed as he wiped his eyes. "I love this! Keep struggling like this. Your futile hope is like sweet wine. The truth will be hard for you to swallow, when I choke the life out of you in the end."

"Truth?" gasped Albert as he rose to his feet once more. "If you swallow any truth whole, you'll choke on it. Use your teeth!"

Albert leapt as Gabriel opened his eyes. He wrapped his arms around the golden man's chest and squeezed with all his might. He sank his teeth into the angel's throat.

Gabriel kept laughing. "Tear out my throat! Yes! Fight! What will it matter? Angels don't need to breathe!"

Albert pushed forward with his legs, throwing them both to the ground. He sat up, straddling the angel, punching him hard in the nose and chin. Hazraphet had assured him Gabriel was capable of feeling pain, but the angel's laughter was starting to worry Albert. From the corner of his eye, he saw Zoe running across the field toward the fight. No matter the plan, he had to warn her to get away.

Gabriel took advantage of Albert's distraction to strike upwards, landing a terrible blow on Albert's chin. Albert fell backward, glad he'd spoken Gabriel's true name already. He'd just lost several teeth, and was unsure if he'd be able to say the name again.

Albert rolled to his hands and knees. Gabriel had risen to a sitting position, but rather than pressing his attack, he was shaking his head to clear it.

"Ah. You do feel pain," Albert said, spitting blood.

"Pain's a novelty," said Gabriel, still shaking his head. "I can see why humans liked to make war. What better fun could there be?"

"You have a lot to learn about humans," Albert said, managing to make it to his feet just as Zoe reached him. Zoe thrust the long, slender package she carried into his hands.

"Go," he said. "You mustn't see this."

"Stay," said Gabriel. "I'll have fun with you next."

"You'll do nothing but fall," said Albert.

"Not to your ilk," said Gabriel. "I haven't begun to show you pain, human. I've watched you kind climb down from their trees. I've studied your kind as ice ages came and went. I know every one of your weaknesses."

"If you know so much about humans," Albert said, "you know we have a fondness for tools."

He drew Hazraphet's sword from the water filled scabbard he had fashioned. The sword burst into flame.

"You said no weapons," Gabriel snarled.

Albert smirked. "I said *you* couldn't use weapons."

19. Funeral Music

Albert returned to the farm late that evening, his body bruised, his right eye swollen. A dozen blisters bubbled and grew on his hands and arms. Most of his hair was singed. Zoe ran to meet him. She said nothing as she leapt into his arms. He closed his weary arms around her and buried his face in her hair. She smelled like cabbage.

"I was so scared," she said.

Albert wiped the tears from her cheeks. "Hush," he said. "There's nothing to fear."

"Is he… is he dead?"

"He can't hurt us now."

"I thought I'd lost you."

"I was worried for a minute myself," he admitted.

"Then you're okay?" she said.

He nodded.

"Good," she said. Without warning, she slapped him. He stood there, staring at her, a little stunned, and she slapped him again.

"What the hell were you thinking, Al?" she screamed. "Why the hell did you fight him after you said his name? That wasn't part of the plan. You put everything in danger!"

Albert rubbed his cheek. It hurt worse than the wounds Gabriel had inflicted.

"I had my reasons," he said, quietly.

"What? What could possibly justify—"

"I needed to hurt him," Albert said. "I needed to hurt him for what he's done, and for what he intended to do. To you. To our children. The look on his face before I bound him—he was joyful. And I crushed that joy."

"Of all the stupid—"

"It's over," he said, placing his hand on her shoulder. "We shouldn't fight. Not now."

She reached for his hand. From the way she grabbed his wrist, he was sure she was about to do some sort of judo flip on him. Her grip slackened, and she leaned in to hug him.

"You're right. We've won," she said. "We can live out our lives in peace."

Albert said nothing. Zoe suddenly grew still. She looked in his eyes and said, "I felt you flinch. Something's wrong."

"Let us go into the house, my love," said Albert.

In the living room, his children were huddled together, staring at him with fear and doubt in their eyes.

"It's okay," Zoe said.

"There's nothing to fear," said Albert. "We must celebrate. Get the instruments." The children ran to fetch Albert's violin and Zoe's dulcimer and their own drums and flutes.

"You're keeping something from me, Al," Zoe said.

"Hush. Let's play." He took the violin his son brought him and looked at it. It was the fifth one he'd made, the first one that sounded approximately right to his ears. No doubt a concert violinist would have found the tone abhorrent, but he'd never been a concert violinist. It did well enough with the songs Zoe had taught him. He took up his bow and burst into *Bonaparte's Retreat.*

Zoe joined in, and Joseph on the flute, with Sissy and Christina keeping time on their small drums. Even little William clapped along. They played for hours, reels, waltzes, even a polka he'd remembered from his childhood. The night grew very late. William fell asleep, his daughters were nodding off, and even Joseph was having trouble keeping his eyes open.

He carried the children to their beds and kissed them good night. He left Zoe to tuck them in, while he went back to the living room, and his violin.

He began to play the song he really wanted to hear, a song he hadn't played in many, many years. Oh, nothing, nothing could weep like a violin.

"Al," Zoe said as she came back into the room. "What's wrong?"

Albert kept playing. Tears were in his eyes.

"You've never played like this," she said, her voice trembling. "It's like funeral music. I don't... I don't want to hear it anymore."

Albert stopped playing.

He put the violin down and placed his arms around her. "I want you to know I love you," he said.

"I know."

"I never wanted to part with you. I can't bear the thought of life without you."

"Al, you're alive. We can stay together for years."

"And then what? We will die eventually. Our children will die. It may not be my specialty, but I know a thing or two of genetics. We cannot be Adam and Eve. There is no hope of repopulating the Earth with a gene pool of two individuals."

"Al, we can't think like that. There's always hope."

"Yes," said Albert. "There's more than hope. Which is why I must save mankind."

20. Sacrifice

"Save mankind?" asked Zoe. "You've saved yourself. You've saved us! Isn't that enough?"

"You break things, you fix them. A wise person once told me that."

"Don't go blaming yourself again for what the Nazis did. You and I both know it's not your fault."

"No matter where the blame lies," Albert said, "only I can fix things."

Their eyes met, and he could see it in her, could see the terrible realization. She'd always been able to understand him as no other person ever could. He wished for the first time that she were an imbecile, a fool.

"I'll find you," she said.

"Perhaps," he said. "I will be old."

"I love you. Age ain't nothing but a number."

"We must do it now. While the children are sleeping."

"Just let me kiss them good-bye."

"No. We must act while we have the strength."

She followed him outside, across the fields. Beneath the shade tree the flaming sword flickered like a torch. Gabriel lay impaled by the sword, pinned to the ground, his arms and legs laying in a pile beside him.

Albert placed the limbs back in their sockets. He wasn't sure this was going to work with his missing teeth, but he had to try. He spoke Gabriel's true name. It didn't come out right. He tried again, fighting past the pain in his empty tooth sockets. This time, Gabriel's eyes fixed on him with a look of hatred, and he knew he'd gotten it right.

"Repair yourself," he said, grabbing the sword by the hilt and pulling it from Gabriel's chest. "Get up."

"If I must," said Gabriel, flexing his limbs as he floated upright.

"You must."

"Come to torture me some more?" Gabriel asked.

"I've toyed with the idea."

"You've surprised me, Albert Einstein," said Gabriel. "I didn't anticipate this streak of sadism."

"One man's sadism is another man's justice," said Zoe.

"Pithy," said Gabriel.

Albert said, "Hazraphet told me you spoke the truth about your abilities. With your wings, you can soar across the curvature of time."

"Yes. And it was you who gave me the map. Why did you doubt this? You're here, aren't you?"

"You're going to take us back," said Albert. "You will return Zoe to her rightful moment in time. My mind, with all my memories, you shall return to my twenty-three year old body. This time, I'll never reveal the Unity theory. I'll do what I can to muddy the theoretical waters to make relativity and quantum math seem even less compatible. Instead of arguing to keep America out of the war, I'll campaign to see that Hitler falls before he ever has a chance to grow strong."

"Twisting history to suit your whims may prove to be more difficult than you imagine, Albert Einstein."

"So be it. I must try."

"And you'd simply abandon your children?" asked Gabriel.

"Eden will keep them safe. One day, I will find a way back to them, perhaps. But, if not, I trade my children for the billions of unborn lives I snuffed out with my careless actions."

Gabriel looked at Zoe. "You can't agree to this."

"He's the genius," said Zoe, sounding unconvinced. Then her eyes hardened. "When I signed up to serve in the war, I was told sacrifices would be required. Leaving my children isn't right. But letting all those people die in those bombs is less right."

"I'll be free if you change history," said Gabriel, looking back toward Albert. "I'll find ways to thwart you."

"But if I don't reveal the Unity theory to the world," said Albert, "God never leaves. Hazraphet assures me that while God paid little attention to humanity, He kept the angels in line."

"God's presence only made me more subtle. Besides, it doesn't matter if you don't solve the unified field equation. It's woven into the fabric of reality. Someone eventually will figure it out. God will leave again. Next time, I'll kill you without bothering with the foreplay."

"Shut up," said Albert. "Obey me. Take us back."

"I'll find you," Zoe said.

Albert kissed her as Gabriel spread his wings.

Albert woke by the roadside, his bike overturned beside him, its wheels spinning wildly. He remembered this road, this wreck, and the amnesia he'd had for the rest of this day. There was no amnesia this time.

Zoe would never find him, he knew. There would be no Second World War. She would never serve in Canada, she would never come to Eden. What had happened would be prevented before it ever affected her, even though it would never change for him. His mind understood the subtle paradoxes that allowed this, and the terrible consequence. Only he and Gabriel could ever remember. But, as Gabriel had carried them back, he'd commanded the angel to forget.

He would carry this burden alone.

Albert died, in 1955, with the quest for a "Grand Unified Theory" more confused than he could ever have hoped.

His death was reported that night on television. Zoe Monroe Miller turned off the television and swallowed hard.

That night she slipped from bed without a word to her husband and climbed into the attic.

She moved among the dust covered boxes to the case that held her grandfather's fiddle.

Only tonight it wasn't a fiddle, it was a violin. She played it as it deserved to be played, like a woman weeping. After a time, she heard her husband's footsteps on the stairs. He came to her side and took her in his arms. He asked, softly, "What's wrong? What's wrong?"

"Ah," she said, half sobbing, half laughing. "You never know."

Queen of Mars

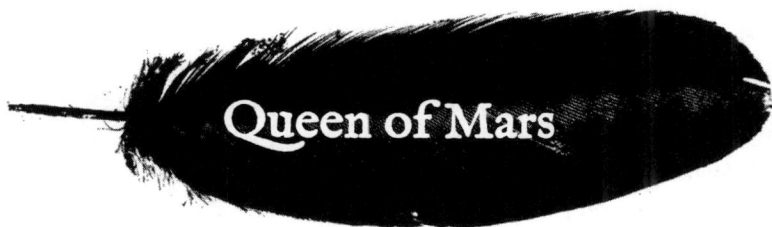

I was dangling by my fingers from the cliff. The dust swirling from the rockslide obscured the ravine below me. Maybe there was a ledge a few centimeters below my boots, or maybe there was a five-hundred-meter drop onto jagged stones. Even in Martian gravity, a fall like that would be fatal.

My rebreather monitor dipped toward red. Air farted through the rip in my suit. I needed to keep calm to save what was left of my oxygen. *Yeah, right.* I was sucking down air in huge gulps.

"Calling Blueford Habitat! This is California Lee!" I shouted. "Cali!" I don't know why I thought it was important to add my nickname. There are, like, a hundred people, tops, at Blueford, and I'm the only fourteen-year-old girl. Everyone knows me. "A cliff sheared off beneath me! Send help! Help! Help!"

I screamed, "Help!" three or five or twenty times until my panic ran its course. There was no response from Blueford. Helmet radios aren't strong enough to get a signal all the way up to a satellite. My radio pairs with the sat-phone on my bike and, of course, my bike was at the bottom of the ravine.

"Mom, I'm sorry," I said, knowing that my helmet video was still recording. "I shouldn't have lied to you. I should have said where I was going with my bike! But you would have said no, which wasn't fair, since I..." My voice trailed off. Why was I arguing with Mom in a message she'd see only after they found my mangled corpse?

I started to speak again, a short, simple, "I love you, Mom," but my voice caught in my throat. A shadow moved across the edge of my vision. I craned my neck and saw it was Deimos! My cat flittered down on those weird wings of his, coming in for a landing next to my fingers on what was left of the ledge. He stared at me, like he was curious as to what, exactly, I was up to.

"Deimos!" I yelled. "Fly down! Find my phone!"

Deimos didn't fly down. He twisted his body and started licking the edge of a wing.

"Deimos! Please! Don't act like you can't understand me!"

Deimos stopped licking his wing and gave me that cat look of, "Why are you bothering me with your mouth sounds?"

My jaw tightened. I was going to die because of my stupid cat.

Or, you know, because I was making stupid choices. I don't mean biking up the cliffs of the Valles Marineris. On my bike, I'm Queen of Mars! Since I've got the only mountain bike on the planet, there's not much competition for the title, but still. No, the stupidity here was wasting air screaming into a dead radio, and asking a cat to be helpful.

The breach was in the right armpit of my suit, judging from the farting noise. For understandable reasons, I was clinging to the cliff with both hands. I forced myself to let go with my left hand. My fingers were numb from hanging, so I mainly relied on sound as I grabbed loose bits of suit and pinched them together. The farting grew louder, then higher pitched, then stopped! I'd burned through a lot of my rebreather catalyst, but if I wasn't actively losing air, I'd bought myself a little time.

Sure. Time to dangle until my fingers failed and I dropped to my death.

Then, *duh,* I realized something obvious. It's crazy, but for the first time I got why some stories are called cliffhangers!

You know what they say about life flashing before your eyes when you're about to die? Maybe there's something to it. I mean, hanging off that cliff, I kept remembering my dog, Bucky. Back on Earth, we lived on the edge of the desert. There were endless single-track trails connecting right to my backyard. Bucky raced along beside me whenever I went out. If I'd gotten myself into a scrape like this one, you can bet Bucky would have already pulled me up from this cliff.

Then Mom got her dream job, and we moved to freaking Mars, and had to leave Bucky with my uncle. And Bluford? What a dump! The whole place smells like a locker room. Our apartment is smaller than my old bedroom, and my new bedroom could fit into my old closet.

The only upside to Mars is that Ron in the fab unit has a crush on Mom and lets me print pretty much anything I can design on the fabbers. I've been playing with 3d printers since I was four, but never had one big enough to print a full carbon fiber bike frame.

Unfortunately, you can't 3D print dogs. Deimos is alright, but he's no Bucky.

Technically, Deimos is a chimera, not a cat. Chimera's are lab animals gene tuned to prove mammals can survive on Mars. His DNA is, like, 95% feline, but the remaining 5% is crammed with DNA from insects, reptiles, and even plants. The purple batwings rising from his back are packed with photoreceptive cells that convert CO_2 into sugars and oxygen. His dense, black fur blocks radiation.

He's also a genius. He knows how to override the biometric locks on our doors by punching in the PIN on the keypad. But, he won't learn tricks, or even come when called. The closest thing we have to a game we play is him hiding my stuff and making me find it. Socks, pens, my STEM medals, all disappear. I find them in vents and behind pipes. One of my scrunchies turned up outside! I still haven't found my holo-bracelet.

When he's not being a brat, Deimos can be sweet, sneaking into my lap while I'm linked to school, watching the screen like he's totally engrossed by my assignments.

Which makes it even more frustrating that, when I was dangling off a cliff, about to fall to my death, he looked so dang bored.

On the other hand, I'd been hanging off the cliff long enough even *I* was getting bored. With my oxygen levels stable, it was time to do something exciting. I could let go and take my chances that I wouldn't drop far. Or, I could try to climb, even though the cliff was obviously unstable, and trying to move might trigger another slide.

I let go of my armpit, ignoring the return of the farting sound. I swung my hand up and groped for a better handhold further back on the ledge. Deimos watched me struggling, then put his paw on my grasping hand. Hooking his claws into my glove, he guided my arm over about three inches. My fingertips sank into a small crack in the rock, the perfect handhold.

Feeling more secure in my grip, I kicked around. Fine blades of stone crumbled beneath my boots. At last, my right boot found a good toehold. With better footing and a firm handhold, I pushed and pulled myself up. My right arm had no feeling at all, but Martian gravity has its advantages. I got my chin up over the ledge. My legs flailed wildly, searching for new toeholds, finding them. I rose higher, straining to reach another crack on the ledge further back. Every muscle trembled as I dragged myself onto the ledge. I rolled to my back.

"Queen of Mars!" I said, pumping my fists in the air.

This caused the farting sound to grow louder. I clamped my hand back into my armpit and sealed the leak. It was nice not to be losing air anymore, but my rebreather catalyst meter was already in the red zone. I had, I don't know, ten minutes? Fifteen?

"Mom," I said, so that my last thoughts would be recorded. "Mom, I love you. I'm so sorry. This isn't your fault. This isn't your fault."

I swallowed hard. I mean, it sucked that I was about to die. But it sucked a million times more that Mom would blame herself.

Mom wasn't thrilled the first time I took my bike outside the habitat, even though people go onto the surface all the time. You need a ton of exercise to stay healthy on Mars, and runners can bound across the landscape like gazelles.

On my bike, I leave runners in the dust, literally. Mom wants me to stay within two klicks of the domes, but riding on flat ground is tedious, especially when you can see the cliff walls not all that far away, begging to be explored. I started pushing out 10 kilometers, then 20. Mom yells at me when she checks my GPS logs, but she knows that biking is all that's keeping me sane on Mars. Luckily, she's never grounded me.

Still, I knew she'd never say yes to my big dream. I spent every night studying satellite maps of the cliff walls. There were some blind spots under overhangs, but I thought I'd found a route up the cliffs. Back on earth, every mountain biking record had been set decades ago. But to be the first person to ride from the valley floor to the rim of the Valles Marineris? *Queen of Mars!* People would remember me forever!

Sure. They'd remember me as the dumb girl who got herself killed.

I forced myself to sit up. I scooted further onto the cliff, bracing my back against the rock wall. I made myself stand, even though my legs felt like rubber. Shielding my eyes, I searched the valley floor. The way the cliffs folded around, I didn't have a line of sight to Blueford. But maybe if one of the runners were far enough out, and I could see them, and use my visor as a mirror…

But there were no runners, only the empty, silent desolation of Mars. If people really did turn into ghosts, this was going to be a lonely place to haunt.

The main reason I was thinking about ghosts was because, the night before, I might have seen one. I'd snuck into the vehicle bay to hide an extra rebreather cylinder in the handlebar bag, and spotted someone crouched next to my bike. I only saw her from behind, but it was plainly a girl, about my height and build. She even had the same haircut. Weird!

"Hey!" I called out. "What are you doing?"

Without looking back, she took off running.

I ran after her. "Stop!"

She dashed down a tunnel. I rounded the corner two seconds later. She was gone! There was no way she'd made it to the hatch at the end of the tunnel, opened it, and resealed it in two seconds. And why hadn't I heard her footsteps when she ran?

A vent cover overhead was slightly ajar. I peeked inside. The vent tube was, like, ten centimeters wide. No way she crawled into it.

I went back to my bike. I examined every bolt and screw. Nothing was out of place. Why would anyone mess with my bike anyway?

I should have asked the bay master to let me review security video. But, he'd want to know why I'd been in the bay to start with. In retrospect, maybe catching a fleeting glimpse of your own ghost is a pretty bad omen.

I sank back down the wall, feeling beaten. Mom was still at work. She's on a gene-team designing a more sustainable microbiome for Martian soil, and when she's at her job she's so busy she never checks in with me. My oxygen would give out long before she got home and realized I was missing. I had a spare rebreather catalyst in my handlebar bag. If I could get to it, maybe I could stay alive until Mom got home and started wondering where I was. I crept forward, stretched out on my belly, and nervously stuck my head over the edge, still worried the whole cliff might give way.

The cliff didn't come crashing down, but my hopes did. The dust had settled, at least enough for me to see my bike. It was just a blurry speck three or four hundred meters straight down. I couldn't jump down and survive, and there was no way my oxygen wouldn't give out before I could climb to the bottom. The fastest way down would be to rappel, and I'd been smart enough to bring along some climbing rope.

In my saddlebags.

On the bike.

Deimos walked to my side, looking down to see what I was seeing. He must not have been impressed by the impossible challenge before me, because he turned back, sat down, and started licking his wings again.

"Can you at least pretend not to be bored by my impending death?" I asked. "I mean, I wouldn't even be here if you hadn't pulled your little stunt."

Deimos stopped licking long enough to give me a nasty look. No matter how much he pretends otherwise, I swear he understands every word I say.

This morning, while Mom was getting ready for work, she asked if I'd seen Deimos.

"Nope." Not that I'd looked for him.

"I'm sure he'll turn up," said Mom. "I've put down fresh water. Fab up some protein nuggets when he comes home."

Like I was going to wait around for the stupid cat. The second Mom was through the door I wriggled into my surface suit. I only had eight hours to make history!

Once I was out on the surface, I tried to pace myself, keeping my legs fresh for the hard climbs, but ten minutes out I was already sweating. To be safe, I'd packed enough spare parts to almost build a second bike.

I finally found my flow. My thoughts were lulled by the steady crunch of dust under the wheels. The sun rolled along the rim, tiny but harsh, like a lamp without a shade. Every little pebble cast dark shadows. You'd think riding on a whole 'nother planet would be exciting, but the valley is kind of monotonous, except for the cliffs.

The Valles Marineris is the biggest canyon in the solar system, a rift valley that cracked Mars right down the middle. Gritty wind has sandblasted every rock face. The cliffs have sheered and settled at different levels and weird angles, making a kind of twisting road just begging to be ridden.

Except, you know, it's not a road, and the jumbled cliffs are separated by ravines. I swallowed hard when I got to the first jump I'd need to make. It was only two meters to the next ledge. That's nothing. But, yeesh, it was a long way down if I missed.

I rode back down the trail, wheeled around, then pedaled like my life depended on it. I overshot the jump by, like, five meters. I squeezed my brakes before I skidded off the ledge beyond. Once my heart started beating again, I pumped my fists. Queen! Of! Mars!

Full of adrenaline, I tackled the next climb. I was huffing and puffing up an incline I'd never have tackled in Earth's gravity. At the top, I leaned my bike against the cliff wall to take a break. I sat at the edge of the ledge, my feet dangling. This was the highest I'd ever been on Mars. The valley was painted a hundred different shades of red, glittering with flecks of mica. I totally needed to launch the minidrone in my trunk pack for a pic against this backdrop.

When I turned back to the bike, my jaw dropped. The trunk pack was wide open and Deimos was sitting in it, staring at me!

No wonder my legs were so shredded. Deimos weighs, like, five kilos. On a hard climb, every gram counts. "How did you even get in there?" I asked.

My heart sank as I realized I had to turn back. It was one thing to risk my neck, but, even if it was his own fault being out here, I didn't want to put him in danger. On the other hand, there was less than half a click to the first overhang, one of the blind spots on the satellite maps. There was only one ravine between here and there. I couldn't turn back without at least scoping it out to make certain the route was viable.

I calmly approached Deimos. "Who's a good kitty?" I rubbed the top of his head as he rose to meet my hand. "Not you!" I shouted as I grabbed him. I jammed him back into the trunk. I zipped the lid shut while he mewed. I had some duct tape in my handlebar bag, the ultimate trail multitool. I wrapped the trunk a few times to seal him inside. Chimeras might be escape artists, but there was no way he was getting out of that.

I got back onto my bike and slowly climbed the skinny ledge that led toward the next ravine. Gravel slipped beneath my tires, threatening to send me over the edge. I didn't have far to go, but it felt like forever before the trail widened and got a little flatter. I had a nice straight shot leading up to the next ravine. This was a five meter jump, slightly more challenging, but I can tackle eight meters or more in Martian gravity. I gripped my handlebars tightly, lifted up from my saddle, and pumped, pumped, pumped! As my front wheel went over the edge, my rear wheel lost traction! The whole bike lurched as a heavy weight landed on my shoulder. It was Deimos!

Maybe he jumped on my shoulder to make sure I knew he'd thwarted my best efforts to trap him. Maybe he was only curious about what I was doing. You know what curiosity does to cats! Thanks to losing traction at the last second, I was dropping faster than planned, on a much flatter arc, until…

WHAM! My front wheel came down on the opposite ledge. My rear wheel dropped, barely catching on the lip. Deimos leapt from my shoulder to safety as I fought for balance. I only needed a few millimeters to get my center of gravity fully over the ledge. "Queen of Mars!" I screamed, as I gave the right pedal all my strength. The rear wheel rolled up the lip. I spun forward another meter on firm ground and stopped. I leaned on the handlebars, gasping for air. I'd made it!

Then the rock ledge I stood on peeled away with a deafening *CRACK!*

I jumped forward, arms outstretched as the ground vanished beneath me. My fingers grabbed hold of the remaining ledge as countless tons of rock tumbled down the ravine. The freshly exposed rock I hung against was sharp as razors. There was a fluttering, farting sound from my armpit as a dagger of stone tore a gash at the seam. The vapor trapped in my suit turned into snowflakes as it swirled in the turbulent air.

So that's why this story starts with me hanging from a cliff. Is it going to end with me running out of oxygen and dying where I might never be found? If only Deimos wasn't such a cat. I looked at him and said, "Bucky would have run to get help by now."

Deimos looked mildly offended. Without warning, he leapt off the cliff.

"No!" I yelled, trying to grab him. He was too far away already, flapping his wings in a zig-zagging flight. He fluttered down the ravine, coming to rest on my bike. I watched as he unzipped the handlebar bag. He pushed his head into the bag, then came out holding something in his mouth. He also used one of his claws to hook onto the roll of duct tape. Climbing, jumping, and flying, he navigated his way back up the cliff in a little under a minute.

Deimos dropped a small tube next to me. My eyes went wide. It was my spare rebreather cylinder! I ejected the old canister and clicked it in. Instantly, my oxygen levels turned green.

I turned back to Deimos. Only Deimos was no longer sitting next to me. In his place was a girl my age. Exactly my age, because she was me! Also, I could see through her, like a ghost.

"You were messing with my bike last night!" I said.

My ghostly double held up her fist and bobbed it back and forth, sign language for "yes." Luckily, ASL is one of the languages I'm studying.

I signed back, "Who are you?"

"Talk with voice," said the girl, still signing. She pointed at her ear, then her mouth. "Hear good. No make people sounds."

"People sounds?" I asked. "Are you an alien?"

The girl rolled her eyes. She said, out loud, "Meow."

"Deimos?"

The girl nodded, lifting a hand to her throat. She vanished, leaving Deimos sitting before me, with his paw touching his collar. Only it wasn't his collar. It was my missing holo-bracelet! He clicked the bracelet/collar once more and turned back into me.

"Could Bucky do that?" he signed as he pushed the roll of duct tape toward me.

"Why do you look like me?" I asked, picking up the tape.

"You in bracelet," Deimos said, with a shrug. "Easy to move around when girl."

"To do what?" I asked, as I tore off a strip of tape.

"Take stuff. No ask old girl who feeds me."

"Old girl? You mean Mom?"

Deimos nodded. "No trust."

"Why not?"

"Scientist. Put in cages. Stick with needles. No good."

"Mom's not like that," I said, sealing the hole in my armpit with the tape.

"No trust," said Deimos. "No tell I talk."

If chimeras could talk, it seemed like something the gene-tuners should know. But, who was I to lecture anyone about keeping secrets?

"My lips are zipped. I won't rat you out."

"Rats?" Deimos asked, his eyebrows lifting. "What rats?"

"It's just an expression."

"Oh," said Deimos. "No rats?"

"I swear I don't have any rats."

The holographic version of me looked crestfallen. Then, Deimos touched his throat and resumed his feline form. He motioned for me to follow him and starting walking along the now tiny remnant of the ledge.

I followed, hugging the rock. Around the bend, we found the overhang I'd been trying to reach. Beneath the overhang was a small opening to a cave, barely a meter tall.

I crawled inside, following Deimos up a gravel slope, into the darkness beyond. I flicked on my helmet LEDs to see where I was going.

I slipped on the first big rock we reached. It was coated in thick black slime. How was anything on Mars slimy? Weird as that was, I was too distracted by the gages on my helmet to bother getting a sample. There was some oxygen in the room. And water vapor! Even weirder, the room was a balmy 2 degrees Celsius. That's chilly on Earth, but crazy hot for Mars.

Crawling down another tight tunnel we reached a small chamber where, somehow, there was an open pool of water. Beside the water was a second chimera, a small tabby with huge eyes. Snuggled up against her belly were three kittens.

"Meow," the female chimera said, plainly alarmed. "Meow! Mew, mew, meow!"

"Mew meow mew," Deimos explained to her. "Meow meow!"

Deimos turned to me and used sign language again, using only his paws. I had to guess at half his "words," but I think he'd explained I was a friend.

I said to the female chimera, "I swear I won't hurt you. How are you even out here, anyway?"

Deimos shifted back into my mirror image to better use his sign language. It was still challenging. His syntax was sloppy and his vocabulary had weird gaps. Like, he kept calling the kitchen fabber the "food thing," and my bike was the "wheel thing."

As best as I could piece together, the chimeras had been exploring the area around the habitat for a while. Deimos and Donut (her name) found this brine seep and decided to turn it into a home for their kittens. I thought I was making history exploring these cliffs, but my cat was way ahead of me.

"Kittens need solid food before long. I hide food thing in wheel thing," Deimos said.

A kitchen fabber isn't much bigger than a toaster. I guess that's another reason my saddlebags felt so weighed down.

Deimos said, "We get wheel thing with snake thing. You go home. Leave food thing."

Snake thing had me stumped until I remembered the climbing rope I'd packed.

"You saved my life," I said. "The food thing is a fair reward."

I gave the bike a quick inspection once we dragged it up from the ravine. My emergency beacon was smashed and my phone was nowhere to be found. As for the rest of the bike, the rear tire wobbled from a broken spoke, but the frame hadn't bent at all. I flew back down the mountain, catching crazy air as I zoomed over the ravine and jumped boulder after boulder. Back on the valley floor, I pedaled like I was being chased by wolves. The sun had long since vanished over the cliffs. Mom had to be tearing her hair out.

I kept watching the skies for search drones. If my phone was back there in the rocks, a rescue party might lock in on it. Drones might spot the cave. I'd betray Deimos and Donut without even meaning too.

I made it to the bay without seeing any drones take off. Mom had to be worried, but apparently she wasn't to the demand-a-search-party stage.

I ran back to my apartment, stopping at the door. I took a second to peel off the duct tape in my armpit, hoping Mom wouldn't notice the rip. I brushed back my sweaty hair, took one last calming breath, then opened the door.

I was maybe ten steps into the apartment when Mom ran at me, babbling, switching between yelling and cooing with each breath. Her words were a confusing jumble of "where were you?" and "thank God!" and "why didn't you answer your phone?"

She didn't pause to let me answer, which was fine. I didn't know what to tell her. I mean, if there was one lesson I should take away from my near death experience, it was not to keep secrets from my mother. On the other hand, there was Deimos, Donut, and the kittens, so maybe the bigger lesson was that some secrets are okay if they're for a good cause?

I emerged from my moral calculations to find that Mom was still talking at me. "I've called you a hundred times! Why didn't you answer?"

This time, she paused. *Uh oh.* She expected an answer.

"I, uh, lost my phone," I said, truthfully.

"Lost it?" she said. "Where?"

"If I knew where, it wouldn't be—"

"Don't get smart with me, young lady."

At that exact second, the keypad on the door went *beep, boop, beep. The* door slid open.

Deimos sauntered into the room, holding my phone in his mouth. He walked into the kitchen, dropped the phone on the tiles, then took a drink from his water bowl.

"I found my phone," I said, managing a half grin.

Mom crossed her arms. She still looked angry, but seemed to be weighing how much of her wrath should be allocated to the cat.

She threw up her hands. "Why would the cat take your phone?"

I shrugged. "Why do cats do anything?"

Deimos stopped drinking, walked into the living room, and flopped onto the rug, instantly asleep.

"Go to your room," Mom said, obviously still needing time to process her emotions.

"Okay," I said. But, before I went, I stepped forward, and gave her a big hug. "Mom, I love you."

"And I love you," she said, returning the hug even harder. "But you're still being sent to your room."

I skedaddled, grateful for the escape. I needed to wipe the video memory in my helmet before Mom thought to look at it and learned about Donut and her kittens. Plus, you know, the whole near-death thing. She'd totally make a big thing out of it. Moms!

I pulled up the virtual interface, grabbed the video file, and dragged it toward the trash icon. I paused. This was the only record of, like, the dozen different ways I'd made history today. What's the point of having an amazing adventure if you can't share the video?

I sighed, then dropped the file into the trash.

I opened up the satellite maps of the cliffs and started searching for a different route. Assuming I wasn't grounded for, like, a decade, I still had history to make.

"Queen of Mars," I whispered, permitting myself a discreet fist pump. "Queen of Mars."

The Map of the Drowned City

Elspeth leaned from the rigging of the *Sea Dragon,* shielding her eyes from the glare of the bay. The ship was eerily quiet. The often boisterous crew had grown listless in the windless heat. The anchor rope groaned as the ship rolled on the gentle swells. The calm was broken by a loud thumping from the forecastle.

Elspeth frowned. Her father was finally awake. She leapt, plunging toward the sea as her father drunkenly called out, "Where's my mermaid?"

With her body straight as a spear, Elspeth sliced into the water. She scissored her legs, swimming deeper. The sun cast her flickering shadow across the sandy avenues that covered the seafloor. On their spring visit to the Drowned City, the storm-swollen rivers that fed the bay had dumped so much silt that she'd barely been able to see her hand before her face. Now, as summer dried the inlands, the innumerable oysters of the bay filtered the waters to near transparency.

She glided over the bejeweled ridges that marked the ruined streets. Enormous crystalline shards, many as tall as houses, jutted at odd angles from rainbow sands of pulverized glass.

She came across the largest intact pane she'd ever seen, a rectangle of silver nearly as long as her ship. She swam closer, watching her reflection glide across the glass. The muted sun painted her skin with shimmering scales of blue and green. Her long hair floated around her in a halo as she drifted.

For a moment, she fantasized that she truly was a mermaid, stolen from her kingdom and forced to live among ship-bound

James Maxey

brutes. Any moment a fish-king with a crown and trident might swim forth to guide her to her castle of coral.

She cherished these quiet moments, far from creaking ropes and thumping sails, safe from surly voices and slurred curses. The distant murmur of surf rolled along her skin, a slow echo of the heartbeat a baby must hear in the womb.

Of course, at eleven years of age, Elspeth was no baby, and she was no mermaid. She was the daughter of Portsmouth Howell, no matter how much she wished it were not so. But wishes would never bring order, safety, or comfort to her world. Hard and cynical before her time, her father had taught her well that all desirable things in life could only be purchased with gold. Turning her face toward the sun, she kicked, rising toward the great, grim shadow of her father's ship.

Elspeth drew breath as she breached the surface. As water drained from her ears, the chaos of the *Sea Dragon* wafted over the waters. Her father still shouted for her, and his rising anger had crewmen racing about the deck, attempting to look busy while avoiding actual labor.

The only motionless figure was Surgeon. The dragon was perched in the rigging, his long, scaly face turned toward her. Surgeon was a tatterwing, a sky-dragon whose wings had been cut to ribbons in punishment for some crime. No one aboard the ship knew or cared what might have earned him such a fate. Nor did anyone care what his true name might have been. The crew called him Surgeon because the beast was, in fact, a competent surgeon. He had an encyclopedic knowledge of human anatomy, and his pills, potions, and poultices cured more maladies than they caused. Despite this, every sailor aboard cursed the filthy beast, though never to his face. Surgeon's claws could slice a man open as skillfully as they could sew a wound shut.

"Where's my mermaid!" her father screamed, his voice echoing in the hold, followed by a loud crash.

Surgeon tossed a rope from the deck down to Elspeth. "You should go to your father before he tears the ship apart."

"Do you know what he wants with me?" she asked.

"What does he ever want you for, other than to dive for treasure?"

For most people adrift at sea, the rope dangling before her would have been a lifeline. She stared at it like a condemned man looking upon a noose.

Surgeon noted her hesitation. "We're only a few miles from shore. I never saw you if you choose to swim away forever."

Elspeth sighed. "Who then would care for my mother?"

She grasped the rope and started to climb.

"Someone bring her to me!" her father shrieked as he came up the ladder from the hold at the same time she swung herself over the railing. Her father had a bottle in his good hand as he waved the hook that capped his other arm. "I want my mermaid!"

None of the men on deck bothered to look in his direction. Portsmouth Howell's captain's coat was unbuttoned, revealing his shirtless torso, pockmarked with festering boils. His long, dark hair hung in tangles around his face. His tricorn hat had blown overboard weeks ago, meaning he had nothing to shield his eyes as he looked into the rigging still seeking Elspeth, staring right into the sun. He winced, closing his eyes as he shook his bottle of liquor at the sky, growling, "Son of the devil!"

As he gesticulated toward the sun, his pants slipped from his boney hips, catching at his knees. He bent to retrieve them, toppling face first to the deck.

"Assassin!" her father shouted, rolling to his back, slashing the air with his hook. "I'll flay the villain that tripped me!"

"No one tripped you, Father," said Elspeth, stepping toward him. She crouched, helping him pull his pants up, steadying him as he rose. Never once did he let go of his bottle.

"Where've you been?" he asked, sounding more confused than angry.

"Swimming," she said, as if the water streaming from her hair failed to make that obvious. "While you slept, we reached the Drowned City." She started to add, "No thanks to you," but held her tongue.

Though she was only eleven, Elspeth had made this journey countless times. Her father's men were the worst Hampton had to offer, louts too dumb, lazy, or degraded to find work on respectable vessels. On any other ship, a captain as abusive as Portsmouth Howell would have been the target of mutiny, but her father had assembled a crew too slovenly and stupid to unite against him.

None of these men could use a sextant or read a map. Elspeth had navigated the *Sea Dragon* along the parlous coast, through the gauntlet of pirates and shoals that lay between Hampton and the Drowned City. While she lacked her father's ability to tongue-lash his disheveled crew into chaotic action, the less dimwitted seamen grasped that Elspeth knew what she was doing. They followed her commands because she was their best hope of returning from a voyage alive.

Elspeth tried to navigate her father back to his cabin but he couldn't keep his legs under him. A shadow fell across them both and she turned to find Surgeon. Wordlessly, the dragon grabbed her father, rudely slinging him across his back like a filthy duffle bag. Surgeon carried him to his cabin and tossed him on the bunk. The dragon doused the captain with the contents of a bucket next to the bed. Elspeth held her breath, sparing her lungs from the reeking fumes.

Her father sat up, sputtering, wiping his face, his eyes wide.

"You've found your mermaid," Surgeon said. "Show her the map."

Portsmouth glowered at Surgeon. "How do you know about the map?"

"You were boasting about it before we ever left port."

"I was?" asked her father. He nodded slowly. "Aye. 'Tis a thing of beauty! I'm going to be richer than Albekizan!" He cast a hateful gaze at the tatterwing. "You'll get your taste, you greedy dog. Now be gone! The map's not for your devil eyes."

"As you wish," said Surgeon, turning away. The dragon's eyes lingered on Elspeth for a long second. He seemed on the verge of speaking, before changing his mind and leaving.

Elspeth was glad he hadn't asked her a question, since she was still holding her breath. Her mother's family, the Bloodsworths, came from the Blades, a chain of long, thin islands far beyond the eastern horizon. Women of these isles fed their families by spearfishing among the reefs of the archipelago. Elspeth had inherited her mother's powerful lungs. Beneath the waves, she could swim for nearly ten minutes before resurfacing. With luck, her father would tell her what he had planned before she had to take another breath in the rancid atmosphere of his cabin.

Her father rolled from his bunk, landing in a crouch, then stood and lurched for his desk. He dramatically swept aside the clutter of empty bottles and scrawled ledgers, then fumbled beneath the desk with his hook, muttering curses.

Elspeth gently nudged him aside, reached beneath the desk, and pressed the latch that popped open the hidden drawer. Her father pulled out a scroll of yellowed paper and unrolled it. "Behold!" he said. "The key to my fortune!"

Her heart sank. She'd seen this map before, or ones like it. In the narrow alleys of Hampton, dealers sold antiquities from the antediluvian world. Long ago, the coasts were cluttered with great metropolises teeming with wonders, including towers of glass that pierced the heavens. Mankind had grown so powerful that they no longer feared the gods. In retribution, the gods caused the sea to rise, destroying the cities.

Elspeth doubted the existence of gods. The sea, the wind, and the sun needed no guiding intelligence to destroy the works of man. Still, the magnificent cities of lore were no myth. When she ran her fingers through the sands of any beach, she pulled up fragments of this lost age, worn bricks and rusted blobs, the occasional coin, and innumerable sand-frosted pebbles of glass. In shallow bays, parallel rows of oyster beds marked out ancient avenues of towns long forgotten. The Drowned City was the largest of these vanished places. When the water was calm and clear, anyone could see the grid of streets covering endless miles of seafloor.

"This street," her father said, tapping the map. "This street was where the banks were."

She didn't understand why that mattered at all. Her father's unsteady finger was pointing to a street that was plainly inland.

The bank where the land bordered the bay was several blocks distant from his finger.

Portsmouth recognized doubt in her face. "I'm not speaking of a shoreline. Men used to store their fortunes in buildings called banks. The vaults of these banks were filled with gold and silver and precious gems. Find even one, and my fortune is made!"

She rolled her eyes, having heard all this before.

"It's different this time!" he said. "There are tons of gold in these vaults! Literally tons!"

The absurdity of his words defeated her resolve not to breathe inside his cabin. She said, "If it truly is a ton, how am I supposed to swim back up with it?"

"Find it and I'll figure it out."

"Have you figured out how I'm supposed to get into a vault?"

"Iron doors will have corroded away," said her father. "The gold will just be lying there, pristine and for the taking!"

"Nothing down there is pristine," she said. "These banks you're looking for collapsed long ago."

"The vaults would be in basements, untouched by the waves."

"If there are any basements, they're filled with silt."

"Not all of them," said her father. "Mary told me of the tunnels she found. She said there's a city beneath the city. This map tells me where to find the entrances to these tunnels."

"I know about the tunnels," Elspeth admitted. "The ones I've found are pitch black. You want me to grope around in the dark? That's your big plan?"

"I've figured that out!" said her father, staggering toward his bunk. He dropped to his knees, thrusting his good arm far beneath his bed. He pulled out a small wooden crate barely big enough to hold a loaf of bread. "Feast your eyes on these," he said, prying the lid open with his hook. He revealed a row of red cylinders, each about a foot long and maybe an inch and a half thick. "Flares! Do you know how rare these are?"

"Oh my stars," said Elspeth, who *did* know how rare they were. Thanks to her father's lust for lost treasures, she knew more than most people about the relics of the antediluvian world. These red cylinders had once been relatively common objects. A flare was full of a substance that burned brightly, even underwater. The passage of centuries had turned these once mundane items into precious rarities. Her father's mad plan was to search for phantom gold using antiquities worth more than their weight in gold.

"How did you get these?" she asked.

"Never mind that," he said.

"You want me to burn through a fortune in rare artifacts for the chance of finding a few gold coins?"

"It's not a few coins we're seeking," he said. "You'll find bricks of gold. Bricks! And diamonds as big as apples!"

"But these flares could pay our debts. The *Sea Dragon* could sail into Hampton without being seized by our creditors. You could get our house back, and— "

"You dream small, Daughter," said Portsmouth. "The devil take my creditors!" He drew up to his full height, straightening his captain's coat, and hitching up his sagging britches. He puffed out his chest as he said, "Those coin-sharks spend their days fiddling over numbers on a ledger, blind to the true riches of this world. When we sail back to Hampton with a ship laden with treasure, they'll erect statues to the force of nature that is Portsmouth Howell!"

Of course, there was already a statue of a Howell standing in Hampton. Elspeth's grandfather was Samson Howell, the legendary commander of the Salt Fleet. Before meeting his untimely death in a storm, Samson had given his young son Portsmouth command of his finest ship, the *Sea Dragon*. Inheriting a well-established trade route and the good name of his father, Portsmouth Howell had been handed a foolproof path toward his own fortune. But, the first time Portsmouth had navigated the *Sea Dragon* from her home port, he set a course not for Sharlston, the contracted destination of his cargo, but for the distant Blades. The beautiful Mary Bloodsworth had rebuffed his drunken proposal two years before, when he was but a lad of seventeen. Returning as the captain of his own ship, Mary saw the young sailor with different eyes, and said yes.

Portsmouth celebrated their nuptials with a voyage to the Drowned City. His cargo was already weeks late. What would another month matter?

The sandbars surrounding the city were treacherous to navigate, but the glittering, glassy ruins were a wonderful gift to a diver like Mary.

Mary discovered statues of long forgotten men, their names and faces blotted out by barnacles. She swam through great, roofless halls, sifting through the bejeweled sand for simple treasures. She found an old tea cup with a gilded rim, a porcelain doll with a painted red dress, and fragile glass tubes bent and twisted to form letters. On the last night of their stay, on a moonlit dive, Mary had dragged her fingers through fine sand and came up holding a glittering gold necklace studded with diamonds.

When Mary had handed Portsmouth the necklace, she handed over a fortune worth more than all the cargo in the hold of the *Sea Dragon*. She didn't know she was also handing over all her hopes and her happiness, to be crushed in his greedy fingers.

PORTSMOUTH HOWELL CLIMBED THE RIGGING with his spyglass tucked beneath his chin. Elspeth had no doubt her father would find this street of banks among the avenues of shells. For longer than she'd been alive, her father had obsessively studied the city. Her two older sisters, long since lost to the sea, had dragged up old street signs, which her father had cross-referenced with his collection of ancient maps. Her family had never found another treasure quite as valuable as the necklace, but they'd pulled up smaller trinkets, wedding bands, earrings and gold nuggets shaped like human teeth. Bowls and plates and glassware emerged from the sand looking new. The antiquities fetched good prices, but never quite paid the expenses of the trips. The worse their finances grew, the more frequently Portsmouth returned to the Drowned City in pursuit of his great fortune.

The loss of two daughters hadn't dissuaded him. Their bodies had never been found. As Elspeth went below deck to the small cabin near the rear of the ship, she found herself thinking of these lost sisters, whether she might one day find their bones among the ruins, or whether they'd taken their chances by swimming for the untamed shores surrounding the bay.

She knocked once on the door of the small cabin. There was no answer. She went inside. A single open window ventilated the small space, with a ragged curtain fluttering before it. Her mother was tucked beneath covers, her hand draped across her eyes. Elspeth could tell that she was awake.

"We've reached the Drowned City?" Mary asked.

"Aye," said Elspeth.

"Your father won't be satisfied until all our bones roll beneath the waves," said Mary.

"This might be the last time we make this journey," said Elspeth. "Father has a map that leads to vaults of gold."

"Then our doom is certain," said Mary, still covering her eyes.

"It might be different this time," said Elspeth. "Imagine if we were rich. We could have a house in Hampton again. We could live comfortably, among respectable people."

"Your father owned a house when I married him," said her mother. "The name Howell was respectable, once." Her mother lifted her head, rising on her elbows. "Help me with the bedpan."

Elspeth moved to her mother's side. She'd been Mary's primary caretaker for the last four years, ever since her mother had lost the use of her legs.

Mary said, "Don't be seduced by your father's dreams of treasure."

"But we've found treasure before," said Elspeth. "And I'm not doing this for his dream. I'm doing it for mine. I want to take you from the chaos of this ship. I want you to be safe and comfortable. The gold that will save us is down there, I know it. I just need a little luck."

"My luck finding that necklace ruined us all."

"You can't blame yourself," said Elspeth.

"I can and I shall," Mary said bitterly. "I'm the one who awakened the monster. One day, it shall devour us."

Elspeth wasn't certain if her mother spoke metaphorically of her father, or referred to the actual sea monster that she claimed dwelled in the subterranean chambers of the city.

"Whatever your father wants, don't swim into the tunnels," Mary warned, which resolved the ambiguity. She was speaking of the actual beast. For the hundredth time, Mary gave her warning of the monster haunting the Drowned City: "The beast that crushed my legs has tentacles thicker than the trunk of an ancient oak. No matter how much your father tempts you with tales of treasure, never swim into the undercity. If I lose you, I'll have nothing."

"You'll always have me," said Elspeth, as she emptied the bedpan out the window. "I swear this is our last trip to these terrible waters. I'm going to buy us a house, hire a nurse, and give you the life of a queen."

Mary's eyes glistened. "It pains me that I chain you down."

"Caring for you is no burden."

Her mother shook her head. "The only reason your father keeps me aboard instead of dumping me at some house of charity is that I shackle you to him. As long as I live, you can't escape."

"I swear, after this trip, all will be different," said Elspeth.

Mary wept uncontrollably at these reassuring words. No doubt her mother had heard them before, from her father's lips.

Elspeth left her mother's tiny cabin, returning to the hold. The exposed ribs of the ship curved around her in the large, dimly lit space, making her feel like she was in the belly of some enormous beast. In the shadows of the far wall, two golden eyes watched her.

It was Surgeon. She shuddered at the sight of him. In the air, sky-dragons seemed huge, with twenty-foot wingspans and powerful chests and shoulders. Stripped of their wings, they weren't terribly fearsome. Surgeon was only a little taller than she was, and his wingless forelimbs were thin, almost skeletal, though inhumanly strong. The dragon's claws would be the envy of any panther, but it wasn't his claws that gave him such a sinister air. There was something about his gaze that made her feel like a mouse staring into the eyes of a cat.

Surgeon said, with a disinterested tone, "Your only escape will be to kill him."

"What?" she asked.

"You could follow the example of the dragon kings," said Surgeon. "They drive away their sons when they reach the age of maturity. The spurned sons either perish in the wilderness, or grow stronger in their exile until they return to slay their father. In this way, the kingdom is always ruled by a dragon of great strength."

"Why are you telling me this?"

"I've lived among humans for a long time," said Surgeon. "I've never before known a child who commanded her own ship."

"This is my father's ship," Elspeth said, clenching her fists. "If you continue to speak with such insolence, I'll have you keelhauled for mutiny."

"Yes," said Surgeon. "You'd take charge of the task yourself. The last three times we've put to sea, your father has barely given an order. The crew waits for your commands."

"They know I speak for my father."

"They know your father babbles and blusters, while you give sensible orders that will return them safely back to port."

"My father has many things on his mind," she said, crossing her arms. "I'm merely helping."

"Such loyalty. You'll never keep the promises you make to your mother while your father still breathes."

"You were eavesdropping?"

"Dragons hear everything," said Surgeon. "Men fear my claws, but it's my ears that have kept me alive all these years."

"Those years will come to a swift end if you continue to speak of mutiny."

"Then let us speak of treasure."

Her curiosity stirred. The dragon was too intelligent to reveal himself as a mutineer unless the payoff was genuine. "What treasure?"

"Look around," said Surgeon. "What do you see?"

She shrugged. "The hold?"

"The *empty* hold," said Surgeon. "The ribs of this vessel should be groaning with the weight of cargo. Your father inherited all he needed to build his fortune. This ship is all that remains, but it's no small prize."

James Maxey

"I don't need you to tell me my family history," she said.

"Then let me tell you your future. Despite all your father has done to besmirch his name, if you take command of this vessel, your Howell ancestry will open many doors."

"You truly believe anyone would entrust their cargo to a ship captained by a girl my age?"

"The audacity of the proposition is what makes it attractive," said Surgeon. "Investors are gamblers at heart. But this need not be a gamble on *your* part. I've the wealth you'd need to pay your debts."

"You? Wealthy?" She'd overestimated the dragon's grasp of reality.

"I haven't always been a tatterwing," Surgeon said, raising his bony forelimbs, shaking the remnant shreds of his wings. "I held a high office at the College of Spires. I studied artifacts and manuscripts from the antediluvian world, a time before dragons even existed."

"Haven't dragons been around forever?" she asked.

"Dragons didn't appear until roughly a thousand years ago. As a scholar of the Human Age, the origin of dragons seems plain enough. Humans mastered the codes that organize non-living molecules into the various forms of life. The obvious conclusion is that humans created dragons."

"Really?" said Elspeth. She had no idea what a molecule was, living or non-living. The only reason she couldn't comfortably dismiss his talk as gibberish was that in all her journeys through the Drowned City, she'd never once found any sign of dragons. Every artifact she'd ever dug up had plainly been crafted for use by humans.

Surgeon nodded, then said, "It was a great honor to be able to study the Human Age. The High Biologian took care in selecting dragons who could be trusted with this scholarship. For many years, I did nothing to betray this trust." He shook his head slowly. "But dragons aren't the only ones who study antiquities. There are isolated communities of humans who cling to the old knowledge. I was eager to learn what they knew. Doing so required clandestine trades of my documents for theirs. My superiors learned of my collaboration with humans... and...." The rest of his story trailed off as he scratched at the ragged scars that marred his limbs. "Your father routinely tosses aside trash brought up in his obsessive search for gold. Within these cast-off clumps of shell and mud, I find remnants of lost technologies."

"I've found old gears and cables," said Elspeth. "But it's all ruined. Useless."

"Who cares about gears and cables?" asked Surgeon. "The greatest machines of men moved information, not cargo. Vast libraries of knowledge could be inscribed on a tiny wafer of silicon. The infusion of so much information into such a compact space brought forth a new form of life, machines that could think."

Elspeth let out a deep sigh. She'd been intrigued by his story, but this latest detail was proof he spoke only of fantasies.

Surgeon didn't notice her skepticism. He continued: "These silicon chips were ubiquitous, embedded in everyday objects. The devices that contain the chips seldom endure beneath the sea, but often the chips themselves were sealed for protection against the elements. My human contacts pay handsomely for these chips. I've accumulated a respectable fortune."

"Yet you still work as a sailor," she said.

"A tatterwing with wealth would draw unwelcome attention. I use human agents to manage my affairs. Your father fears his creditors will seize the *Sea Dragon*, never suspecting that I'm his primary investor. His journeys to the Drowned City have been very helpful to me."

"If you're benefiting from my father's actions, why speak of mutiny?"

"Your father wearies me. He's too unreliable and too greedy to be trusted. If you were in command, our partnership would prove most fruitful."

"I would hardly be trustworthy if I betrayed my father," she said.

"You're only betraying yourself if you continue to serve him. You want order, safety, and comfort for your mother. Your father stands between you and your needs. I can help you. In return, you can help me obtain the one thing I truly desire."

"Which is?"

"Revenge!" said Surgeon, his eyes flashing as he gazed upon his ruined wings. "My fellow dragons thought I was dangerous. I intend to prove them right!"

"You're as mad as my father," said Elspeth.

Before Surgeon could say anything to dispute this, her father's voice rang out from above, calling for his mermaid. She turned from Surgeon, fully intending to recount this conversation to her father. Yet, before she reached the deck, she decided to say nothing. Order, safety, and comfort. Could Surgeon's tiny treasures truly purchase these things?

It was late afternoon. The air was thick and menacing, ripe for a storm though there wasn't a cloud in the sky.

"By the stars, I've found it!" her father said from high in the crow's nest, bidding her to climb the rigging to join him.

From the heights, she studied the waters. The grid of long, straight avenues of the ancient city could be seen in rows of light and shadow.

"Remember the stone towers we found?" her father asked.

She nodded, remembering the bulky structures, evenly spaced in a straight line that ran nearly a mile.

"Bridge posts," Portsmouth said, tapping a line on the map that crossed a finger of blue. "And if the bridge was there, the waterfront was yonder."

She nodded again as he pointed. She'd swam in that area before, finding an old seawall, with ruins on one side and deep water beyond, and concrete pilings that might have once supported docks.

"And if that's the waterfront, then we're over the street of banks!" He drew a long, loud sniff. "The treasure is so close I can smell it!"

"If you say so," she mumbled.

"That's my girl!" he said, wrapping his hook arm around her shoulders in an awkward hug.

They climbed back down to the deck so that her father could get the flares. Her father went into his cabin while she waited on the deck. When her father stepped back through the doorway, Surgeon hopped down from the rigging, landing face to face with the man.

"Demon!" her father growled, reaching toward his scabbard. His fingers closed around empty air where a hilt should have been. Drawing back his shoulders, Portsmouth said, "You're lucky I didn't run you through. Have a care!"

"Care is in short supply these days," said Surgeon. "Don't you know where we are?"

"Of course," said Portsmouth. "I brought us here, did I not?"

"I don't doubt your navigation, only your memory," said Surgeon, pointing toward the distant shoreline. "We can't be more than a hundred yards from the area where your mate was attacked. Let's find safer waters to explore."

"You ungrateful turd!" Portsmouth's spittle sprayed across the dragon's face. "You were a starving beggar when you came crawling to me! I didn't bring you aboard to question my orders! Get out of my sight or I'll use your sorry hide for a new pair of boots!" Her father raised his hook, looking as if he intended to slash the dragon. Surgeon didn't retreat.

Her father lowered his arm, "To hell with you! Keep your damned snout out of my business."

Surgeon looked at Elspeth.

She said, "I'll dive where my captain tells me to dive."

Surgeon nodded, then stepped aside.

Elspeth looked toward the distant shore. She'd been so young when her mother had been hurt. Was this the place? The land looked identical to hundreds of other miles of feral coastline. Her jaw tightened as the memories of her mother's screams came back to her.

Then she was in the water, swimming along avenues of glass, alone in the magnificent desolation, a mermaid princess surveying her kingdom of shells. It was an empty kingdom, but still more of a home than the ship, where she was orphaned by her father's madness and her mother's grief. The temptation to never again rise toward the air crept into her mind, lingering only a moment, before she chased it out like an unwelcome guest.

Clutching the rake she carried more firmly, she weighed the conflicting desires of her mother and father. Her mother wanted her to stay out of the tunnels. Her father wanted her to search for treasure in the undercity.

Her father's plan, despite the risks, held the most appeal. Order, safety, and comfort — Surgeon had diagnosed her needs well. Her father's bottomless greed could never be satisfied, but gold, properly spent, could purchase the better life she craved.

She stood in the center of the avenue. Her weighted belt and heavy rake pressed her outstretched toes into the glassy sand. In pale ghost light beneath shimmering waves, she could imagine the city at twilight, with candles and lanterns flickering in windows. Anemones bloomed where flowerbeds once stood, as lazy nurse sharks swam in and out of doorways where merchants and maidens once strolled.

She wondered if the deluge had come as a single wave, or inch by inch, over decades. The people who lived here might have watched the waters claim one cobblestone at a time, year after year, until endless loss became the normal course of life, and none could remember that the streets had once been dry.

Walking slowly, raking at lumps, she turned up fragments of old junk. An intact saucer caught her eye and she stuffed it into the sack slung over her shoulder. She continued her journey, making discoveries with each sweep of the rake, dismissing all she found as worthless. Bottles, buttons, encrusted bolts and nails. Her tines caught an odd bit of yellow rope that couldn't be pulled free, so she moved on. She found a battered orange cone trapped beneath a flat rock that cracked apart when she lifted it. The cone was made of stiff rubber, with a large open top surrounded by a flat, square lip and a hole at the narrow end big enough to stick two fingers in. What the container might have held eluded her. She tossed it aside.

She kicked back to the surface for another breath. Her father called her name, then shouted out the direction he wanted her to swim. She dove without acknowledging him. She sank next to a relatively straight and flat wall. In a few stray spots not covered by shellfish, loops of green paint fluoresced in fingered rays of sunlight. Gliding around the broken wall, she found a deep pit with a series of shallow ledges descending through the sand. It was an old staircase, leading underground. She drifted downward until she reached the ghost of a door, a paper-thin barrier of lacy lime and fragmented rust. Beyond was darkness, black and formless.

She pushed her rake through the remnant door, tearing it to pieces. She probed the darkness, sweeping side to side, up, down, until the tines hit the floor. She pulled the rake across a surface that felt like tile. She waved away the swirling sediment dragged out by the tines. Something yellow flashed among fragments of shell. She snatched it up, unable to believe her eyes. Gold! A whole rod of it, thinner than her little finger, but nearly as long as her hand. Only, it didn't weigh as much as it should. It was a hollow tube, not a solid rod. Similar tubes littered the seabed throughout the city, though this was the first she'd found made of gold. Sometimes there were words on the shaft, like "Bic" and "Sharpie." This one bore the words "Elijah Industries." It must have been sheltered in darkness ever since the city flooded. Gold didn't corrode in seawater, but even faint sunlight would hide gold beneath a crust of lime.

She raked into the room once more, straining to fully extend her arm. She felt the tip push against a few bits of rubble, some heavy, some she could move around. She dragged out a fist-sized lump. It proved to be a figurine, an orange cat, sitting with its hind legs splayed out before it, holding a big cup against its belly. Some of the glaze had flaked off the ears, revealing white ceramic beneath. The ceramic would have turned green if light ever penetrated the room.

She decided the room beyond was worth a closer look. She had two flares tucked into her pants, though they would have to wait. Her lungs were full of needle pricks. Turning her face upward, she scissored her legs and rose.

When she reached the surface, gulls were all around. Over their cries, her father called out, "Have you found my gold, mermaid?"

She swam toward the ship, holding up the ceramic cat. Her father lowered a basket for her to put it in. She could see the disappointment in his eyes. She kept the golden tube, to add to her private stash of easily hidden loot that might one day purchase order, safety, and comfort.

High overhead, in the crow's nest, Surgeon's inhuman form was a silhouette against a white sky.

Elspeth dove. It took less than a minute to return to the stairs. With a final kick, she glided into the darkness beyond, a flare held tightly in her hand. With clenched teeth, she pulled the cap free.

Instantly, she was blind. She turned her face away, her eyes clamped shut. Bright red filled the interior of her eyelids. Her hand started to burn as the flare boiled the water near the tip, forcing her to drop the light.

She kept her eyes closed until the glow faded, wasting a precious minute of air. When her vision returned, the light surrounding her was hellish red, with her shadow a looming devil cast upward by the flare. Despite the odd lighting, she could make out the contours of the room well enough. To her great surprise, there was a wooden desk near the far wall, and beyond it was an open doorway. She'd never seen anything made of wood survive in such perfect condition before. She kicked, drifting toward the desk, until she hovered over it. On the far side, she saw drawers, including a long center one slightly ajar. She reached out to open it further.

The second her fingers touched the wooden handle, the whole desk collapsed into a cloud of loose, brown, gelatinous fragments that looked like diarrhea. As the cloud calmed, glints caught her eye. Coins! They were tightly sealed in a transparent bag. She picked up the bag, which felt, vaguely, like a sausage casing, thin and tough. There were several dozen coins within the bag, of four different sizes. Three of the sizes were made of a dull silver, but the most common coins within the bag were brown. All were stamped with the heads of men, proof of their antiquity. Modern coins bore the visages of dragons.

Further sifting through the brown muck produced a picture frame, with a ghostly family imprinted on the glass. She found a small, round mirror, cracked in half, and more of the hollow tubes, though none were made of gold.

She turned her attention to the doorway. If there had been a door once, it had long since rotted. She poked her head inside. Unfortunately, the flare behind her failed to cast much light into the room. She could barely make out a boxy shape about two yards inside the room. She threw the tines of her rake across it and dragged it closer. It turned out to be a large flattened rectangle made of a tough, shell-like material. Despite being large enough for her to curl up inside it, the object weighed practically nothing. The sealed case obviously had air trapped within, leaving it neutrally buoyant. The face of the case had raised letters that matched those on the golden tube she'd found: *Elijah Industries.*

She ran the strap of her canvas bag through a handle along the edge of the case then slung it over her back. Her lungs tingled. She needed to return to the surface. Curiosity overpowered caution, and she leaned into the darkness of the doorway, her rake outstretched as far as it could go.

Instead of striking a second case, her rake fell upon something firm but yielding, as if she was pushing the tines into a featherbed. No, it was more like the time they'd found the freshly beached whale, the way the skin had felt when poked with driftwood.

Without warning, a swirl of water tossed her backward. The rake tore from her hand. Her head banged against the upper frame of the door as the violent current carried her back into the first room, where the flare danced and skittered across the floor, casting turbulent shadows. Her eyes fixed on the door she'd just been forced out of. Something was moving across it, like a dark, mottled gray curtain, fluttering and flapping. The rolling gray halted, leaving a single shape centered in the doorframe. An eye! The size of a wagon wheel, with a copper and teal iris surrounding a pupil dark as the abyss.

Terror seized her. She kicked and twisted, her arms windmilling, her whole body writhing in uncontrolled panic. Her disjointed motions brought her no closer to the stairs that led to escape. She'd turned in a full circle, and was now facing the interior door again. The eye was gone, as was the gray curtain. Had it only been her imagination? A hallucination brought about by a lack of air?

Then a tentacle groped from the doorway, thicker than a yardarm, covered in large, grasping suckers. It probed blindly toward her, until the tip brushed against the burning flare.

Instantly, the tentacle drew back.

She fought to control her fear. It was only an octopus! True, it was the largest she'd ever seen, but that was in her favor, wasn't it? Nothing that big could possibly fit through the door.

As soon as she had the thought, the octopus proved her wrong, as its boneless body started flowing through the gap. She decided not to wait to see if all of it could really make it through. She whirled, swimming for the stairs.

All at once, everything went black. Had the flare burned out? She reached back and grabbed the second flare. She held it tightly as she pulled the cap free. Nothing! No light at all.

Before she tossed the useless flare away, some voice in the back of her mind screamed not to do so. The door to the staircase should have been a rectangle of light no matter what the flare was doing. The water around her hand was growing hot. She couldn't see the door or the flare because the octopus had filled the water with ink.

Fortunately, as the huge beast flowed into the room, water flowed out, tumbling her through the door and up the stairs, the water growing grayer, until at last she could see the dark hull of the *Sea Dragon*. She unfastened her weighted belt. She tried to slip off her bag, ridding herself of the bulky case, but with all her panicked twisting she'd tangled the strap and had no time to waste trying to get free. Straining every muscle, she swam for the surface still holding onto the flare. The octopus had recoiled from its heat. As long as she kept moving, the hot water flowing across her hand was bearable.

Just as she was most hungry for a lifesaving breath, something wrapped around her leg. With the surface mere inches away, she was jerked down. Her leg felt like it was being torn from her hip. She cried out in agony. Life sustaining air undulated toward the surface in silvery bubbles. Beneath her, the octopus expanded across the sea floor. The beast looked large enough to swallow a whale. The tentacle grasping her leg had to be at least fifty feet long. To her relief, her leg was still connected to her body.

Despite the surprise attack, she'd kept her desperate grasp on the flare. She jammed the blazing tip against the tentacle that trapped her. The tentacle released her, its raspy suckers tearing moon-shaped chunks of flesh from her leg as it recoiled. Despite the pain, she swam for the surface, trying to ignore the gushing clouds of pink pulsing from her leg.

With a final push, her head popped above the surface. She gulped precious air. The fresh breath left her giddy. She'd survive this yet! She spun in the water, searching for the *Sea Dragon*. The ship bobbed in the breeze, its sails unfurling. She heard her father screaming, "Faster, you scurvy dogs, faster!"

She furrowed her brow. She appreciated her father's sense of urgency in wanting to save her, but the ship was fifty feet away. They didn't need to raise the sails, they only needed to toss her a rope.

Her eyes found her father, leaning out over the side of the ship. He wasn't looking at her. He was looking into the depths. He cried out, "'Tis the kraken! He'll swallow us all if you laggards don't snap to!"

Her father hadn't raised the sails to rescue her. He was saving himself! Did he think the creature had already swallowed her? Did he care if she was alive or not?

She tried to swim but her leg, bloodied and half-wrenched from its socket, wouldn't cooperate. She stopped flailing as a triangular fin cut an arc through the water not more than twenty yards off. It was a bull shark, and a big one. She swam among sharks all the time, but never while bleeding. She called out to the ship, but there was no sign anyone heard her.

She hung in the water, motionless and silent. She let the flare drop from her fingers. Between the octopus and the shark and the bulky case threatening to pull her under, all her fears collided, then collapsed, producing a curious calm.

As clarity settled over her mind, she thought of the people of the Drowned City, of whether the waters killed them swift or slow, and whether that mattered at all. The world offered no safety and no comfort. But order? Order had ruled her all along. Her life followed the same grand plan all humanity must follow. She'd been born, she would die, and all that happened in between meant nothing at all to the sun, the wind, and the sea.

Then a lifebuoy splashed into the water only a few feet away.

Surgeon stood at the rail near the rudder, clasping the buoy rope. "Grab hold!"

She splashed her way toward the buoy, flopping like a wounded seal. She reached the rope and twisted it around her forearm. Surgeon braced himself against the rail, straining as he pulled the rope.

"Blast you!" her father screamed as he ran up to Surgeon. "I sent you to the wheel! Move or I'll flay your accursed hide!"

Surgeon ignored the captain. Portsmouth grabbed a belaying pin and brandished it menacingly. Surgeon kept to his task, dragging Elspeth through the water with all the speed his inhuman muscles could summon. In seconds, Elspeth was close enough to the hull to touch it. Surgeon tried to pull her from the water. The instant the case strapped to her back cleared the waves it lost its buoyancy and turned into an anchor. The rope slipped from Surgeon's grasp and she splashed back into the drink.

Before Surgeon could attempt to haul her up again, the unfurled mainsail caught wind at a bad angle. The ship rolled toward her. The looming bulk smashed into her, the barnacles of the hull hooking into her face and shoulders like the claws of a thousand cats, dragging her beneath the surface. The rope still wrapped around her arm had fallen slack, but jerked taut as the ship rolled in the other direction, lifting her from the water. She lost her grip on the rope and tore her hands attempting to halt her slide across the barnacles into the churning waves. One second, she was in the air, the next, her world turned into bloody foam and rainbow bubbles, dazzling light and indecipherable darkness. Sweeping her arms, she managed to push away from the ship, getting distance from the barnacles, but was still tossed by swells that lifted her and plunged her down.

Righting herself in the water, she craned her neck to see if the shark was any nearer. It was. The predator was no more than ten feet away, shooting straight toward her. The gray fin rose nearly a yard above the water, a true behemoth of a shark.

The sea mounded. A gaping, toothy cavern opened, sucking her toward her death. Then, the shark came to a sudden halt. It whipped into the air, revealing a body at least thirty feet long. Wrapped around this body was a massive tentacle. The shark wriggled as a mountainous form rose beneath it. With a jerk, the shark vanished beneath the surface. The swirling water pulled Elspeth under. Through the churn she saw the shark shoved beneath the mantle of the octopus. Her eardrums rang as the creature's beak snapped shut on its struggling prey.

As the octopus gulped down its meal, the creature fixed its wagon wheel eyes upon Elspeth. She stared into the twin voids of its pupils, looking for mercy, finding only hunger.

Before the tentacles could grasp her, something sharp and strong clamped onto her shoulder. She was yanked from the water, then clasped roughly against Surgeon's boney ribs. The dragon dangled from the buoy rope, which had been swiftly lashed to the rail.

"You weigh… more… than I expected," Surgeon said through gritted teeth. "What's in that chest?"

"I hope we find out!" she said.

At that moment, there was a loud *WHACK*. Above them, her father had finally found his cutlass. He chopped at the rope, muttering a string of guttural curses about mutineers and dragons and bait. She was too breathless to call out. If he'd known about the case on her back, certainly his greed would overcome his fear of the octopus. As Surgeon climbed, Elspeth held out hope that her father's drunken aim would keep him from cutting the rope. At that moment, Portsmouth's sword found its mark.

The limp rope dropped across her shoulders, but she didn't fall. Surgeon's talons dug into the hull. With heaving breath, he climbed. As he neared the rail, she stretched to grab it. She tried to lift herself but the weight of the case threatened to drag her back into the sea. With an animal cry of pain and rage, she tapped into a frightful strength that delivered her inch by inch toward the deck. Just as she was certain she couldn't hold on another second, she flopped over the rail and onto the deck, limp as a dead codfish.

Still clinging to the hull, Surgeon let out a yelp. Elspeth at last wiggled free of the entangling weight of the case. On trembling legs, she managed to look over the rail. The octopus had wrapped a tentacle around Surgeon's torso. Surgeon's muscles bulged in sharp relief, his scales bristling, as he kept his hold on the boards. Tentacle after tentacle slapped against the hull, rolling the ship toward the enormous cephalopod. Wooden pegs shot from their holes as boards twisted and splintered. The *Sea Dragon* in her prime might have withstood the weight of the beast, but with so much maintenance neglected under her father's command, the ship seemed fated to snap in half.

Elspeth had lost track of her father, but now he returned, brandishing a gaff pole. He leaned over the rail, trying to knock Surgeon loose. "Let go, you devil!" he screamed. "The beast wants your carcass and I aim to let him have it!"

"No!" Elspeth screamed, limping along the rail to grab her father's arm. He looked at her with confused eyes, baffled as to where she'd come from, then roughly pushed her away.

"He saved my life!" she screamed.

"He'll save us all by giving the monster something to chew on!" Her father's eyes were wild, bloodshot with inebriation.

She wasted no further words, hopping and limping toward her father's cabin. She stumbled inside, falling to the floor, thrusting her hand under the bed. Her groping fingers found the box of flares. If the octopus didn't like the touch of a single flare, it definitely wouldn't enjoy a dozen shoved down its gullet.

She hobbled her way back toward the rail. Surgeon's claws had left long gouges in the hull as the octopus dragged him ever closer toward its snapping beak. Many of the more cowardly crew members had thrown themselves into the water, swimming for the distant shore.

She pulled out a single flare and tore off the cap. It burst into white smoke and intense cherry light.

Her father screamed at her. "Those are for treasure, damn you!"

As he spoke, an enormous tentacle rose behind him.

"Move aside!" she cried.

"You worthless brat!" Spittle flew from her father's lips as he swung the gaff hook toward her.

She ducked beneath its drunken arc as she dropped the lit fuse into the box with the others. She jammed the lid shut. "You want them? Catch them!"

She threw the box as hard as she could. Her father dropped the gaff and caught the box against his chest as smoke erupted from every seam. He stumbled back against the rail as the gaff skittered across the deck and stopped at Elspeth's feet.

As the octopus had demonstrated with the shark, sometimes the only way to be rid of a monster was to feed it to another monster. She grabbed the gaff and skillfully hooked it behind her father's ankles.

His drunken eyes snapped into sudden sobriety. "Daughter?" he said, his voice suddenly calm. "What are you doing?"

"Giving the monster something to chew on," she said, pulling her father's feet out from under him so that he fell backward atop the rail. He hung in the balance, his good hand still holding the smoking box of flares to his chest as his hook hand flailed desperately to snag a rope.

Instead of a rope, the hook sank into the rubbery flesh of a tentacle. The slithering arm encircled her father's torso, pinning the box of flares against his chest. With a crunch, both box and ribcage were crushed. Her father's face went purple. The black smoke pouring from the fractured chest gave way to blinding light as the collective flares erupted in a maelstrom of hideous flame.

The ship lurched as the octopus released it. Elspeth was thrown from her feet, tumbling across the deck as the ship pitched away from the beast. She caught herself at the far rail, and found her footing a moment later as the ship groaned back toward an even keel.

She looked to where she'd last seen her father. He was gone, leaving only a faint haze of smoke where he'd tumbled over the rail. Surgeon's face was visible through this haze as his quivering limbs at last brought him to the deck. She limped to his side and gazed over. The water around the ship was black as coal.

She didn't see her father, or hear him shouting over the cries of the craven sailors who'd lost faith in the ship, all now vanishing beneath the waves as countless shark fins darted and dashed about. The storm she'd felt earlier was drawing nearer. Somehow, the mast hadn't snapped, and the mainsail still flapped in the rising wind. The storm front would carry her far from these cursed waters.

Elspeth picked up her father's fallen cutlass. She turned to gaze across the deck. The eyes of a dozen desperate seadogs sized her up carefully. She met their stares one by one, until each man blinked, or turned his face.

"Don't just stand about!" she called out. "You four! Trim those sails! You, and you! Get hammers! We'll have to make repairs on the move!" She shouted more orders, until every hand was busy, save for Surgeon.

"Don't think that saving my life means you'll get to slack off on my watch," she said, folding her arms behind her back. "Take the wheel!"

"Aye, Captain," Surgeon said, loud enough for the whole crew to hear. "And where are we heading?"

"Hampton," she said, as she saw that none of the crew was going to raise an objection to Surgeon's use of her new title.

"And what of your discovery, Captain?" Surgeon said, eyeing the case.

"Stow it in my cabin. We'll look it over together, if we make it through the storm in one piece."

Surgeon nodded, and dragged the case toward the captain's quarters.

With all the crew too busy to notice her, she sagged against the mast. She slid the cutlass into her rope belt. The hilt was sticky and wet. She stared at the literal blood on her hands.

It took a monster to slay a monster. The sun, the wind, and the sea, would never judge her.

The *Sea Dragon* lurched across the waves, chased by thunder, as she limped toward her new cabin. Before she went inside, she watched her crew hard at work. There was nothing like the terror of death to put a little life into them, and whip them into order.

Surgeon was now at the wheel, steering the ship past the sandbars toward the relative safety of the open ocean.

Closing the door behind her, she collapsed onto her father's bed.

Her bed.

Wind swirled through the window, washing her with fresh, clean air. For a moment, at least, she was comfortable.

She stared at her ravaged hands. She closed them into fists. Gore oozed between her fingers. She clenched them even tighter.

Order, safety, comfort.

The price, all along, was blood.

Life in a Moment

A long mile after mile of fields full of dry cornstalks, crows wheel through the reddening sky, guiding me. As night settles the crows fade into the growing gloom. On the horizon there's a glow. My old eyes strain to make sense of what I'm seeing. Finally I make out the Ferris wheel. I'm driving toward a county fair. The symbolism of a wheel, of coming full circle, is almost too on the nose. The Void Dweller isn't even trying for subtlety.

Of course, maybe I'm reading too much into this. Sometimes a crow is just a crow, and sometimes what looks like an omen is only a distraction. I've come out to the boondocks to commit an unspeakable crime against a lonely old man. I've got a few hours to kill before he goes to bed.

The parking lot is nothing but a big field of packed dirt. The night air smells of hot oil churning out fried dough as I leave my car. In the distance, above the noise and clatter of the rides, the song "Wagon Wheel" is playing. Another hint that things are coming back to where they started. The song is coming from the open windows of a pick-up truck where three teenage girls sit on the hood, smoking cigarettes. This is the version of the song performed by Old Crow Medicine Show. There's no way my arrival here is by accident.

I buy my ticket and move among the crowds. No one looks at me, even though I'm the only person wearing a suit. Ten years ago I still turned the occasional head, but age has caught up to me. As I casually read the minds of people passing, most register my face as little more than a pale blur. I stop at the nearest food trailer and order a funnel cake. I don't even plan to eat it. I just crave the smell. It helps me remember clearly how I started on this journey. My memories have become a jittery, scratched up, black and white film, the soundtrack fading to static, but the funnel cake brings back the first time I met Oscar with almost painful clarity. The taste of powdered sugar on Oscar's lips is something that will be with me to the end.

Ignoring the barks of a man offering to guess my weight for a dollar, I pull the engraved silver lighter from my jacket pocket. The fairground neon dances on its mirrored surface. I permit myself the faintest smile.

It's almost six decades since I came to the fair with Oscar and discovered that everything I knew was wrong. When we stepped onto that Ferris wheel I was a shy, awkward college freshman confused by my own desires. Then Oscar, dashing Oscar in his uniform, kissed me and opened my eyes to magic. Which is how many people describe their first love, but they probably mean it metaphorically.

One aspect of magic Oscar taught me was an awareness of synchronicity. Things I once assumed to be coincidence I understand as the future working its will on the past. The universe didn't steer me here to satisfy my sentimentality. I've been waiting for my replacement to enter my life for a long time.

I notice a line of people near the Tilt-a-Whirl, but they aren't facing the ride. This line leads into the shadows. Everyone in the row has a sickly green fog around them, a common aura for people who don't know where to turn. Where they're turning now is a dark tent with a painted sign of an old gypsy crone in a colorful scarf. *Madam Neva, Palm Reader.*

Neva. One letter away from raven, backward. The Void Dweller hasn't been this ham-fisted in a long time. Maybe it knows I'm not as sharp as I used to be.

I walk along the line, back to front, gently touching each person on the base of their skull, stealing the memories of where they've heard of Madam Neva. They shuffle off, forgetting why they're in line, forgetting also that I've touched them. I hold their stolen memories at a distance, hearing them as distant murmurs. *"It was like she saw right into my soul. You have to see her,"* some random voice whispers in testimonial. Another witness mumbles, *"Everything she said came true. She'll be able to help you."*

The unseen beast that lurks in my shadow opens its maw and the memories vanish down its throat. It gets like this, nipping and pecking at every little crumb of memory when it knows I'm about to feed it with a human sacrifice.

As the last of the line meanders away, I step into the tent.

I raise an eyebrow. Madam Neva is a teenager, not a crone, with far more tattoos than I'd consider advisable. I've got nothing against body art, but a person shouldn't run out of canvas before they're old enough to legally drink. I see the tips of tattooed black feathers along her wrist and feel certain that beneath her black blouse the feathers continue up her arm and cover her back. The Void Dweller has been guiding her to this moment for a long time.

Neva glares at me. Her aura is red and spiky, like a wall of fiery spears. She's holding the hand of some balding farmer in overalls. Give him a straw hat and he could be an extra on *Hee Haw*. His vague aura swirls as he flashes through a rainbow of emotions, settling into pink whirlpools of embarrassment.

"Get back in line and wait your turn!" Madam Neva yells at me.

I pull out my wallet and hand the farmer several hundred dollar bills. "You came here looking for advice, so here it is. Your wife's never going to forgive you, but some nice jewelry will help her decide against leaving. Now, beat it."

Madam Neva stands up, fists clenched. "Who the hell do—?"

She stops as Hee Haw makes a beeline for the tent flap.

"Hopefully you got paid up front," I say.

She hesitates for half a second, her aura flickering white as inspiration strikes. She crosses her arms. "You owe me a hundred bucks."

"People really pay that these days?" I place a few bills onto the table in front of her. "That's an easy way to make a living." Her aura spikes red again, but before she can correct me I hold up my hands. "Joking. It's a shitty way to make a living. You're the real deal. You hold their hands and their secrets flow right into you. The misery you see... not many people can handle it. Most of the genuine psychics become junkies or drunks to silence their talents."

"It helps to hate all mankind," she says, picking up the money, eying it skeptically. "I expect the worst of people, so nothing surprises me." She folds the money and puts it in the pocket of her jeans as she gives me a nasty look. "Nor am I surprised by assholes who think that throwing money around gives them the right to do whatever the hell they want."

"My apologies for barging in without a proper introduction. I'm Alistair Daw," I hand her my business card. "I'm a wizard."

She furrows her brow as she studies my card. "This says you're an accountant."

"Look again."

She does, then flips the card back and forth before deciding her eyes aren't playing tricks.

"Not just wizard, but master wizard," she says, reading the card. "Humble."

"I've been doing this a while. I'm part of an elite consortium of mystics sworn to protect mankind. We're always looking for new talent. I'm on my way to thwart the apocalypse. Care to tag along?"

"I'd be more intrigued if you were on your way to *start* the apocalypse," she says. "You're on your own. I've got a line of customers outside."

I push open the tent flap, revealing no one waiting. "You've got a free evening."

"What the hell did you do? I was set to bring in five grand!"

"With a little training, you can drop into any poker game in Vegas and walk away with more money than you'll know how to spend. Right now, you need physical touch to read others. I'll help you scan people just by looking at them."

"You're bat-shit crazy."

"I know it's a lot to swallow." I glance at my watch. "But, if we can skip ahead to you believing me, it would save a lot of time."

"If you're in a hurry, don't let me keep you."

"Let's cut to the chase," I say. "We both know you have the ability to tell if I'm the real deal."

I hold out my hand, palm up.

I suspect she's as surprised as I am when she reaches out to take it.

It's a little after ten when we crunch through the leaves covering Harlan's yard. I head right for the front door.

"I suppose you're going to unlock the door with a spell?" Neva asks, her hands on her hips.

"That's not necessary," I say, turning the knob. "Welcome to the magic of a small town."

I push the unlocked door open slowly, holding my fingers to my lips, though we probably don't need to be too quiet. There's a loud voice coming from somewhere in the house. Someone is ranting about illegal immigrants. Harlan's fallen asleep with his television on.

Neva follows me into the house, an unassuming ranch probably built in the late fifties. The living room is tiny by current standards, with a couch, recliner, and coffee table hiding most of the scratched up hardwoods. Photographs cover the walls. Across the room, there's a fireplace, painted white. Above it hangs the painting that might destroy the world. The energy surrounding it is bright yellow, swirling like leaves in a vortex.

"I can't see anything," Neva whispers, squinting.

"Right," I say. "Sorry. Wizard stuff. I see in the dark. You'll learn it."

"When?"

"Now's good. May I touch you?"

"Touch me where?"

"Your forehead. Your third eye."

"Oh Lord," she whispers, rolling the two eyes she already knows how to use really well. "Whatever. Sure."

I lick my finger, stick it into the pouch of dried blood in my jacket pocket, and touch her about an inch above her nose.

"Open," I say.

"Open?" she whispers. "That's the magic word?"

I shrug. "The universe understands English."

She frowns as she closes her biological eyes. The red spikes grow sharp as needles. She's pissed off that she's falling for whatever joke it is I'm playing on her. But, under the red spikes, there are blue waves. She wants what I'm saying to be true.

Suddenly, she does it. Her third eye opens, then her original pair, wide in wonder.

"Holy shit," she says.

I put my finger to my lips again, reminding her to keep her voice down, then whisper, "Look at the painting over the fireplace."

She does, seeing it as I see it. On the surface, the painting is unremarkable. It's two hands, male and female, one laid across the other, showing wedding bands. The background is tan and blue with a few blotches of white near the top, representing a beach.

Neva steps toward the canvas. "Tell me what I'm looking at."

"Judging from the pedestrian brush strokes and flat perspective, I'm guessing it's something Harlan's wife painted in a community college art class."

"Harlan?"

"The guy we're here to take care of."

She cocks her head to the side, looking like she's about to say something snarky, but I interrupt by answering the question she really meant to ask. "The energy you're seeing is a nexus of memories."

"So you see it too," she whispers, running her hand through the air around the painting. "It's like... fire, but there's no heat."

"I don't see fire," I say. "More like yellow leaves swirling."

"Okay," she says. "I see that. What's it mean?"

"The painting is based on a photo taken on Harlan's honeymoon in October 1962. Now that his wife is dead, this painting is where his memory of that day has taken residence. Harlan's almost ninety. His brain's been leaking memories for a long time. But this painting has become a totem that returns him to the past, dangerously close to another memory of what happened a few days later."

"Which was?"

"A nuclear holocaust. The Cuban Missile Crisis didn't end well originally. The navy sank a Russian ship, the Russians sank one of our submarines. Eight hours later a tenth of the world's population was dead. More than half of the survivors of the initial war died in the nuclear winter that followed."

"History wasn't my favorite subject," she whispers, "but I'm fairly confident that never happened."

"Exactly," I say. "Once we're done, it will continue never happening."

The red spikes around her bend toward me as she prepares to hurl some rather salty language in my direction. Before she can unleash her rage, her forehead wrinkles as she studies the air in front of her. "What's this red stuff?"

"Like a wall of bloody spears?"

"Yeah."

"Your anger. You've been bristling with it since I met you back at the fair."

"Jesus," she whispers, holding up her arm, studying the hostile energy jabbing out of her. "This is badass. I look like a monster!"

"Indeed," I say. "And now you'll need to act like one."

"What do you mean?"

"We need to destroy this memory. It's the last spike pinning Harlan to reality. Once it's gone, he'll be gone. His body might stagger on a few more years. He might have whole days when he's lucid enough to watch a TV show. But anyone looking into his eyes will see he's hollow. Just old meat, dying slowly, as every trace of who he was ebbs away."

"That's horrible," says Neva.

"Monstrous," I say.

"But you can't... I mean, you can't really—"

"You're right. I won't destroy what's left of Harlan's life. You will."

"No," she says.

"So you don't hate all mankind," I say with a smirk.

"I don't want to hurt some random old guy I don't even know. What's he ever done to me?"

"He's no paragon of virtue," I assure her. "If you dig through his memories, you'll find reasons to hate him. Maybe he's cheated on his wife, or beat his kids. Hell, maybe he murdered some hobo and hid the body in the cellar." From the television in the bedroom, I hear a second talking head join in on the immigrant bashing. "I can also say with some confidence you'd find his politics abominable."

"I don't understand any of this," she says.

"Excellent. Mapping the contours of your ignorance is the first step toward learning."

I again hold my fingers to my lips, then motion for her to follow me down the hall. Not that we really need to worry about being heard. Harlan must be nearly deaf, judging from the volume of the television. Harlan sleeps with his bedroom door open, the better to reach the bathroom in the hall. I feel a flicker of sympathy. I'm the master of a thousand mystical arts and even *I* don't have a spell strong enough to get me a full night's sleep without getting up to pee.

Harlan tosses in his sleep. His aura is dark and smoky. In his dreams, the world around him is nothing but ash and ruins, the streets full of blistered corpses, the air stinking of burnt hair. Only, of course, Harlan's not dreaming. He's remembering.

I sprinkle a line of salt from a packet I grabbed at McDonald's across the threshold of his bedroom. The angry speechifying from the news show goes quiet, unable to cross the barrier. I turn to Neva and speak in a normal tone. "We don't need to whisper now. He can't hear us."

"Good," she says. "Because, you know, I have a few questions."

I nod. "Would you like some coffee?"

"What?"

"Coffee," I say, heading for the kitchen. "The civilized, proper way to hold a conversation about the nature of reality is over a cup of coffee."

"I think that's more a conversation for weed," she says. "Lots and lots of weed."

"Ayahuasca would be an even quicker way to get past the veil of illusion that we mistake for truth," I say with a smile. "But I suspect the best we can hope for in Harlan's kitchen is coffee."

Next to his coffee pot, Harlan's got a big basket full of pill bottles. I open the cupboard to hunt for a coffee can. Neva starts looking through the medication.

"So," I say, grabbing the coffee. "You manage with pills."

"I'm not an addict," she says, reading labels. "I share a tiny RV with five other girls. I take pills sometimes to sleep while the idiots yammer."

I pop the lid from the coffee can, my nose wrinkling. I'm something of a snob when it comes to coffee, but this will have to do. I measure some grounds into the filter. "Opioids help you forget the darkness you've witnessed in other people's souls. It's not easy to sleep when you see people as they really are, and not just their public masks."

"I've been seeing people the way they really are my whole life." Her eyes brighten as she finds a bottle of oxycodone. "My dad ran off before I was born. My mom died of cancer when I was seven. Spent most of my life in foster homes being raised by people who pretended to care about me, not knowing that every time they touched me I could feel their pity and disdain." She shakes the pill bottle, and her aura is full of white diamonds when she hears the clatter of a full month's prescription. Then the diamonds vanish as she hides her excitement from herself. "Seriously, pills aren't a problem for me. I run into a lot of addicts. I'm not one of those losers."

"For a born empath, you don't have a lot of empathy."

She stuffs the bottle into her jacket pocket. "What you said about the old guy, Harlan. You're right. I don't know the specifics since I haven't touched him, but it's true. It's true for everyone. He's done horrible things. He's hated, cheated, lied. I turn nineteen next month and already I'm burned out. Everyone sucks."

"All have sinned and fall short of the glory of God."

"You're a religious nut?"

"Hardly." I find us some cups as the water gurgles through the filter. "Just stating an old and obvious truth. I can only tell you to be patient."

"Patient?"

"It takes a while to see it. Everyone's awful, but somehow the sum of humanity manages to be better than the parts. An individual coffee ground is bitter and gritty. Get a bunch of them together and add water and heat and you wind up with the greatest achievement of mankind. In time, you'll see that the world is quite a beautiful place."

"You and I must live in different worlds."

"Same world, different perspectives," I say, pouring us each a cup. "I've seen alternatives to our present existence. Back in 1962, I died from radiation poisoning."

"You got better, apparently." She pours an unethical amount of sugar into her coffee. I suppress my urge to comment.

"Much better, thanks to Oscar." I pull out my wallet and take out a small, black and white photograph of a clean cut young man in a naval uniform. "When I went to the fair tonight, it brought back memories of the most wonderful night of my life."

She takes the picture and looks at it, her face showing no emotion.

"Oscar and I shared our first kiss at the top of a Ferris wheel. No one could see us. The fairground lights spread out beneath us like some fairy kingdom. For the briefest moment it felt like the world had no choice but to approve the love we felt for each other. Euphoria left us careless. We held hands as we rode down, certain no one could see us. We were wrong. A gang of teens spotted us holding hands. They confronted us as we went into the shadows behind a tent to sneak another kiss. One of them had a knife, another had a bat. I had my fists clenched, ready to fight like hell. But Oscar just held up his hand and said, 'You never saw us.' Suddenly, they all looked confused, like they couldn't remember why they'd come behind the tent. They wandered off without even hurling a slur at us. That's when I discovered that Oscar was a wizard at more than just kissing."

She hands the picture back to me. "So, what? He wizarded you out of death after a nuclear war?"

"He wizarded the world out of death." I pause to sip my coffee, properly lightened with only a single spoon of sugar and a few drops of cream. "With some help, of course. The real mastermind was a witch named, no kidding, Sabrina. Not a teenager, though. She says she's three hundred years old, but I don't think she looks a day over two-fifty. She claims she'd saved the world from destruction three times before 1962. I've worked with her twice since then to undo the end of civilization."

"This some sort of time travel bullshit?"

"Not time travel, per se. We manipulate the past by destroying memories." I pause, uncertain if I should tell her yet that we destroy memories by feeding them to a beast that lives in the void that enfolds our reality, an entity older than time itself. Too soon, I decide. "When Oscar robbed those thugs of their memory of seeing us holding hands, he changed their reality. They simply never saw us."

"But he didn't really change the past. You still held hands."

"True. But I would have forgotten if Oscar hadn't shielded me. What if we'd both forgotten? Would it truly have happened?"

"Of course," she says. "Things happen or they don't. There's no middle ground."

"Actually, there's nothing but middle ground," I say. "Look, I'm going to use a scientific metaphor, but this isn't science. Understand that my explanation is only a shadow of the truth. Once you're immersed in that truth, you won't need the metaphor anymore. But, right now, it's the best tool I have for explaining what we do."

She rolls her eyes. "I understand how metaphors work."

"Let's say a scientist puts a cat in a box with a vial of poison."

"Because that happens all the time."

"All the time." I nod. "It happens when countries build arsenals of atomic warheads that can vaporize most of the northern hemisphere. It happens when politicians fly private jets across oceans to make toothless vows to reduce carbon emissions. It happens when the citizens of a wealthy, literate nation decide to stop vaccinating their children."

She stares at me, then shrugs. "I retract my sarcasm."

"Back to the cat in the box. A scientist comes in the next day and opens the box. There's a fifty percent chance the cat is alive, and a fifty percent chance the cat is dead. He writes down the answer on a clipboard, closes the lid, and goes home."

"Which is it?"

"Who knows?"

"The scientist."

"Didn't I mention? He has Alzheimer's. When he goes back into his lab the next day, he sees the closed box and doesn't remember that he ever opened it. With the lid closed, and no memory of what he saw, the cat is no longer definitely alive or definitely dead. It's back to being both and neither."

"But he wrote down the answer on a clipboard."

"True," I say. "Except I snuck into the lab in the middle of the night and stole the clipboard and burned the notes without looking at them."

"If I'd snuck into the lab, I'd have freed the damned cat," she says.

"If you open the box, you might find it dead."

"Someone eventually has to open the box or the cat will starve, poison or no."

"Yeah, the box has to get opened eventually. But, if the scientist forgets he opened the box and found a dead cat, the next time he opens the box he might find a live one."

"So, what? Oscar and Sabrina and maybe Merlin and Dumbledore all teamed up to make everyone forget a nuclear holocaust, which means it never happened?"

"Dumbledore's not real," I say. "And Merlin's a dick all the other wizards steer clear of. If you ever meet him, run, since he's a walking *#metoo* moment. But, yes, you've got it. Wizards team up, cast a world-wide forgetfulness spell, and history gets a redo. Simple."

"I can't decide what's more stupid," she says. "Your story or me kind of believing it."

"That's the whole third eye thing," I pour myself another cup of coffee. "While it's open you can't be deceived by untruths."

"Okay," she says. "Let's pretend I believe you. Why, exactly, are we here?"

"Cleanup work. Oscar used to do this stuff but he died, and kept dying, no matter how hard I tried to undo it. That's something you should know. Eventually, you'll hit an apocalypse where every way out is a terrible choice. We undid an AIDS plague that killed close to a billion people, but only by finding a path where mere tens of millions of people died. Sometimes you open the box and find the cat puking and blind. That counts as alive."

"Oscar died of AIDS?"

"Throat cancer. He smoked like a damned chimney. No one's immortal. Except Merlin, and he's bitter about it. Back to the mission: Harlan's bleeding memories. For some people, as memories of the life they've lived fade, memories of alternate lives start bleeding in. Harlan remembers the nuclear war more and more. Which isn't a problem if it's just one old man remembering, but memories can be contagious. Maybe he'll get put in a home where he talks to other people his age. Suddenly there are two people remembering the war, then ten, then twenty, and, BOOM, some threshold in the cosmic consciousness is crossed and we're all living in a post-apocalyptic landscape. At least, you are. I'm dead, remember?"

"What's that painting of the hands have to do with any of this?"

"That painting is Harlan's nexus," I say. "Sometimes mundane objects become totems as people imbue them with meaning. Over the years the painting has become a reservoir for his memories. Even as his brain decays, the nexus endures to refresh his recollections every time he stands before it. Without it, he'll forget everything. He won't recall his dead wife's name, won't recollect how they met, and definitely won't remember how she died from the fallout of a nuclear war. He won't be a danger anymore."

"It would be more merciful to kill him."

"If you don't mind getting your hands dirty. You ever smother someone with a pillow? The movies make it look like it takes thirty seconds. It's more like a half hour, and if the bastard breaks free for even a good gasp, you've got to start all over again."

"Couldn't we, you know, shoot him?"

"You are surprisingly blood thirsty. But, no. Guns are iron. Iron negates magic so wizards steer clear of them. Trust me, it's less messy to siphon the memories in the painting."

She takes a long drink from her coffee. She sits the cup on the counter and gazes into the brown film in the empty cup. The look on her face is one I've seen on lesser mystics trying to divine the future from tea leaves.

She looks back at me, her eyes hard and cool. "I'm in."

"I know."

"What do we do?"

"Follow me."

Back in the living room, I take the painting down from the wall. The swirling memories feel like raindrops running down my arms. I hand her the painting.

"Weird," she says. "It even smells like a beach. I swear, I hear waves crashing."

"Good," I say. "You're a natural. Now drink them in. Imagine you're a memory vampire, draining the memories from the canvas."

"Vampire? Am I supposed to bite it?"

"Funny. No. Something slightly harder. You have to embrace these memories. You have to lower all the barriers you've put in place that keep you from feeling other people's emotions. Harder still, you have to break through the shell of your own cynicism. You have to genuinely feel what he felt if you want to take the memories away from him. Only once you've taken control of these memories can we guide them to, um, where they need to go."

Her brow furrows. She's balanced between skepticism and acceptance. For a moment, the yellow leaves of memory swirling around the canvas snag and tear at the red spikes surrounding her. My heart sinks. She's young, but she's already seen too much of the world, and hardened herself to it. I don't see how she's ever going to let anything touch her emotionally. For the first time, I wonder if I'm wrong about her. Perhaps the barriers she's built to protect herself from others will never be breached.

What's so hard is that she's doing it alone. When I was eighteen, I was surrounded by the same red spears of anger. It's not easy being gay in the current world. Maybe ninety percent of the world has no problem with this aspect of myself, or, if they do, are too polite to show it. But, not even a year ago, I was called a fag right to my face. I hear schoolkids routinely refer to things they don't like as gay. Politicians proudly campaign to protect good citizens from my perverse desires to pledge myself to a partner, or care for children. Neva's hardly some rightwing bigot, but she assumed that Oscar had died from AIDS. And this is today.

I grew up queer in the fifties. There was absolutely no one I could talk to about my feelings. My school library didn't have a single book explaining my desires. There were no celebrities proudly standing up as role models for love in the way I wanted to be loved. So, yes, I put up some walls. Then Oscar came along and I had to knock down those walls to let him in. It was and is and always will be the most terrifying thing I've ever done.

Neva shakes her head. The memory vortex hasn't lost any energy at all.

"I can't do this." She places the painting back onto the wall. "What if... what if he wasn't so bad?"

"I promise he was. That night that Oscar and I almost got the shit stomped out of us? Harlan was the one with the knife. His return to my life is just the wheel of my existence turning a full circle. He would have left me bleeding all because he couldn't stand the thought that two men might love one another."

"You're just saying that the man we need to destroy just happens to be... I mean... what are the odds?"

"100%. These coincidences happen all the time, only they aren't coincidences. Everything is tied together by strings most people never see."

"Fine," she says, taking the painting down from the wall again. "But, I still don't know how to do it."

"Will you let me help you? It will mean touching you in a way you might find uncomfortable."

She furrows her brow, but nods. I step behind her and reach around to place one palm on her throat and another on her buttocks, pressing against the base of her spine. You might recognize these as the root chakra and throat chakra. She'll be using them a lot in her new role as guardian against the apocalypse.

She stiffens at my touch but doesn't try to pull away. I massage these spots carefully, and suddenly she understands exactly how she's supposed to absorb the memories. Her grip tightens on the painting, like she's squeezing the memories from it. They start flowing into her and she gasps. She laughs, delighted to discover her new power. And then the memories become real to her and she whispers, "No." Then she cries, "No!"

There's no turning back. All I can do is hold her as the memories tear through her. I didn't tell her the full truth. It's not her job to destroy these memories. She's just a conduit. For a brief moment, she's become a door that opens onto the void.

And within that void, the Dweller, the Devourer. The void is always hungry to consume life, hungry to devour the past, the future, eager to eat everything and everyone until nothing remains. This is the bargain Sabrina and Oscar and the others made. We feed this eternal destroyer unwelcome realities in order to protect the one world that's tolerable to live in.

Though Neva's eyes are now open to the void, this isn't why she's screaming. It's not nothingness that's slicing up her soul. It's the somethingness. It's the full reality of Harlan's life. Since I'm touching Neva, I see what she's seeing as the memories flow through her. It's the most terrible thing that anyone can ever see.

It's in there, like I knew it would be, the hatred. Harlan once served on a jury, giving not a second thought to acquitting a deputy who'd shot an unarmed black teen driving a stolen car. I hear Harlan shouting at the TV, angered at some news story about a celebrity telling the world they'd been born the wrong sex. Then an older memory, a shameful one, of Harlan cursing at his own child, calling him stupid, calling him a disappointment. These spiteful memories are easy to throw down the gullet of the Void Dweller.

But now Neva sees Harlan's wife Becky as he saw her. Neva feels the genuine love Harlan had for Becky, the gentleness he showed her, his protectiveness, his pride, his joy. She remembers the children they had together, two boys and a girl, and feels his pain when the older boy dies without warning in the middle of a basketball game, the victim of an undiscovered birth defect in his heart. Neva sees Harlan weeping at the funeral, sees the changes he went through after that, how he devoted so much time to his church, how he started doing yardwork for his elderly neighbors.

She remembers how he always carried a toolbox in the back of his truck and would stop to help anyone in distress on the side of the road, black, white, rich-looking, poor, it didn't matter. In contemplating what Jesus would do, Harlan somehow concluded that Christ would carry jumper cables and a gas can wherever he drove. He was probably right.

There's more. Every song Harlan ever sang. Every piece of cake upon his tongue. Every Band-Aid that comforted a bleeding child. Every clean sheet he slid beneath to find the waiting warmth of his wife. Every sunny morning. Every star-filled night. Every joy. Every sorrow. All the rage, and all the love, and every laugh, and every tear.

We live it all, a life in a moment, its beauty blinding.

And we've destroyed it.

The deed is done. The canvas looks exactly the same, but the energy around it has vanished. It's now only a mediocre painting that strives for romance and lands on clunky sentimentality.

The canvas slips from Neva's grasp. She falls to her knees, weeping.

"He... he held... he held his wife's hand all night as she was dying." Her voice trembles. "He wouldn't leave her side. But... I mean... I felt his hatred, too. But, he wasn't a monster. He was..."

"He was human," I say. "We don't have the luxury of only doing this to bad people. The worst person you'll ever rob of memories will have lived a life full of wonders and joys and kindness that will be heartbreaking to behold. This is the most important thing I can teach you tonight. We don't do this to punish anyone. I didn't come for revenge against Harlan. We do what we must to save the present from the past. We do it because every life we save is worth saving. Do you understand?"

She nods, wiping her cheeks. "Kind of." Then she looks at me. "What the hell was that thing? I saw... something... big and black and... it ate the memories as I freed them. It... it felt like it was ravenous enough to eat the entire fucking world!"

"Yeah," I said. "That's the Void Dweller. People see it as different things. Oscar saw it as a dark angel. Sabrina swears it's a dragon. I've always seen it as a black crow whose wings are wider than the sky. It's—"

"It's going to eat me one day," she whispered.

"It's going to eat all of us. I'm sorry I didn't warn you, but it wouldn't change your fate if I had," I say, not knowing if this is any comfort at all. I kneel before her and offer her my handkerchief. "You must have a strong stomach. I threw up the first time I glimpsed the Void Dweller."

"Yeah," she says, her voice shuddering as she fights to regain her composure. "I've got good guts."

I rise, offering her my hand. I help her back to her feet, then put the painting back on the wall.

"What happens now?" she asks as we move toward the front door.

"To Harlan? He'll wake up tomorrow unaware that anything has changed. He might feel that something's missing, but, like I said, he's been bleeding memories for a while. With his nexus drained, the last traces of his old self won't last long. He's now the exact opposite of a ghost. He's a body without a spirit."

She shakes her head. "I meant, what happens now to me?" She looks up at the glow from the fairgrounds as we step outside. She crosses her arms over her chest, tucking her hands in her armpits. It's dropped ten degrees since we went inside. "I can't imagine going back to reading palms."

"Now we'll do a magical mystery tour," I say. "I'll introduce you to Sabrina. She'll take over your training."

"You won't be training me?"

I shake my head. "Unlike Sabrina, I've never even tried to master the art of extending my own life. Tonight I've held things together pretty well. But, like Harlan, my memories aren't what they once were. Honestly, without my own memory nexus, I might not function for long. Once Sabrina decides I've become dangerous, she'll have you sneak in while I'm sleeping and feed me to our feathery friend."

"I wouldn't do that to you," she says.

"You'll have to," I say. "And you'll do it with my blessing. The world only moves toward tomorrow by surrendering its yesterdays. I won't feel a thing. Just like Oscar didn't feel a thing."

"You... you mean...."

I nod and pull out the silver lighter. "His nexus was this lighter. It was the first birthday present I gave him. He used it his whole life. But, his throat cancer spread. He had tumors in his bones, and in his brain. One day, he was talking about the first nuclear war, the one in 1959, a war I'd never known about. I knew it was time. I couldn't throw the lighter away after I was done. Eventually, the lighter became the nexus for my own memories."

"I don't know how you could possibly have been strong enough to do that to someone you loved," she says.

"You're stronger than you know. A lot stronger than those pills you're relying on."

"I don't know," she says, taking the pills from her pocket. She studies the bottle. I see her aura flutter through a dozen shades of green as she doubts herself. Then, the red starts pushing through again. She's angry that she wants the pills. Anger is more than destruction. It's power. "Whatever," she says, as the red pushes away the last of her doubt. "I should put them back."

"Good call," I say.

I gaze at the lighter as she goes back inside. My breath comes out like smoke in the cold air. I open the lighter and flick the wheel. It's a hard thing to look at, the little flame, trembling in the chill night, like it knows it will soon flicker out.

But that's the very nature of flame. The source of its brevity is the source of its beauty. The act of burning destroys the fuel that allows it to burn.

Once you've seen a life in a moment, you understand that's all life is. Only a moment, fleeting, futile, a brief burst of heat and light, fated to go out. It's the most wonderful thing that can ever be, a feeble little flame against the backdrop of the terrible, all-consuming void. One day soon all that remains of me will go dark. For a little longer I flicker on, facing the long night with a defiant smile.

About the Author

James Maxey's mother warned him if he read too many comic books, they would warp his mind. She was right. Now an adult who can't stop daydreaming, James is unsuited for decent work and ekes out a pittance writing down demented fantasies.

Readers interested in sampling Maxey's odd ramblings might enjoy his science-fantasy *Bitterwood* series, the secondary world fantasy of his *Dragon Apocalypse* novels, his two superhero series *Lawless* and *Whoosh! Bam! Pow!* (aka the *Nobody Gets the Girl* series) or the steampunk visions of *Bad Wizard*. His short fiction has appeared in *IGMS*, *Asimov's*, and over a dozen anthologies, with the best of his work appearing in the collections *There is No Wheel, The Jagged Gate,* and *Life in a Moment*.

He also occasionally delves into non-fiction, with books like *Write! Daydream, Type, Profit, Repeat!* and *Cryptids: How We Know They are Real.*

James lives in Hillsborough, North Carolina with his lovely and patient wife Cheryl and too many cats. Cheryl joins James as co-editor and publisher of Word Balloon Books anthologies for kids, including *Beware the Bugs! Rockets & Robots,* and *Paradoxical Pets.*

To sign up for his newsletter, visit jamesmaxey.net, or use this QR code. He can also be found on Facebook by searching for the group Dragonsgate: The Worlds of James Maxey. Or, follow him on Twitter @JamesAllenMaxey.

Links

Review this book!
Follow the QR code to the Amazon listing for this title.

Read more by James Maxey!
Follow the QR code to his Amazon Author page.

Made in the USA
Middletown, DE
19 September 2024